Patrick's Seduction is a work of fiction. Names, characters, places, and incidents are the products of the author's imagination and are used fictitiously. Any resemblance to actual events, locales, or persons, living or dead, is entirely coincidental.

Copyright © 2025 Tina Folsom

All rights reserved.

Scanguards® is a registered trademark.

Published in the United States

Cover design: Leah Kaye Suttle

Author Photo: © Marti Corn Photography

BOOKS BY TINA FOLSOM

Samson's Lovely Mortal (Scanguards Vampires, Book 1)

Amaury's Hellion (Scanguards Vampires, Book 2)

Gabriel's Mate (Scanguards Vampires, Book 3)

Yvette's Haven (Scanguards Vampires, Book 4)

Zane's Redemption (Scanguards Vampires, Book 5)

Quinn's Undying Rose (Scanguards Vampires, Book 6)

Oliver's Hunger (Scanguards Vampires, Book 7)

Thomas's Choice (Scanguards Vampires, Book 8)

Silent Bite (Scanguards Vampires, Book 8 1/2)

Cain's Identity (Scanguards Vampires, Book 9)

Luther's Return (Scanguards Vampires, Book 10)

Blake's Pursuit (Scanguards Vampires, Book 11)

Fateful Reunion (Scanguards Vampires, Book 11 1/2)

John's Yearning (Scanguards Vampires, Book 12)

Ryder's Storm (Scanguards Vampires, Book 13)

Damian's Conquest (Scanguards Vampires, Book 14)

Grayson's Challenge (Scanguards Vampires, Book 15)

Isabelle's Forbidden Love (Scanguards Vampires, Book 16)

Cooper's Passion (Scanguards Vampires, Book 17)

Vanessa's Bravery (Scanguards Vampires, Book 18)

Patrick's Seduction (Scanguards Vamipres, Book 19)

Lover Uncloaked (Stealth Guardians, Book 1)

Master Unchained (Stealth Guardians, Book 2)

Warrior Unraveled (Stealth Guardians, Book 3)
Guardian Undone (Stealth Guardians, Book 4)
Immortal Unveiled (Stealth Guardians, Book 5)
Protector Unmatched (Stealth Guardians, Book 6)
Demon Unleashed (Stealth Guardians, Book 7)
Ace on the Run (Code Name Stargate, Book 1)
Fox in plain Sight (Code Name Stargate, Book 2)
Yankee in the Wind (Code Name Stargate, Book 3)
Tiger on the Prowl (Code Name Stargate, Book 4)
Hawk on the Hunt (Code Name Stargate, Book 5)
A Touch of Greek (Out of Olympus, Book 1)
A Scent of Greek (Out of Olympus, Book 2)
A Taste of Greek (Out of Olympus, Book 3)
A Hush of Greek (Out of Olympus, Book 4)
Venice Vampyr (Novellas 1 – 4)
Teasing (The Hamptons Bachelor Club, Book 1)
Enticing (The Hamptons Bachelor Club, Book 2)
Beguiling (The Hamptons Bachelor Club, Book 3)
Scorching (The Hamptons Bachelor Club, Book 4)
Alluring (The Hamptons Bachelor Club, Book 5)
Sizzling (The Hamptons Bachelor Club, Book 6)
Reversal of Fate (Time Quest, Book 1)
Harbinger of Destiny (Time Quest, Book 2)
Eyewitness (A Thriller)

PATRICK'S SEDUCTION

SCANGUARDS VAMPIRES #19

SCANGUARDS HYBRIDS #7

TINA FOLSOM

1

"Where are you guys today?" Patrick asked.

He sat in his office at Scanguards' headquarters in the Mission district of San Francisco looking into the computer monitor from which his mother smiled back at him.

Delilah, beautiful and forever young, her age frozen in the mid-thirties, stood on a balcony. It was mid-morning in San Francisco, and the sun was up, but behind his mother, it was dark except for the Aurora Borealis that illuminated her surroundings. Shades of pink, red, green, and yellow were painted on the sky as if waves of different colors washed over the heavens. The sight was breathtaking.

"We're still in Fairbanks," she replied just as his father, Samson, came into view, putting an arm around her shoulders as he looked into the camera.

Samson had been turned into a vampire over two-hundred-and-fifty years ago, but looked no older than thirty-five. And though Delilah was human, she didn't age, because she was blood-bonded to Samson, whose blood kept her looking and feeling as young as the day they'd bonded almost forty years ago. And just like their good looks hadn't waned in all those years, their love for each other hadn't either. Instead, it had grown deeper with each year that passed. When he'd been a teenager, he'd always felt embarrassed watching their public displays of affection, but now, as an adult, he looked at them and wished that one day, he would find the same kind of love with his partner, whoever she might be.

"It's an amazing sight, the Northern Lights, don't you think?" Samson asked, smiling.

"It's stunning, Dad!"

Delilah winked at him. "Your father is taking full advantage of the fact that we only have four hours of sunlight up here. I can barely keep up with him."

Since his father was a pure-blooded vampire, he couldn't brave the sunlight. It would reduce him to ash in mere moments, while Patrick, as a vampire hybrid, didn't have that weakness. He had all the other advantages of being a vampire: preternatural strength and speed, immortality, and the fact that he didn't age. In fact, he'd stopped aging at the age of twenty-one, even though he could see changes in himself when he looked in the mirror.

He wasn't the wide-eyed kid anymore who did everything for a chance at adventure. He was more mature, weighing up all pros and cons, and had become less impulsive. In his eyes, he could see the years of knowledge and experience he'd gained, and the man he'd become, despite the rest of his face remaining free of the ravaging signs of aging. People who didn't know him might believe him to be too young to bear any kind of responsibility, but in the eyes of his family and friends at Scanguards, he could see that they saw him as a confident man with strong ethics and boundless energy.

Samson chuckled softly, pressing a kiss to Delilah's temple. "It's a trip of a lifetime."

"How are Maya and Gabriel enjoying it?"

"They can't get enough of the snow," Samson replied.

"They're cross-country skiing right now," Delilah added. "I had to pass on that. That's way too exhausting for me." She glanced at Samson. "You could have gone with them if you wanted to."

"I'd much rather spend time with you, sweetness."

"I should let you go," Patrick said, recognizing that his parents had that look in their eyes that they always had when they wanted to be alone. He didn't need to be a psychic to know what they did when alone—after all, a vampire's sex drive didn't diminish with age, nor did that of his blood-bonded mate.

"How's everything at Scanguards?" Samson asked quickly. "Any issues?"

"It's all running smoothly."

"And the jeweler's convention? Any problems with providing the extra security for them?"

"They're all happy with us. Everybody feels safe. No thefts or even attempted thefts. We've got this."

The door suddenly opened, and Nicholas, a vampire hybrid three years his junior, barged in. "Patrick, we've got a body in the Presidio."

"What's going on?" Samson asked, instantly alert, his sensitive vampire hearing having picked up Nicholas's words.

Nicholas approached and looked at the screen. "Didn't mean to interrupt, Samson, but Patrick is needed."

"Go, son," Samson said quickly. "Call me later and tell me if I can help."

Patrick shook his head. "I won't, Dad. You're on vacation, and I can handle Scanguards. That's why you put me in charge while you and Gabriel are away. Trust me, I have all the help I need right here. Right, Nicholas?"

"Totally." Nicholas gave a quick nod, puffing out his chest in a show of confidence.

"Alright." Samson sounded reluctant, but then he nodded. "I trust you."

"Bye, Dad, bye, Mom."

Patrick disconnected the video call and rose from his chair, looking at Nicholas.

"Give me the details," Patrick demanded, already heading for the door, leaving the office.

Together they marched down the corridor.

"We got a call that the body of a jogger was found in the Presidio, near the Lyon Street steps. There was a lot of blood," Nicholas reported. "Anita checked it out right away and restricted access by SFPD."

"She suspects that a vampire did this?" Patrick asked.

Anita Diaz-Montgomery wasn't only married to his fellow vampire hybrid, Cooper Montgomery, she was also the liaison officer in charge of assigning investigations of any crimes to Scanguards in which vampires or other supernatural creatures were suspected to be involved. She reported directly to the Chief of Police as well as to Samson—and in Samson's absence to whoever was in charge at Scanguards. She was a very capable police detective and had been instrumental in taking down a vampire serial killer a few years earlier.

"I only spoke to her briefly, but yes, that's her gut feeling," Nicholas confirmed. "Buffy should already be at the Presidio securing the body so she can do a preliminary examination."

"Who else is on scene?"

"Anita is still there. And Benjamin was in the area, so I sent him to assist Buffy and wait for us."

Patrick nodded, pleased that all preliminary measures had already been set in motion. "Good."

Over the last few years, Nicholas had turned into a dedicated and competent investigator and bodyguard ready to conquer the world, if given only half a chance. He still had something to prove, not necessarily to himself but to his strict father, Zane, a pureblooded vampire. He'd inherited a fierce sense of justice from Zane, who'd survived the Holocaust. Zane had hunted down his Nazi tormentors for over six decades until he'd meted out the appropriate sentence for their crimes: death. Even today, he still had a penchant for violence, though he only directed it toward the bad guys.

"Do we know the identity of the victim?"

Nicholas opened the door to the underground garage and looked over his shoulder. "No. We only know it's a male jogger."

Patrick followed him into the garage, where they headed to a black SUV with tinted windows. Nicholas jumped in on the driver's side, and Patrick took the passenger seat. Moments later, they shot out of the parking garage and merged into heavy mid-morning traffic in the colorful Mission district with its trendy restaurants and bars.

While Nicholas concentrated on driving, Patrick let his mind wander. He knew that his father was ready to give him more responsibilities, but did he really want that? Running Scanguards meant less time in the field and more in the office. While he was okay with overseeing certain things at Scanguards, he excelled at fieldwork: protecting humans, investigating crimes perpetrated by members of his own species, and saving the innocent. He couldn't imagine spending all night at headquarters getting reports that required action, only to delegate those cases to others, when all he wanted was to get his hands dirty and take action himself.

In a way, he wasn't so different from his father. On more and more occasions, he could see in his father's eyes that he too wanted to carry out missions. But after Samson had been kidnapped and nearly died five years earlier, he'd learned to suppress the urge to join the most dangerous missions for Delilah's sake. The fear of almost losing her husband sat deep in her bones, visible to anyone who cared to look. His parents had grown even closer now if that was at all possible. Their love had grown in the presence of danger.

He sighed. Would he ever find a woman he could love the way Samson loved Delilah? And one who loved him like that in return?

"Something wrong?" Nicholas asked with a sideways glance.

Patrick shrugged, deflecting from his thoughts. "Do you think people will ever stop killing each other?"

"Doubt it. It's in everybody's nature. We're all capable of it. We just need the right catalyst."

Surprised at Nicholas's wise words, he nodded to himself. "Well, then let's see what the catalyst was this time."

Nicholas pulled to the side of the road and parked at the Eastern edge of the Presidio, where the Lyon Street steps led down to the Marina, and an iron gate that stood open led into the Presidio where the wooded area was interspersed with walking trails, bike paths, and narrow streets.

The fog still hung low in the park, an unusual occurrence for January. Normally, during the winter months, the days were clear without fog, and only the occasional rain clouds blocked out the sun. But today, even the sun hadn't peeked through the thick fog yet. As if she didn't want to shine a light onto the unfortunate man who'd met his end while jogging.

Upon getting out of the car, Nicholas opened the trunk and took out a large black bag. Patrick was aware of its contents: a forensic kit with which to collect evidence at a crime scene.

They had to walk only four or five hundred yards before reaching the crime scene, an area with several tall trees and a few bushes along the walking trail. By the looks of the broken branches and trampled plants, it appeared that the victim had tried to get away from his attacker. But the chase had been a short one, indicating that the victim's speed had been no match for the perpetrator's.

The smell of blood became more intense with every step that brought them closer to the dead body. Benjamin nodded at him and Nicholas as they approached, his gaze sweeping the area for any unsuspecting civilians, so he could keep them away from the gruesome scene. Benjamin was one of the twin sons of Amaury, the pure-blooded vampire who was Samson's best friend. Benjamin's twin, Damian, had found his mate a few years earlier, leaving their joint apartment to move into a house in the Marina with Naomi. Benjamin always claimed that he wasn't ready for matrimony. However, Patrick couldn't help but wonder whether Benjamin secretly envied his twin for having found his soulmate, while he still lived the life of a womanizer who had suddenly lost his wingman.

Patrick's gaze was drawn to Buffy, the 26-year-old black human stepdaughter of John Grant, a pure-blooded vampire in Scanguards' employ. She crouched down next to the dead jogger, examining what was left of him. He admired Buffy for how calm she was at handling this important task, collecting forensic evidence off the body and its immediate surroundings. She'd assisted Maya, Scanguards' own physician, many times, administering not just emergency medical care but also performing autopsies. This would be the first autopsy she handled on her own during Maya's absence.

Next to Buffy stood Anita. The tall blonde was beautiful and acted as their liaison with the SFPD.

Patrick stepped closer. "Hey, Buffy. Hey, Anita."

"Patrick." Buffy looked over her shoulder, her face serious. She let out a breath.

To one side of her rested a gurney with a body bag on it, waiting to transport the corpse to HQ once it was ready to be moved.

"Thanks for coming so quickly," Anita said. "I've never seen anything so brutal." She pointed to the body on the ground.

Patrick stared down at the corpse. The man's jogging suit was soaked in his own blood, his face smeared with it, his forearms showing long cuts as if somebody had sliced through the flesh using multiple knives. The worst was his torso. It was ripped open, the chest cavity exposed, ribs sticking out at odd angles.

He couldn't stop his fangs from extending, an automatic response to the massive amounts of blood that impregnated the air. The chest cavity itself was filled with blood and dirt, even some leaves from the bushes around the area.

"Buffy, any idea how long he's been dead?" Patrick asked.

"A couple of hours, maybe longer. The body is already feeling cool, and rigor mortis has set in. I should know more when I can take the liver temperature back at HQ."

Benjamin approached. "So, he was killed before the sun came up?"

Buffy nodded. "Quite likely."

Patrick exchanged a look with Benjamin and Nicholas. They were all thinking the same.

"Could have been a vampire attack." He looked at Anita. "Thanks for keeping SFPD away. The fewer people who see the body, the better."

"You think we've got another serial killer on our hands like a few years ago?" Anita asked.

For the length of a breath, Patrick held her gaze. "God, I hope not."

Nicholas placed his forensics bag on the ground and started unzipping it. "Guy looks like he was mauled pretty bad."

Patrick grunted to himself. "Looks like it. But given that we don't have bears or mountain lions in the Presidio, it sure looks like a vampire attack. A pretty brutal one."

He forced himself to be all business despite the horrific sight. He was in charge here, and it was time to get everybody organized.

"Nicholas, I need you to scout the area for footprints, tire tracks, and anything else that could lead us to the perpetrator. Search the immediate surroundings to see if the killer could have lain in wait."

"Sure," Nicholas said and began following his instructions.

"Benjamin, you'll help Buffy transport the body to HQ, and assist Nicholas if he needs any help. But your first priority is to keep humans away from the scene. There are bound to be other joggers and people walking their dogs in the area."

"I've got it covered," Benjamin assured him.

"Anita," Patrick continued, "go back to SFPD. Keep your eyes and ears open for any reports of physical altercations, assaults, stalkers, and the like. You know what to look for. Anything out of the ordinary that could point to a vampire."

"Alright. I'll see what I can find."

Patrick acknowledged her reply with a nod, then ran a hand through his hair. "We need to find out who the victim is. That might give us a lead as to who did this."

"Patrick, I found this on him," Buffy said from her crouching position.

He bent down to her and took the small item from her hand. It was a hotel key card. He turned it over and read the name of the hotel. "Hotel Drisco."

"That's only two blocks from here," Benjamin said. "Pretty expensive place."

"I'll go there. They'll be able to scan the card to see which room it belongs to," Patrick announced. "Nicholas, I'll take the car." He glanced at Benjamin. "Can he ride back with you?"

"No problem, bro," Benjamin said. "We'll be a little while longer anyway before we can move the body."

With a nod, Patrick acknowledged Benjamin's words. "I'll see you all at HQ later."

Confident that everybody on his team knew what they were doing, he turned his back to them and headed to the car. An uncomfortable chill crawled up his spine, and he stopped for a moment, freezing in place, slowing his breath and his heartbeat to concentrate on the sounds around him. Was the killer still in the area?

2

"Dr. Doyle?"

Fallon Doyle looked up from the microscope she'd been hunched over in her lab at UCSF, a medical university in San Francisco, where she conducted research on epigenetics and aging.

In front of her stood one of the administrative assistants of the department. She'd met the woman a few times but couldn't remember her name. Her brain was too preoccupied with her research that she'd never made the effort to learn the names of department employees she didn't see on a daily basis.

"Oh, hi," she said quickly. "Is there something you need?"

The woman cast her an apologetic smile. "I'm sorry, but I just wanted to remind all your lab assistants that their union meeting has been moved to the large assembly room in the annex up the hill."

"Oh, I forgot about that." Fallon glanced at the clock on the wall. "When does it start?"

"In twenty minutes."

"Oh, okay." Fallon turned on her stool and rose. "Everybody, listen up! Your union meeting starts soon. You'd better leave now."

Her five lab assistants, two men, and three women, rose to their feet.

"We still have time," Clara protested, pointing at the pipettes and petri dishes on her workbench. "I can't just interrupt this experiment."

The administrative assistant cleared her voice. "I'm sorry, but the meeting is mandatory."

"Clara, I can continue your experiment," Fallon offered. "But you'd all better leave, or you won't make it up to the annex in time."

"Would you?" Clara replied with a hopeful smile.

While Fallon gave Clara a reassuring nod, there were low levels of annoyed grunts, but her five employees finally made their way to the door of the laboratory.

"I don't know why we even have to attend," Brian grumbled. "They never do anything for us anyway."

When the door finally shut behind them, silence and calm descended on the lab. This was a rare occurrence. For a moment, she closed her eyes. The only sound in the large space was the humming of the freezers and refrigeration units, which contained a multitude of tissue and blood samples. Since these samples were vital to her research, the freezers as well as the refrigerators were equipped with alarms that sent an automatic message to her cell phone should the power go out or the temperature change, so she could take measures to save the contents from spoiling.

For a few moments, she just stood there, enjoying the silence and peace she'd been missing for the last few weeks. Finally, she had the feeling that her life was returning to normal. She walked to Clara's workstation and looked at the petri dishes and the handwritten notes her assistant had made. Since she'd given Clara this assignment, it wasn't hard for Fallon to continue where the lab tech had left off.

Just as she was about to transfer one of the petri dishes to the slide beneath the microscope, the sound of a door closing made her snap her head in its direction.

Her heart stopped only to begin pounding uncontrollably, her breath catching in her throat, while her body activated her fight or flight mode. She felt her hand holding the petri dish tremble, and set it down, forcing herself to maintain her outer calm, when inside, she was twisted into knots, annoyance quickly transforming into anger.

"You haven't replied to any of my messages or gifts," Cameron said, his tone accusatory, his dark eyes pinning her as he approached. "It's not polite. Especially not when you treat your boyfriend like that."

"We broke up two months ago," she managed to squeeze out with the little breath still in her lungs.

"We didn't break up." The words were hard and cold, a dangerous undercurrent accompanying them.

This wasn't the man she'd dated for three months, not anymore. The fun, carefree Cameron Gallagher she'd met at a bar after her friend had canceled last minute, was nowhere in sight. He'd been charming and romantic, and he'd swept her off her feet, making her feel like the most important woman in the world, or at least in *his* world. Too late, she'd seen past the handsome facade of dark hair, dark eyes, a chiseled chin, the athletic torso, and the strong, muscular arms that had held her tightly. His tall body, which he knew how to use to every advantage had been such a turn-on. She'd ignored the warning signs until it was too late.

But now, she saw him for what he really was: an arrogant, possessive, egotistical jerk who thought he could control anyone he set his sights on. And he'd set his sights on her. After she'd realized two months earlier what kind of violence he was capable of, she'd broken it off with him.

Clearly, he wasn't accepting this fact.

"It's over, and you know it," Fallon said firmly.

"I say when it's over. And it's not over," he ground out. "You're mine."

At the possessive words, an ice-cold shiver ran down her spine into her tailbone, sending her heart rate spiking. She felt her Apple Watch vibrating, alerting her to her elevated heart rate, but she ignored it.

"I'm not yours. Leave, before I call campus security!"

He made a few more steps toward her. Only Clara's workbench was between them now. With his long arms and his upper body strength, he could easily reach for her and grab her. Inside, anger suddenly collided with fear, the two emotions battling for supremacy. She stepped back, fixing him with her eyes, worried that he would get physical and hurt her. Yes, she saw it in his eyes. He was capable of physical violence. He'd proven it two months earlier, though back then it hadn't been directed at her.

"Get away from me!"

"You need me."

"I don't need you. And I don't want you. It's over. It's been over since the moment you hurt Hank."

Cameron scoffed, though he didn't go as far as admitting that he'd hurt one of her lab assistants in a jealous rage. "Oh, please, Fallon, you're blowing things out of proportion. I'm just protecting what's mine."

She gritted her teeth. "Nobody owns me. Least of all you!"

"You will be mine, soon! Because you'll need me. You'll see. You're not leaving me a choice, you know that?" He grunted to himself, his face distorting into a mask of anger and rage. And ugliness. She'd never thought that a handsome face like Cameron's could turn into such an ugly mask.

"Soon, you'll beg me to let you come back. You'll need me because I'm the only one who can help you. Mark my words."

The threat hung there in the empty lab, and for a few seconds, only the sounds of their breaths filled the silence.

"Never," she vowed.

A bitter laugh was his answer. "Soon, my dear Fallon, soon, you'll be mine."

He turned on his heel and stalked out of the lab, the door slamming shut behind him. She was frozen in place, paralyzed by his words. This wasn't just an ex-boyfriend who was pissed off that she'd ended it. No, he'd turned into a stalker. For two months now, he'd bombarded her with gifts, text messages, and voicemails. He'd now graduated to coming to her place of work, all in an effort to make her change her mind about him. But her mind was made up. Cameron was neither good for her, nor treated her the way a man in love ought to treat a woman. He wanted her as his property. And she would never be any man's property. It was time to make him understand—once and for all—that it was over between them.

It was time to ask the police for help. Maybe Cameron would accept her decision when it came wrapped in a restraining order.

3

"Patrick, you need to come down to the med center and see this," Buffy said on the phone.

"Are you done with the autopsy already?"

Patrick rose to his feet and headed out the door from his office, his cell phone pressed to his ear.

"No, just the prelim stuff, but you need to see this."

"Alright, I'll be down in a minute."

Outside the office, he almost collided with Nicholas.

"Got a minute?" Nicholas asked.

"Walk with me. Buffy needs to see me."

Nicholas joined him walking to the elevator, which opened a moment later.

As they stepped inside, Patrick asked, "Did you find anything?"

"Yes. I found footprints and drag marks on the ground near the crime scene. It looks like whoever attacked that guy dragged him off the path so that he wouldn't immediately be found by other joggers. Guess the perp didn't count on anyone letting their dog run off leash."

"Makes sense," Patrick agreed. "Did you speak to the dog owner who found the body?"

"Yeah, older woman who lives in the neighborhood. Nothing suspicious about her. Her dog found the body. There were paw prints too, but I'm not sure they were from her dog. She's got one of those little yapping dogs, and the paw prints I found belong to a bigger animal. It's possible that there were other dogs in the vicinity, but their owners never investigated what their dog was sniffing."

"So, you think other dogs could have contaminated the crime scene?"

"Yeah, totally possible. Plus, there could have been strays too. Or coyotes." Nicholas shrugged.

"Did you take impressions of the prints that were salvageable?"

"Yeah, pawprints and footprints. Just in case."

"Good work," Patrick praised.

The elevator doors opened, and they exited on one of the lower levels that housed Scanguards' mini medical center.

"Did you find out who the victim is?" Nicholas asked.

"I was gonna call the team together to bring everybody up to speed just when Buffy called. But, yes, I got his identity. Malcolm Broadmore, 42 years old, from Cincinnati. He's here for the jewelry convention."

"You think theft might have been a motive?"

Patrick swiped his access card at the door to the morgue and pushed it open.

"That's for us to find out," he said as he and Nicholas entered.

Dressed in green hospital scrubs, Buffy stood over the body, which was laid out on a cold steel operating table, strong lights shining down on the naked corpse. By the looks of it, Buffy had started cleaning the dirt and blood off the body to reveal all wounds.

"Hey, guys," Buffy said, letting a breath escape slowly through her nostrils.

"So, what did you want to show me?" Patrick asked.

Buffy grimaced. "Well, it's not so much what I want to show you but what I *can't* show you."

Surprised at her cryptic remark, Patrick followed Buffy's outstretched hand pointing to the victim's chest cavity.

Patrick leaned in and noticed that Buffy had removed a lot of the blood and debris from the open wound and had used a rib stretcher to allow her to widen the opening for better access. He stared into the chest cavity. The stench of death wrapped around him, and for once, he wished that he didn't have the superior sense of smell that all vampires and vampire hybrids were gifted with. However, there was nothing he could do about that, so he tried to ignore it, and instead, focused his eyes on the exposed organs. A few seconds later, he reared back, stunned.

"Oh my God."

"What?" Nicholas asked, and squeezed past him to look into the dead man's chest cavity. "Oh fuck! Somebody cut his heart out?"

Buffy instantly shook her head. "Not cut. The edges of the large blood vessels leading to and from the heart are jagged. It wasn't cut out. It was ripped out. With bare hands." She paused for a moment. "Or claws."

"And the heart? Was it in there?" Patrick asked, even though he already guessed the answer.

"No."

"It wasn't near the body either," Nicholas now added, "or I would have found it when I took impressions of the footprints."

"Fuck!" Patrick cursed. He knew what this meant. "Only a vampire has the strength to rip somebody's heart out with his bare hands."

He glanced at Nicholas, who instantly lifted one hand. "We all know that."

"Thanks to your father."

"Huh?" Buffy asked. "Nicholas's father? Zane?"

Nicholas nodded. "He once ripped a rapist's beating heart out."

Then he looked at Patrick. "But my father had nothing to do with this."

Patrick lifted his hands in a show of surrender. "Hey, I know that. What I'm trying to say is that the killer has to be a vampire. If a human had done this, he would have had to use a knife or a scalpel to cut out the heart."

"But why take the heart with him?" Buffy asked. "It's not like he could eat it. Maybe suck the blood out of it, yes."

"Could be a fetish," Patrick mused. "Could it be that the heart was torn out later, I mean once the guy was already dead? Is it possible that a coyote could have eaten the heart?"

At least that theory would suggest a less gruesome murder, not that it changed the outcome: a man was dead.

"Not sure yet. I'll have to examine all the claw marks and other injuries on the body. I've also found hair and other tissue, which I still have to test to see whether it belongs to the victim or the killer. That'll take a while."

Patrick nodded. "Okay, we won't take up more of your time. Call me when you have news."

Buffy nodded. Patrick and Nicholas left the morgue.

"What now?" Nicholas asked.

Patrick contemplated his answer. He was the boss right now. He was supposed to have all the answers, yet he didn't. Finding a killer who seemingly had no relationship to the victim was one of the most difficult crimes to solve.

"Let's get some people out there to check whether there are any cameras in the area, both traffic cams and private ones. There are a lot of mansions on the street leading to the entrance of the park. Most of them will have outside security cameras. If we're lucky, they captured somebody following our victim."

"But the cameras don't capture a vampire's aura."

"I know. But we can use facial recognition to see if it's anybody in our vampire database."

"That's a long shot."

Patrick grimaced. "I know. But that's all we've got right now."

Somewhere out there, a murderous vampire was roaming the city, perhaps already looking for his next victim. And all they had was the victim's name and a missing heart. Well, to be precise: they didn't *have* the heart.

4

Fallon wanted to scream. She'd spent the better part of the afternoon at the police station closest to her apartment in Laurel Heights, trying to get somebody to listen to her, and had been handed from one police officer to the next, each one giving her a different reason as to why she couldn't get a restraining order against Cameron. No wonder most women didn't bother going to the police. They weren't helpful at all. She'd been naïve thinking that they would listen to her complaint and immediately recognize that Cameron Gallagher was a danger to her. Instead, they treated her like a hysterical woman who was seeking attention. As if she was making this up!

"You're saying your ex-boyfriend has never hit you?" the young male police officer asked for the second time, his forehead furrowed.

"As I said before," she emphasized, forcing herself not to raise her voice, "so far, he hasn't hurt me. But he threatened me."

"What were his threats exactly?"

How should she describe Cameron's threats? He'd been vague, but that hadn't diminished the fear she'd felt when he'd lashed the cold words at her: that she was his. His what? His slave? His property? His to do with what he wanted? In that moment, she'd seen that he was capable of anything. It was a gut feeling. But if she said that to the police officer, he'd think she was overreacting.

"He said that I would regret leaving him, and that he would punish me for doing so." Well, those weren't his exact words, but the intent was there.

"And you have witnesses that can confirm those, uhm, threats?" The last word sounded as if he'd put quotation marks around it, making it sound just as doubtful as his facial expression underlined.

Fallon cleared her throat. "No, not exactly. He came to my lab at UCSF when everybody else was at a meeting. I was alone when he threatened me. He must have waited until everyone was gone so that he could catch me alone."

"Hmm." The police officer hesitated.

She knew that look. He was trying to find an excuse to palm her off on somebody else, or to get rid of her altogether so he wouldn't be stuck with the paperwork.

"I'm telling you: Cameron is dangerous. I don't feel safe. He knows where I work, where I live. He can get to me anytime he wants to."

"I understand, Ms. Doyle—"

"Dr. Doyle," she interrupted him. "So, what else do I need to do to get a restraining order? I mean, isn't that what it's for? To protect women like me from violent ex-boyfriends?"

The young officer swallowed hard, his Adam's apple bobbing in his throat. "Well, in theory. If you had any proof of his violence, then we could certainly do something."

Fallon gritted her teeth. "Damn it, he's stalking me! Does he have to hurt me first before the police will do something to keep me safe?"

"Please calm down, Dr. Doyle."

"Calm down?" she scoffed. Nobody had ever calmed down just because somebody had told them to calm down. On the contrary, it got her even more agitated. "I'm scared. For the last two months this man has stalked me, sent me messages, bombarded me with phone calls at all hours of the day and night, and sent me unwanted gifts. I told him it was over, but he wouldn't give up. He's a stalker."

"Dr. Doyle, I know this is—"

"Officer Friedman, why don't I take over here?" A woman dressed in civilian clothes appeared next to the police officer and put a hand on the man's arm.

"Are you sure, detective?" Officer Friedman asked with a quizzical look on his face as he stared at the badge that hung on a lanyard around the detective's neck.

"Yes. I've been assigned to assist with any stalker cases." She looked directly at Fallon for a moment, before adding, "And this looks like it fits the criteria."

"Be my guest, detective." Officer Friedman nodded and turned away, clearly relieved.

Fallon stared at the pretty blonde woman who was taller than her, but around her age. She seemed out of place in the police station, dressed too casually for a detective, yet exuding an authority that inspired instant confidence in her abilities as a cop. There was a kind smile on her lips and warmth in her eyes.

"Dr. Doyle? I'm Detective Anita Diaz-Montgomery. I was alerted that you're dealing with a stalker. I've come from police headquarters to see if I can help you. I'm sorry that you've been getting the runaround here, but luckily, one of the officers here sent me a message."

Was this woman serious? A detective was getting involved in issuing a restraining order, when this was police grunt work at best?

"Detective? Uhm, will you be able to help me get a restraining order against my ex-boyfriend?"

"Why don't we go into one of the interview rooms, so we can talk without being disturbed?" She glanced around, indicating the busy station where everybody talked over each other, and the noise level increased by the minute.

Fallon hesitated. Was this another attempt at making her understand that her experience with Cameron didn't warrant a restraining order? That she was overreacting? That she was reading too much into her confrontation with her ex?

Detective Diaz-Montgomery seemed to sense her hesitation and put her hand on Fallon's forearm. There was something comforting in the gentle touch.

"If you feel threatened by your ex, I will make sure that you're safe. Whether that's by having the court grant you a restraining order, or by getting you protection via other means. I promise you that."

For the first time in hours, Fallon felt that somebody was really listening to her concerns and was taking them seriously. Was it because this was a woman? Did she know firsthand that verbal threats could instill just as much fear in a woman as physical violence? Had she seen the consequences of the police's inaction in other cases? Had she seen women getting hurt because nobody believed them? It didn't matter why this detective was willing to help her. It only mattered that she did.

"Thank you, detective. I appreciate your help."

5

Patrick downed the blood in one big gulp and set the glass down on the bar, nodding at the vampire bartender who was on duty in the V Lounge, the large room on the ground floor of Scanguards HQ, where vampires and vampire hybrids could relax in between their shifts and drink blood. Like in a regular pub, there was a multitude of taps—though they dispensed blood sorted by blood group rather than beer. This was a service free of charge for any employee or visiting vampire to discourage them from drinking blood directly from humans.

Of course, not everybody partook of the free blood. All vampires blood-bonded to a human never touched the stuff, because they could only drink from their blood-bonded mate. All other blood would make them sick and eventually kill them. And then there were those vampires who had never gotten used to the bottled blood, and preferred to drink directly from the source—from a living, breathing human.

"Another one, Todd," Patrick said, pointing to the empty glass.

"Stressed?" Todd asked with an understanding glance.

"Do I look it?" he deflected.

He'd been burning the candle at both ends, working double shifts since his parents had left for their dream vacation. At most, he got three or four hours of sleep in a twenty-four-hour period. To make up for the lack of sleep, he drank more blood than usual, feeding up to three times daily, when normally, he only needed one meal a day.

Todd shrugged while taking back the empty glass. "Just figured with you running the show here, you must be exhausted."

Before Patrick could answer, he heard somebody approaching.

"There you are," Anita said. "I was looking for you."

Patrick turned to her. "Hey, Anita. Any news?"

"Didn't mean to interrupt your dinner," Anita said, tipping her chin toward the bar, where Todd was filling the glass.

For a human, Anita wasn't squeamish about blood at all. There were two reasons for it: she was a police officer who'd seen her fair share of blood at crime scenes, and she was blood-bonded to his friend Cooper, a vampire hybrid, which meant that Cooper was drinking her blood at least once a day. At that thought, Patrick felt a twitch of envy travel up from his belly. The idea of feeding from a woman he loved was something he'd never experienced, although he'd bitten women before. He could only imagine the high Cooper experienced from this intimate act, drinking from his soulmate while making love to her.

"You're not interrupting." He approached Anita. "Did you get my update on what Buffy found during the autopsy?"

"You mean what she *didn't* find? Yeah, got your message. But it's not about that. At least not directly. A case just dropped in my lap."

Patrick listened up. "And you think it might be connected to the murder in the Presidio?"

"It's possible."

"A physical assault?"

Anita shook her head. "No, a stalker."

Somewhat disappointed, Patrick said, "Give me the gist of it."

"This female doctor, Fallon Doyle, came to the station today to ask for a restraining order against her ex-boyfriend. He won't leave her in peace. He's threatening her."

"Verbally?" Patrick interrupted.

"Yes, but I get the feeling that he's capable of violence. She doesn't feel safe."

"Well, that alone isn't really much. Any guy who got dumped might try to get her back. That in itself doesn't mean that he'll get violent."

"True, but the things he said to her..." Anita shook her head. "You know how vampires get when they fall for a woman?"

"Meaning?"

Anita rolled her eyes. "They get all possessive and territorial. I got that same vibe when I talked to Fallon. He said to her that she's *his*. No human talks like that."

"You think he's not human?"

"Not the way he's talking."

"Did you ask her the right questions to find out whether she's seen him outside during daylight hours?"

"Yes, and he was outside at daylight with her—"

"Then he can't be a vampire."

"He can still be a hybrid like you," Anita countered.

She was right. But there wasn't much to this case. Just a verbal threat. No violence—yet.

Patrick sighed. "I really don't see that this case rises to the level where we should get involved. If we had to protect every woman whose ex-boyfriend is still obsessed with her, we'd never be able to do the work we're hired for."

"Scanguards' mission is to protect the innocent," Anita stated.

Patrick ran a hand through his thick dark hair. "And that's what we're doing. But with everything that's going on, the jewelers' convention, and the murder in the Presidio, I don't see how we can spare somebody to protect this doctor. I'm sorry."

Anita braced her hands on her hips. "Then maybe you should tell her that yourself. Because I don't have the heart to tell this woman that we don't believe that her ex is capable of hurting her. I don't wanna get a call in a few days that she's been hurt, and have to regret that I didn't fight harder to get her the protection she needs."

"Damn it, Anita! Maybe you can talk Cooper into anything you want him to do, 'cause he's clearly pussy-whipped, but I've got a company to run. I have to use our resources where they have the most impact, and right now, that means I have to find the Presidio killer before he strikes again. Because I don't wanna get another call about a second body with the heart ripped out."

Anita shot him an annoyed look. "You're just as stubborn as your father! Though at least he has the guts to take risks. Clearly, at your young age, you haven't gained enough experience yet to see when to take a risk."

Patrick narrowed his eyes. He recognized what Anita was doing. And he didn't like it one bit. "You're trying to manipulate me. Let me tell you something: it won't work."

6

"He said no?"

Fallon's heart sank. She was out of options. Tears welled up in her eyes as she looked at Anita. During their talk at the station, the blonde detective had asked her to call her by her first name, and she'd felt a connection to her, knowing they could become instant friends if the circumstances were different.

"What am I gonna do now? I'm scared."

"I have one last idea." Anita took a deep breath. "You'll have to talk to him yourself to get him to take your case."

Confusion spread in Fallon's chest. "But you just said he won't talk to me."

"He will if he has no other choice," Anita said cryptically. "We can still catch him."

She felt Anita's hand on her arm and allowed her to usher her to the door leading into the hallway, leaving the luxurious lounge, where a buffet of food and drinks of all sorts invited the guests, behind. It looked like the lounge of an exclusive hotel, or the first-class lounge of an airline—not that she'd ever flown first class.

In the hallway, Anita stopped, forcing Fallon to stop too. Anita turned to her and lowered her voice.

"He should be coming out of that door any moment now," Anita whispered. "Let's just pretend that we're still discussing things, so that it doesn't look like we're waiting for him."

Fallon felt odd about this situation. She didn't like to trick people, and had she not felt that desperate to get protection against Cameron, she would have never taken part in what Anita was suggesting now. But she was desperate. She was afraid of Cameron, and the thought that she'd once believed that their relationship was a promising one, made her sick to her stomach. In the three months that she'd dated him, she'd been carefree and happy. They'd had fun together, and the sex had been hot. She could admit that to herself, although now she shuddered at the thought of Cameron ever touching her again. Disgust rose in her. No, she would never again allow a man like Cameron to touch her.

"Just act natural," Anita said, pulling her out of her thoughts.

"Am I causing trouble for you?" Fallon asked. "I mean, he's already told you that he won't take my case. Why would he change his mind?"

"Because it's harder to say no directly to a person who needs help rather than an intermediary like me. Trust me."

Before she could say anything else, the door Anita had indicated opened, and a young man stepped out. The door fell shut behind him.

This couldn't be Patrick Woodford, the boss of Scanguards. For starters, he didn't look older than twenty-five, and he was far too handsome—with model-like looks to be exact—to be running a large company like this. Anita hadn't told her much on the drive over here, only that this was one of the best security companies in the US, and that her husband was a bodyguard here. In addition, Anita had divulged that Scanguards had a large contract with the

City of San Francisco acting as an additional law enforcement organization.

"Patrick," Anita said. "I was just showing Dr. Doyle out."

Fallon knew that her words were simply meant for Patrick Woodford to know who she was, and for Fallon to be introduced to him. Stunned that this man was truly the Scanguards boss who'd declined to take her case, she stood there, paralyzed. Her eyes were the only parts of her body moving—yes, those, and her thundering heart.

Patrick wasn't just romance-novel tall, dark, and handsome—and definitely her type—no, there was something else about him. There was a poise in him, a self-assurance, a presence that she was surprised to see in a man so young. He was dressed in dark pants and a casual shirt that didn't hide his muscular torso. Somehow, she'd expected the Scanguards boss to wear a suit and tie to project the authority of his position when his age was definitely not lending him that attribute. But to be honest, she couldn't imagine him in a suit and tie. There was something about him that didn't seem to belong in a suit. He had an untamed, rugged look about him, something that seemed to be more at home in the dark streets of an urban jungle. It was an odd thought, but she couldn't shake it. Mesmerized, she let her eyes roam, taking in every inch of this man. And with every inch, her heart beat faster and louder, her pulse drumming beneath her skin, making it prickle with anticipation.

When she heard the clearing of a throat, yet Patrick hadn't moved or spoken, she realized that Anita had been the one bridging the silence between them. How long exactly had she been staring at him?

"You're Dr. Fallon Doyle?" Patrick asked. His voice carried a surprised undertone.

She noticed something else now. He was running his gaze over her in much the same fashion she'd done before. Was he assessing her now? Wondering if she was worth being protected from her ex-boyfriend?

This was the opportunity Anita had spoken of. This was her chance to change his mind. And if she had to use her feminine wiles to achieve that feat, she wouldn't lose sleep over it. Or maybe she would, because just looking at this man, at his virility, his intensity, she wanted him to be the main character in her dreams, helping her chase away her fears, making her forget the last few months entirely. He would keep her safe, if only she could convince him that the danger she faced was real.

"Mr. Woodford," Fallon started. "Anita said you can't take my case, because you're short-staffed." She took a step closer to him, while he still stood there, not having moved an inch.

"Mr. Woodford is my father. Please call me Patrick," he said to her surprise.

He didn't smile, didn't move, made no attempt at extending his hand, yet his voice was an invitation to something. She just didn't know to what.

"Patrick," she said, letting his name roll over her tongue. "I wish you would reconsider. I don't feel safe anymore. If I could move away from San Francisco to get away from him, I would. But I just received a large NIH grant, and I can't leave. My research…"

She looked down at her feet, feeling unshed tears brim in her eyes. She'd worked too hard and too long to get this far. And she wouldn't allow a man to destroy all of this. But she had to pull herself together. No man liked a crying woman. She had to be stronger than that. She swallowed away her tears and marshaled all her strength.

When she looked up again, she noticed that Patrick was now standing only two feet away from her. She hadn't heard or felt him approach. But now she did. It was as if a breeze of a warm Santa Ana wind was sweeping into the corridor, heating the air around them.

"I'm sorry, I'm not normally someone prone to tears, but I'm at my wit's end. I'm afraid of what Cameron will do next."

Patrick's hand was suddenly on her forearm. "Why don't we sit down and talk?" He motioned to the door of the empty lounge that she'd just exited with Anita.

Did this mean that he would help her, or would he let her down softly without any witnesses to her humiliation and disappointment?

"Anita, thanks, I'll take it from here," Patrick said, dismissing Anita without turning his head.

7

Against his better judgment, Patrick ushered Fallon into the H Lounge, the lounge where Scanguards' human employees and guests could help themselves to free refreshments and snacks. He knew what he was doing had nothing to do with his responsibilities toward Scanguards, the city, or its inhabitants, and everything to do with his libido.

Fuck!

One glance at Fallon, and he could understand why any man who'd dated her would have serious trouble letting go of her. He was drawn to her like a moth to the light. Even before she'd uttered a single word, he'd known that her voice would sink deep into him, heating his blood, sending it racing through his veins. She was beautiful with her long black hair, grey eyes, and red lips. She looked a little flushed, but he liked that look. It made him imagine her lying in bed, satin sheets draped around her naked body, breathing hard, and feeling spent after an afternoon of lovemaking.

Damn! His cock was hijacking his mind, taking it for a joyride. And he stood there, unable and unwilling to grab the steering wheel and right the course.

He wasn't one to be charmed by a pretty face so easily. Sure, he got laid whenever he wanted to, but he'd always kept his personal and his business lives separate, never slept with anyone employed by Scanguards, nor with any client. And though Fallon Doyle wasn't a client, at least not yet, he knew he had to treat her like one, which meant one thing: hands off. Apparently, his cock wasn't getting the memo. Because it was his cock that had initiated this scenario. He'd been ready to tell Fallon that he was sorry, but that he didn't have the staff to take on her case, but his cock had been faster, inserting itself into the conversation without shame in the hopes of being rewarded by offering to help her with her problem. Rewarded with sex.

Not only was this unethical from a business standpoint, but also unfair to the woman now sitting across from him on one of the big sofas in the H Lounge. The deserted H Lounge, he noticed immediately. Things couldn't get any worse: if he followed his base instinct, there would be nobody to stop him, nobody to remind him of the manners his parents had instilled in him.

All that left him with was to force himself to concentrate on business, and not on a tumble in the sheets with the tempting woman who was seeking his help.

"So, uhm," he started, clearing his throat, trying to shake off the lust that was gripping him like a fisherman's net ensnared an unsuspecting dolphin. "Why don't you tell me what's been happening with your ex-boyfriend?"

"Cameron and I were dating for only three months, when I broke up with him. But for the last two months, he's been pestering me, constantly leaving messages, sending gifts, flowers, in the hopes that we'll get back together. But it's over. I made it clear to him. At first, I thought, he'd finally leave me alone, but today he came to my lab at UCSF. He's trying to intimidate me so I'll take him back."

"But you're not interested in him anymore?"

She shook her head. "He's not the man I thought he was."

"What do you mean by that?"

She hesitated for a moment. "He's jealous and possessive. He treats me like his property. But I'm not anybody's property."

Patrick could hear her pulse quickening, and he noticed her breathing become irregular. She was agitated. "Fallon... uhm, may I call you Fallon?"

"Yes, of course."

"Why did you break up with him?"

"As I told you, he's jealous and possessive."

"I understand. But there must have been something specific that made you break up with him. Did you have a fight with him? Was he violent toward you? Did he hit you?"

Fallon shook her head. "No, he didn't hit me. And he wasn't violent, not toward me. He's the kind of guy who uses words to make someone afraid of him."

"Are you saying he was emotionally abusive?" When she nodded, he remembered what else she'd said. "You said he wasn't violent toward *you*. Are you saying he was violent toward somebody else?"

Again, there was a slight hesitation in her before she answered, "I believe so, though he didn't admit it outright."

"Tell me what happened."

"It was two months ago. I got this big NIH grant for my research, and my lab assistants and I were really happy about it. So, we all went out for drinks after work. I'd told Cameron about the grant, and I might have mentioned that my coworkers and I would go for a quick drink. He showed up at the bar. We were just celebrating, you know." She looked straight at him, her eyes meeting his, looking for understanding. "But Hank, one of my lab assistants, he'd had too much to drink, and he was so relieved that we got the grant, because that meant he could keep his position. You know, without the grant I would have had to let him, and a couple of the others, go."

Patrick nodded. "I understand. So, what happened?"

"Hank hugged me, thanking me. It was very innocent, believe me. He's a tactile person. He hugs everybody. Sure, maybe that's not appropriate coming from a coworker, but that's just the person he is. And it's never bothered anyone at the lab. Besides, he's not interested in me that way. I'm his meal ticket. It would be stupid if he made a pass at me when I can easily fire him, right?"

Patrick wondered how she could be sure that Hank wasn't interested in her. Did she not realize her own appeal? What man with a pulse could resist such a temptation? Fallon exuded sexual energy like it was going out of style. Everything about her was sensual: the way she lifted her lids, her long lashes almost crashing against her eyebrows, the way she moistened her lips every so often while speaking, the way her chest heaved, pressing her nipples against her tight blue turtleneck sweater. Even though she showed virtually no skin—like so many San Franciscans during the wet winter months—her body invited all kinds of fantasies that filled his head. Fantasies about undressing her slowly and exploring her body. Fantasies about kissing every inch of her glorious body.

When he suddenly realized that there was silence between them, he forced the thoughts out of his mind.

"So, he hugged you. What happened then?"

"Cameron showed up right then. He saw it. And I've never seen so much hate and fury in somebody's eyes than when he stared at Hank." Fallon swallowed hard. "Cameron made me leave early. He said he'd made a dinner reservation for us, and claimed he'd told me, which I'm absolutely sure he didn't—just so he could get me away from my coworkers."

"And you went to dinner? Did Cameron say anything about the incident?"

"No, he didn't. He was just very intense that night. Like he was trying to suppress something. I can't explain it. When I went to work the next day, Hank called in sick. I didn't think much of it right then, because I thought maybe he had a hangover. But then he didn't come in the next two days either, and on the following day, when I was the only one left in the lab, working late, he showed up to pick up his personal items, and handed me his resignation." Fallon closed her eyes for a moment, before continuing, "He looked like he'd been beaten to within an inch of his life."

Patrick wanted to curse. A man who was so jealous and possessive that he would beat anyone coming near his girlfriend was bad news. Anita's gut had been right. Cameron Gallagher was trouble. "Did Hank tell you who'd beaten him up?"

To his surprise, Fallon shook her head. "He claimed he'd fallen down the stairs. But…" Her voice trembled now. "I could see the fear in his eyes. He lied to me, probably too scared that I might tell Cameron." Her breath hitched. "Hank was beaten up because of me. I couldn't have that on my conscience."

"Go back a moment. Did Cameron even have an opportunity to hurt Hank?"

"What do you mean?"

"After your dinner, did you go back to his place or to yours to spend the night together?"

"He brought me home, and…" She hesitated. "We had sex. But this time, he didn't stay the night, which was unusual."

"Does that mean he normally stayed the night?"

"Yes. But he said he had an early meeting, so he left."

"Okay. So, after Hank resigned, did you talk to Cameron about Hank's injuries?"

"Yes, of course. I mean, I couldn't just let this pass. He hurt somebody because of his jealousy. But when I asked him point-blank if he beat up Hank, he kind of denied it and admitted it at the same time."

Confused, Patrick asked, "What exactly did he say?"

For a moment, Fallon seemed to contemplate her next words. "He said: you should be glad that he resigned. Better for both of you." She shook her head, tears brimming in her eyes. "When I asked him what he meant by that, he said: nobody touches what's mine."

No human talked like that. But he knew creatures who did: vampires and vampire hybrids. Their possessive streak was legendary when they found their mate. They didn't like to share the object of their affection. However, in Cameron's case, Patrick wasn't sure whether it was affection or just plain obsession that drove him.

"And when Cameron came to my lab today, he said it again. He said that I was his, and that I would need him, and come crawling back to him. And the way he said it, I could feel that he was prepared to do anything to have me back. Including using violence." She sniffled. "I'm scared that he might abduct me and lock me up so he can do whatever he wants with me."

Patrick exhaled. There was nothing concrete that proved that Cameron had beaten the lab assistant, though, given the circumstances, it was definitely possible. And Cameron's words could send fear into any woman, certainly into a woman like Fallon, who evidently liked her independence and was dedicated to her job.

"Was that the only reason why you left him?"

"The only reason? Isn't that enough?"

Fallon felt disappointment spread inside her and couldn't stop it from seeping into her voice. Did Patrick not believe her? Did he think that leaving a man who was verbally abusive and trying to control her wasn't a valid reason? Was he taking Cameron's side? Was she wrong about this man too? Just like she'd been wrong when she'd thought Cameron was a good man?

"I'm sorry, I didn't phrase that right. What I mean is, were there any other red flags that made you want to break up with him? Before that incident?"

She looked at him intently, trying to find the truth in his green eyes. Was it understanding she saw shimmering in those deep pools that looked like she could get lost in them? For a few seconds, there was silence between them, and she felt calmer.

"Yes. Little things. He always wanted to know where I was, what I was doing. Whenever I got a text message or a phone call, he wanted to know who it was from and what it was about." She felt an icy shiver run down her spine at the thought of how he'd reacted each time she'd told him that she couldn't see him because of work. He'd always questioned her. His constant suspicion as to whether work was truly the reason why she couldn't see him as often as he wanted to or whether she was hiding something from him had worn her patience thin.

"I felt as if I was being controlled. As if I had to ask permission to talk to other people."

"Were you exclusive? I mean, you and Cameron had sex. Were you going on other dates?"

His remark about sex caught her off guard. Yes, they'd have sex. But it wasn't something she wanted to elaborate on. She'd told Anita, but then, Anita was a woman and a police officer. Patrick was a man, a man she felt attracted to, although she shouldn't even be able to think of any man right now, no matter how handsome and friendly he was. Cameron had been friendly too. And handsome. And yes, the sex had been good. Maybe that was the reason she'd overlooked his other faults, his jealousy, his possessiveness. Because she'd interpreted them as affection, as desire. And what woman didn't want to feel desired?

She pushed the thoughts aside, realizing that Patrick was still waiting for an answer to his question. "Other dates? No, of course not. I barely have time to date one guy."

"So, there was no reason for Cameron to get jealous?"

"No. Absolutely not." And that was the truth. While they were dating, she'd never flirted with anyone. Never so much as looked at another man.

"Did you make it clear to him why you broke up with him?"

"Yes, I told him that I believed that he hurt Hank, and that I'm sick of his jealous and controlling behavior."

"So, there's no chance for him to think that you might change your mind and come back to him?"

"None." She'd made that clear to him several times, at first by replying to his voicemails and text messages, then by ignoring him, in the hope that he would finally stop contacting her. But he hadn't stopped, as if he wasn't even listening, as if he was living in a different reality.

"I want him out of my life. Please, help me."

Patrick met her gaze, and there was understanding in his eyes. "Alright. I'll look into him to see whether I can make him understand that he needs to leave you alone."

"Thank you."

"Write down how I can reach you. I also need Cameron's details, full name, contact info, and the like, same for Hank. I want to talk to him too. Maybe I can convince him to tell me what really happened."

Patrick rose and walked to a sideboard. She followed his movements, her eyes darting to his backside, his muscled butt shifting beneath his well-fitting black pants. There was something so confident and self-assured in his walk that drew her to him. He snatched a notepad and a pen from the sideboard and turned back to her.

She quickly averted her eyes, pretending to admire the floral arrangement on the coffee table in front of her. Patrick handed her the pen and paper before he sat down again—this time not on the armchair opposite but next to her on the sofa. Close enough for her to feel his heat, and smell the faint scent of his shampoo or maybe the body lotion he used. Her hand trembled at first when she started to write down the information that Patrick had requested.

When she was done, she handed it back to him, while he was reaching for the pad at the same time. Their fingers touched for a brief second, making her gasp involuntarily and jerk back quickly. Her eyes shot to Patrick's face, and their gazes met.

"I didn't mean to..." she stuttered, embarrassed about her reaction to his touch.

"My apologies, Fallon. I didn't mean to startle you." His voice was calm and collected, even soft as if he was speaking to a frightened child. "I know that the emotional turmoil you're experiencing is making you jumpy. It's normal. I just want you to know that you're safe here."

She nodded quickly, casting her eyes to her hands that now rested in her lap. He'd interpreted her reaction incorrectly, but she wouldn't correct him. It was better that he didn't know that the reason for her reaction was the jolt of pleasure that his touch had caused. Because a reaction like this would only cause more trouble, more confusion. And she had no intention of jumping from the frying pan into the fire. The risk of landing in another relationship that ended badly was just too great, because men who were too handsome and sexy for their own good, almost always came with a fatal flaw.

She was sure that beneath Patrick's flawless exterior lay personality traits that she didn't like either. And just like Cameron's flaws had bubbled to the surface, eventually Patrick's would emerge too. Nobody was as perfect on the inside as on the outside. There was always a catch.

8

Back in his office, Patrick replayed his conversation with Fallon in his mind. From everything she'd told him, he realized that if he followed the desire of the vampire inside him, it would lead to nothing but problems.

Fallon wasn't a woman to readily accept a man she'd only just met, a man she knew nothing about. She was more careful, more contemplative, weighing up the pros and cons of a relationship. Hell, judging by the bad experience she was going through with Cameron, he doubted that she'd be ready to date anyone for a long time. And why wouldn't she take a break from men after having to deal with Cameron's jealousness and possessiveness? It was smart.

Unfortunately, this meant he couldn't act on his desire to kiss her. Hell, he shouldn't even have that desire. He prided himself in being more restrained than his fellow vampires when it came to women, and in the past two years, he'd only had the occasional one-night stand. He hadn't really felt the need to be in a relationship. He wasn't looking for a mate yet, despite having celebrated his 35th birthday not too long ago. He was happy with the way things were.

He had a great relationship with his parents and siblings, and he loved his job and his colleagues. Life was pretty perfect.

Fuck! He wished he'd never laid eyes on Fallon, at least then he wouldn't know what he was missing: a woman who stirred up all kinds of new feelings in him. None of which she'd be willing and able to reciprocate, not in the vulnerable state she was in. He couldn't take advantage of her like that, no matter how much he desired her. The best thing was to lock that part of himself away, before he did something that he would regret later. He had to be patient. First, he needed to remove Cameron from the equation, then he had to let Fallon heal. Only then could he show her that he was interested in her.

Determined to work on the first step, he started his research into Cameron Gallagher. Luckily, because of Scanguards' contacts with the San Francisco Police Chief and the California governor, he had access to all kinds of databases to help him with background checks. He pulled up Cameron's driver's license from the California DMV. It had expired a few months earlier. The man staring back at him from the picture was good-looking, he could admit that. Cameron was over six feet tall, with dark brown hair and brown eyes, a stubble beard, and a cleft in his chin.

So, this was Fallon's type? Well, at least that meant she probably didn't find him unattractive either, after all, Patrick too was tall, had dark, almost black hair, and had inherited his parents' good looks, and his mother's green eyes. Of course, that would also mean that Fallon might be reminded of Cameron every time she looked at him. That would be a turnoff. Maybe she'd choose a blond surfer dude as her next boyfriend, just so she wouldn't be reminded of her ex.

When he looked into Cameron Gallagher's social media presence, he found several persons by that name, three of them women, since the name was unisex. The two men who had social media pages weren't the right age and race. According to his driver's license, Cameron was thirty-eight years old and white. He checked several other social media sites, but the search was a bust.

This wasn't entirely unusual, particularly if his assumption was correct that Cameron was a vampire or a vampire hybrid. Nobody in his extended Scanguards family had a social media presence. It wasn't advisable for a vampire to leave a digital footprint where photos would eventually confirm that none of them aged.

Since Fallon hadn't written down where Cameron worked, Patrick made a note to have Thomas and Eddie, Scanguards' resident IT geniuses, hack into the IRS and the Social Security Administration to find out more. However, before he could dig into more about Cameron, his phone rang. He recognized the internal number and picked up.

"Hey, Buffy. What's up?"

"I'm done with the preliminaries. Can you come down? Benjamin and Nicholas are already here, and I don't want to have to say everything twice."

"I'm on my way."

It took him less than five minutes to reach the autopsy room, where his colleagues were waiting for him. It was cold in the room to preserve the dead body for as long as possible before decomposition set in. The door closed behind him, and he nodded at Benjamin and Nicholas, then gave Buffy an expectant look.

"I'm still waiting for some tests, but I've found something that leads me to believe that it wasn't a vampire who attacked our vic."

Patrick's forehead furrowed. "Not a vampire? But the heart—you said yourself that it wasn't cut out with a knife. It was ripped out."

"And I stand by that," Buffy said calmly. "Somebody or something ripped his heart out. No doubt about that. But I found something else." She motioned him and his colleagues to step closer, and lifted the dead man's arm. "You see these defensive wounds?"

"Yeah. He fought his attacker," Patrick said with a shrug.

"He did. I swabbed the wounds as well as his fingernails. Guess what I found?" It was only a rhetorical question, since she continued immediately, "Strands of hair. Short, coarse black hair. I looked at it under the microscope and compared it to other hair samples in our database. The hairs aren't human or vampire."

Patrick pinned her with his gaze. "What are you saying?"

"He fought with an animal."

"No, that can't be," Patrick said, shaking his head. "You can't tell me that an animal attacks a human with such precision that it rips only the heart out and leaves all other organs intact."

"I'm with Patrick," Nicholas said. "Could it be that a wild animal came upon the dead body and that's how the wounds got contaminated with animal hair?"

Buffy rolled her eyes and huffed. Clearly, she didn't like her findings being questioned.

"If I'd only found hairs in the defensive wounds and the open chest wound, I'd be inclined to agree with you. But hair doesn't get stuck deep beneath the fingernails, unless the victim gripped his attacker. Ergo, our vic was alive when he came in contact with the animal."

Patrick stood there, stunned and silent for a moment, just like Benjamin and Nicholas. They exchanged surprised looks. "And you're sure it's animal hair?"

"Absolutely."

"Any chance you can narrow it down to a specific animal?"

"Not yet. I'm still going through samples, but my best guess at the moment is that it's either a coyote or a mountain lion. Those are really the only kinds of wild animals in San Francisco."

"A mountain lion? In the city?" Benjamin asked.

"A couple of them were spotted in Golden Gate Park last month," Buffy claimed. "And there are plenty of coyotes in the city. Buena Vista Park has a den somewhere. That's why people avoid walking their dogs there after sundown. But as I said, I haven't found a match to a specific species yet. It could also be a rabid dog."

Slowly, Patrick nodded. "Good work, Buffy." Then he turned to his two colleagues. "That complicates our investigation. Assuming that a wild animal doesn't just go for the heart without chowing down on anything else, there's the possibility that somebody attacked our victim and then made it look like an animal attack."

Buffy shrugged. "If that's what you wanna go with."

"I'm sorry, I don't mean to discount your findings, Buffy, you're doing an exceptional job," Patrick said putting his hand on her forearm. "But if you're right, this whole thing is going to be so much harder to solve."

She nodded in agreement, accepting his apology.

He turned back to Benjamin and Nicholas. "Find out if there have been any other so-called animal attacks in San Francisco, down the Peninsula, on the East Bay, and in Marin County. I want to see whether these attacks have a common denominator. Maybe it'll shed a light on what's really going on here."

Benjamin nodded. "Consider it done. What about the victim himself? Since we know he's one of the jewelers in town for the convention, do we know if he had any enemies?"

"I've already asked Ethan and Damian to make inquiries," Patrick replied. "They are on security detail at the convention." He glanced back at Buffy. "Call me when you've identified the hair sample."

"I'm on it."

Patrick acknowledged her reply with a nod, his mind working overtime. Who had the skill to use a wild animal to make it look like this had been an animal attack and not cold-blooded murder by a person, be it human, vampire, or any other supernatural species? How had the perp done it and why?

9

Standing in her darkened bedroom, Fallon stared out of the window, looking over the rooftops of the neighboring houses. The moon was not quite full yet, but its light was nevertheless enough for her to make out a person with their dog walking in the narrow alley behind the apartment building that connected to a small neighborhood park, even though no streetlights illuminated the path.

The fog from earlier in the day had lifted, and the night was clear. Despite the comfortable temperature in her flat, she shivered and wrapped her arms around her torso. After leaving Scanguards, she'd returned to the lab for an hour to check on one of her ongoing experiments, making sure everything was in order. She could have taken the bus home, but the closest bus stop was three blocks from her apartment building, and she was too scared to walk those blocks on her own in the dark. Therefore, she'd taken an Uber home. She'd asked the driver to wait until she was inside the building, giving him a tip in cash, and he'd complied.

It had made her feel somewhat safer. Not that anything could truly dispel the fear that sat deep in her bones, anchored there, unwilling and unable to leave her body. Would she ever feel truly safe again? What would it take for Cameron to leave her in peace once and for all? What could anybody do to stop him from stalking her, from threatening her?

Still shivering, Fallon walked into her brightly lit kitchen. Maybe a cup of herbal tea would make her feel better. She reached for the kettle to fill it with water when her eyes fell on the bottle of red wine tucked into the corner next to the toaster. Maybe a glass of wine would calm her down better so she would be able to sleep for a few hours. She placed the kettle back on the counter without filling it, and instead poured herself a glass of wine.

She took a sip, inhaling the rich aroma, tasting its bouquet, a mixture of cherries and chocolate. Yes, this would help. She took her glass and walked into the living room, where she switched on only one standing lamp, keeping the lights subdued, and took a seat on the sofa. She leaned back and rested her bare feet on the coffee table, closing her eyes.

Fallon breathed evenly, listening to her heartbeat, willing it to slow so that a calmness could descend on her. She'd always meditated when she'd been in medical school and during her residency, combatting the stress and the long hours of work. It had always helped her feel refreshed and ready to face her next challenge. But tonight, she couldn't get into it. Her thoughts drifted off every few seconds to focus on her problems. She wanted her normal life back, the way it had been before she'd met Cameron.

She'd been content, dedicated to her research, and had enjoyed spending time with her colleagues. She'd moved from Boston to San Francisco for her fellowship and had been lucky to be offered a position to stay on as a researcher. Her future looked promising, and everything had been perfect.

If only she'd never gone to that bar in Cow Hollow, where she'd waited for a girlfriend who'd called last minute only to tell her that there'd been an emergency with one of her patients. Fallon had already ordered a drink, and stayed to finish it, when Cameron had come to the bar and started flirting with her. If only she'd left, leaving the drink on the bar, she would have never met him. But there was no such thing as a do-over.

Fallon gave up on trying to meditate and instead, drank more of the red wine until the glass was empty. She was about to set the empty glass back on the coffee table when the shrill sound of the doorbell spooked her and almost made her lose her grip on the glass. She shot up from the sofa, her pulse rising, adrenaline shooting through her veins. Fear instantly gripped her by the throat, making her gasp for air.

Who was at the door? Was it Cameron? Fuck! With the living room windows facing the street, anybody from below could see that the light was on, even though they couldn't see her. Who else but Cameron would dare show up at her doorstep so late? She glanced at the clock over the TV. It was close to ten p.m.

Her knees shaking, she walked to the door and pressed a trembling finger on the speaker to communicate with the late-night visitor.

"Go away, Cameron!" she ground out.

There was a rustling coming through the line, then a male voice said, "I'm sorry, Fallon. This is Patrick Woodford. I know it's late."

"Patrick?"

"Yes, from Scanguards. May I talk to you?"

She drew in a breath. "Yes, of course." She pressed the buzzer.

With trembling hands, she smoothed down her top. Why her hands were trembling, she didn't want to examine. Anybody's hands would be trembling if an unexpected visitor showed up at their home at such a late hour. It didn't have to be because she was attracted to said visitor.

She had to push that thought firmly out of her mind. After all, why would a man like Patrick—who seemingly had everything in the looks and career departments—be even remotely interested in a woman whose life was a complete mess? Besides, she wasn't looking for a relationship. She was done with men for a while. She needed time to breathe, to find her peace of mind again, to get her life in order and her priorities straight. Not drooling over another pretty face. Look where it had gotten her! Clearly, she couldn't trust her instinct when it came to men.

She looked through the peephole and saw Patrick approaching. Taking another steadying breath, she unhooked the chain and flipped the deadbolt, then pulled the door open.

"I'm sorry to disturb you so late," Patrick apologized again, a hesitant smile on his face.

"No, it's alright, you're not disturbing." She stepped aside and let him enter.

He squeezed past her in the narrow foyer, before she closed the door and flipped the deadbolt, then reached for the chain when she stopped herself. She caught his gaze.

"Sorry," she said hastily. "Just a habit. You must think I'm strange…" She released the chain.

Patrick tipped his chin toward the locked door. "Don't be sorry. It's a good habit. That's where security starts."

"I wish it was all it took to feel safe," she said as she ushered him into the living room.

There, he turned toward her but remained standing. "I spoke to Hank. Unfortunately, he couldn't corroborate your story. He insists that he fell and that he's never met Cameron. And—"

"But he's lying!" Fallon cried out. "He met Cameron at the bar. And I'm sure—"

Patrick put his hand on her forearm, stopping her. "We can't prove it."

Pushing back the rising tears, she looked at him. Did this mean he didn't believe her? Was he not going to help her? She couldn't find any words, worried that if she spoke, she'd break down in tears, and she didn't want to be the hysterical woman who cried. No man wanted to deal with a hysterical woman.

"I looked into Cameron, and I couldn't find much on him," he added. "His driver's license expired a few months ago, which is odd, but other than that, he doesn't have a record. No domestic violence, not even a speeding ticket, nothing. His record is squeaky clean."

"But that doesn't mean he's not capable of hurting—"

"I know that," he interrupted, his voice soothing. "But we have nothing on him."

Was this where he would tell her that absent of any prior crimes, he couldn't help her? That Cameron first had to hurt her, before Patrick could protect her from him?

She stepped back and took a breath, steeling herself for the words that would crush her hope that Patrick would stop Cameron from harassing her. There was a deep furrow on his forehead, and he shifted his weight from one foot to the other.

"Are you saying you don't believe me?"

"No, I'm just saying that if he's violent, if he's done something like this before, he's been careful."

"*If...*" She emphasized the word. "That's it, isn't it? *If* he's violent?" She thrust her chin up, looking straight at him, disappointment surging inside her. "Does that mean I have to wait until he hurts me before anyone will do anything? Is that why you came?"

"I'm saying it doesn't give me a lot of options of how to get him to stop stalking you. If we had anything on him, anything you can prove... But our resources aren't unlimited."

"So, you're here to tell me to my face that you can't help me? What do I have to pay to get help? Because if it's about money, I can get enough to—"

"It's not about money."

"Then what do I have to do so you'll help me? Anita said that your company is the best. That I could trust you to help me. Whatever it is I need to do..."

She caught his gaze then, just as he was lowering it to her lips, then her neck and torso, before quickly lifting it back to meet her eyes. The entire action hadn't taken more than a second, and maybe she'd imagined it, but the look he was giving her now had changed. Something in his eyes was different. They were still green, but there seemed to be a golden ring around his irises. A trick of the light most likely, but it made him look more approachable. As if she'd somehow uncovered his soft side, his weak point.

She must have taken a step toward him, because she suddenly stood only a couple of feet away from him, close enough to touch. She wetted her lower lip, while she felt a pleasant warmth rise to her cheeks.

"Please, take my case," she whispered, not knowing when she'd made the decision to beg him for help. But somehow, she sensed that he could help her, if only he would agree to it.

"Fallon, I shouldn't be here…" Yet he made no motion to head for the door.

She suddenly sensed the electricity between them, felt it dancing on her naked arms, her neck, her bare feet. At the same time, it paralyzed her, making her unable to step back from him, to pull herself from the draw he had on her. As if he was a magnet, and she a mere nail. But that thought was stupid. Maybe it was the glass of wine she'd downed that was hitting her empty stomach now, making her unable to think straight or command her muscles to move.

She leaned in, tilting her face up, unable to stop herself. His chest was suddenly brushing against hers, and his face was only inches from hers. His lips parted, and she couldn't stop herself from resisting the desire that welled up inside her. She bridged the last few inches separating them and kissed him.

THE MOMENT his lips touched Fallon's his brain stopped working. Because if it had been working, he would have severed the contact instantly, knowing this was a bad idea. But his brain had shut down, and now another part of his anatomy was doing the thinking. Hell, if he'd been thinking at all, he would have never let it come this far. He would have never stepped closer to her. He would have stayed at least ten feet away from her so he wouldn't be tempted to touch her. Clearly, that had worked out well—*not*.

He could have easily called Fallon on the phone, updating her as to what he'd found out so far. It hadn't been necessary to visit her at home. Instead, he'd made excuses for himself, reasoning that it was best to see what security precautions she was taking at home, so he could make suggestions of how she could protect herself better.

Bullshit! You wanted to visit her to be close to her, you horny, selfish bastard.

Yeah, well, the damage was done. He couldn't back away now, couldn't stop this kiss when it had barely started. A kiss that he'd been hungering for since the moment he'd laid eyes on Fallon. A kiss he should have never initiated.

Fallon's lips were warm and smooth, her response to him immediate, without hesitation. Patrick slid one hand to her nape while he wrapped his other arm around her waist, drawing her closer. Her soft breasts pressed to his chest, and he noticed that she wasn't wearing a bra underneath the casual T-shirt. He could feel her heart drumming against his chest, her hot blood pulsing in her veins.

Her tongue met his as he delved into her mouth to explore her. He tasted the bouquet of red wine on her breath, making him aware even more of how vulnerable she was. But instead of this fact stopping him, it drove his desire for her to a more urgent level. She was all woman, sin personified, vulnerable to the core, and his vampire side rejoiced at that revelation.

Fallon should have pushed him back by now, should have asked him to stop, but when she didn't, he deepened the kiss, drinking in her scent and her taste. Just kissing her and feeling her respond so openly to him, made him hungry for even more. And hungrily, he took what she was giving him, kissing her more passionately, pressing his groin to her sex, making her aware of what she was doing to him, how quickly he was getting aroused.

Fuck, he was harder than a crowbar and only moments away from tearing her clothes off to sink his aching cock into her. At that thought, he ripped his lips from hers and reared back, releasing her as if he'd burnt himself. And in a way, he had. Because he had no right to kiss her, to touch her, and to want even more from her. She'd asked for his protection, not for him to make love to her. If she tossed him out now, it wouldn't surprise him. He'd acted like a selfish prick, letting his needs and desires take over and practically assault her.

"I'm sorry. I should have never..." he stammered, swallowing hard, her taste running down his throat, sending little bolts of pleasure through his heated body.

He lifted his eyes to face her, expecting her to glare at him furiously, but instead, her cheeks were reddened, and her eyes cast downward, evading his gaze. Her lips looked bruised, reminding him of how intense their kiss had been.

"I apologize, Fallon, I don't know what came over me." He paused, not sure how to interpret her silence. "I should have never taken the liberty... I can promise you that it won't happen again. You're vulnerable, and you don't need a stranger practically mauling you. I can assign somebody else from Scanguards to your case if you feel uncomfortable around me now."

Though it would be a hard decision to make, because he wanted to be the one to keep her safe. "Please, Fallon..."

Finally, she lifted her eyes and looked at him. "It's my fault. I, uhm... I made the first move."

He shook his head slowly. Why would she blame herself, when it was absolutely clear that he'd been the one who'd stepped over the line and initiated this kiss?

"I'm not like that," she added. "Not normally. I'm more reserved... I'm sorry, I didn't—"

"You have nothing to apologize for," Patrick interrupted. "I behaved in an inexcusable manner."

She inhaled audibly, before she answered, "So you're not giving up my case? You'll help me with getting Cameron to leave me in peace?"

"Yes, of course."

How could he say no to her now, even if he wasn't sure how much of her story was true? He wished that Hank had corroborated her story. But that didn't matter right now.

"Do you want me to assign your case to one of my guys? Then you won't have to deal with me anymore."

He waited, dreading her answer. What if she said yes? Then he had no reason to see her again.

"Please, if you can handle this yourself, I think I would be more comfortable with you than having to trust somebody new."

Surprised and elated, he nodded. "Thank you. I'll check into a few other things regarding Cameron tomorrow." He motioned to the hallway. "I should leave now, and let you get some rest."

She nodded, a hesitant smile on her lips. "Thank you."

Without another word, he left her flat. Outside, he let the cold, damp night air engulf him as he walked to his car. As much as he wanted to, he couldn't bring himself to regret kissing Fallon. And his promise that it would never happen again had been a blatant lie. Because already now, he knew that he wouldn't be able to resist the temptation should it present itself again. And it would present itself again.

The fact that Fallon hadn't been angry with him and hadn't reprimanded him for the kiss, could only mean that she hadn't hated it. Had she enjoyed it? Would she allow it a second time, knowing what her body pressed to his was doing to him? How she was turning him on? It was impossible for her not to have felt his erection pressed against her soft stomach. Knowing this now, how would she react the next time? Because he was certain there would be a next time despite his assertion to the contrary. Because he knew the vampire deep inside him would get his way.

And the vampire wanted Fallon.

10

After Patrick's unexpected visit, Fallon had trouble sleeping. Their kiss replayed in her mind as if on an endless loop. He'd apologized for it, and she should be happy because that meant he wasn't like Cameron. He was more thoughtful and concerned for her wellbeing. But it also threw up many questions that she couldn't answer.

Had he really thought that he was the one who'd initiated the kiss? Or had he wanted to spare her the embarrassment by taking the blame onto himself? She'd never been so confused in her entire life. He'd promised that it would never happen again. Was he warning her in a subtle way that it was best if she never tried to kiss him again, because next time he would reject her kiss outright? Maybe she should be happy about the warning, so why wasn't she? Why was she disappointed that he'd promised it would never happen again?

For the first time in over two months, she'd felt happy and safe, and for just a few short moments, all her problems had faded into the background, vanished into thin air. She wanted to hold on to that feeling for a little while longer, bathing in the warmth of his embrace and the tenderness of his lips, but she couldn't. Her life was still a mess, and the tender kiss of a stranger who promised to help her couldn't change that fact.

She tossed and turned in her bed, finally finding sleep. A loud noise awakened her, making her sit up with a start. Everything was dark around her. Only the moonlight shaved off a little bit of the darkness where it entered the room through the half-closed blinds. She turned her head to the clock next to her bed. Two-seventeen, it showed in large red numbers. The same shrill ring as before sounded, and she realized what it was: an alarm coming from her cell phone.

She reached for it and read the alert: *refrigerator E3 is malfunctioning*.

Fuck! She was fully awake in a millisecond. Refrigerator E3 was a fridge in her lab at UCSF, which held the most vital tissue samples needed for her current research. If they weren't kept at an exact temperature, they would spoil within a short couple of hours. Each of the refrigerators and freezers was connected to a sensor that was set to send an alarm to her cell phone to inform her of any temperature fluctuations or a power outage.

Fallon jumped out of bed, put on a pair of jeans and a T-shirt, slipped over a thick sweater, and put on her boots. Ten minutes later, she sat in an Uber that drove her to Parnassus Avenue, where her lab was located within UCSF's medical sciences building. She had to enter the complex by the main entrance to the hospital because all side entrances were closed at night. She showed her ID to the security guard on duty. She hurried through the corridors that connected the various buildings, using her access card to open several doors until she got into the elevator to take her to the ninth floor. It felt like the elevator was taking forever, but finally, it stopped, and she was able to get out on her floor. The corridor was well-lit, but deserted.

The sound of her footsteps echoed in the hallway as she walked to her left, then made a turn to the right into the next corridor, until she reached the door to her laboratory. She swiped her access card and heard the familiar beep. Pushing the door open, she entered the dark space and reached for the light switch to her right. She flipped it, but nothing happened. The light didn't come on. Was there a power outage in her entire lab? If that was the case, she would have received an alert for each of the refrigerators and freezers, since they were all connected to the same power source. This was odd, to say the least.

She pulled her cell phone from her pocket and tapped on it, found her flashlight app and switched it on. The small beam from the app was sufficient for her to make her way through the lab without running into any equipment. The refrigerator in question was located in one of the corners of the laboratory, away from the windows looking out toward the hill where tall Eucalyptus trees—not native to California—provided shade in the summer months, and made the interior of the lab dark even during daytime hours.

She heard the humming of the refrigerators and freezers as she approached, her own footfalls accompanying it, when there was a third type of sound. She froze instantly, holding her breath, but there was nothing else, only the humming of the appliances and her heartbeat thundering in her ears.

Damn it, she was too jumpy these days, too nervous, too anxious. She'd never been afraid of the dark, even as a child. On the contrary, she'd loved the night, looking at the stars, admiring the moon. But ever since Cameron had started stalking her, she felt afraid in the dark. As if he was hiding behind every corner. It was ridiculous, of course, particularly here in her lab. Not only was the building secure, but the door to her lab could only be opened with an access card. She was safe here, maybe even safer than in her own flat.

With her cell phone light, she swept the floor in front of her, making sure there was no obstacle, and continued walking toward the refrigerators. As she passed a tall metal shelving unit containing various containers with fluids used in her research, she spotted what was wrong with refrigerator E3: its door was ajar, evidenced by the light streaming out from its interior. How in the hell had that happened? Had there been a minor earthquake during the night, shifting something inside it to force the door open?

Fallon quickly marched toward it and opened the refrigerator door wider to look inside. Everything looked fine. Nothing had spilled or fallen over. Relieved, she shut the fridge door, then assured herself that the doors to the other refrigerators were closed properly. They were. Happy that she'd been able to fix this issue without much effort, she turned around, ready to leave.

A sound to her left startled her, sending a chill down her spine. She perceived a movement, a big shadow approaching. All blood froze in her veins, paralyzing her with fear. With a shaking hand, she tried to direct her cell phone light toward the shadow, when she knocked her elbow on a shelf and the phone fell out of her hand. With a loud noise, it landed on the floor, the light pointing upward to the ceiling, throwing a sliver of light on the figure rushing toward her now. She tried to turn, tried to run, but she stumbled over her own feet. In mid-fall, she reached for the metal shelving unit to regain her balance. But before she could grip it, a hand snatched her shoulder from behind, jerking her back. As the intruder spun her around, her eyes perceived him clearly.

"No!"

A scream tore from her throat, before pain shot through her body, and her brain shut down, protecting her from the horror of the attack. Darkness wrapped around her as if to protect her, even though she knew instinctively that nothing could protect her from what was happening to her. Because she didn't have the physical strength to prevent it, nor anybody who would save her.

11

Patrick pulled his car to the curb, parking it in the red zone in front of the hospital. He jumped out, his heart racing, his entire body coiled in worry. Was Fallon alright? How bad were her injuries?

Clicking the car's remote to lock it, he was already racing toward the hospital main entrance, when a voice stopped him.

"Hey, you can't park there!" The police officer gave him a stern look.

The reprimand pearled off him like water off a Teflon pan. "Run my license plate, and you'll find out that I can."

After all, all Scanguards-owned vehicles had the same parking privileges as police cars, an arrangement they had reached with the police chief who knew of the existence of vampires and had been keeping their secrets for decades.

Inside the hospital it was busy, which wasn't unusual for midmornings. Patrick rushed toward the emergency room. It was hectic, with most of the treatment areas occupied by patients, doctors, and nurses attending to them. He swept his gaze through the large room, when the curtain to one of the treatment bays was shoved aside by a nurse, and he got a peek at the patient behind it: Fallon.

He hurried to it and entered. "Fallon!"

He was at her side, before she could even say a single word.

"Patrick..." She attempted a smile, but he could see that she was in pain.

There was a band-aid on her temple, and she had cuts and bruises on her arms, but she was propped up on the gurney, sitting almost upright, wearing a clean T-shirt and baggy jogging pants. He approached, wanting to take her into his arms to assure himself that she was alright, but of course, he couldn't do that. He wasn't her boyfriend or her lover, and he didn't want to make her feel uncomfortable.

"What happened?" he asked instead, his gaze ping-ponging between her and the nurse.

The nurse, a feisty-looking woman in her fifties, put a reassuring hand on Fallon's hand. "Her colleagues found her in the lab this morning. One of the shelving units fell on her. Luckily, her injuries are only superficial." She nodded at Fallon. "The doctor wants you to stay here today for observation, just in case you have a concussion."

"But I already told him I'm fine," Fallon protested.

Patrick looked at the nurse, glancing at the embroidered name on her scrubs. "Nurse Millie, why don't I speak to Fallon? Maybe I can get her to change her mind."

Nurse Millie sighed. "Well, good luck, young man. She's a stubborn one." She turned to the curtain, pulling it aside so she could slip out.

"I heard that," Fallon grumbled under her breath.

Patrick rested his hip against the hospital bed and took Fallon's hand. Her skin felt warm and the contact sent a pleasant shiver through his body, but he tried not to show what the touch did to him.

"Tell me what happened."

"I was attacked," Fallon said, then sniffled.

Patrick's heart raced. "Where? How? When?"

"I was called into the lab at around 2 a.m. And when I—"

"Who called you into the lab in the middle of the night?" Patrick shook his head, incredulous that Fallon would leave the safety of her home during the night after everything she'd told him about Cameron. "Why would you—"

"Nobody called me, I mean, an alarm went off." A whiff of impatience and annoyance colored her words.

"An alarm?"

"Yes, one of the refrigerators with the tissue samples for my research had a large temperature fluctuation. So, I got the alert on my cell phone. It happens when the power goes out."

Her words made him feel a little bit calmer. "And was that it? The power was out?"

She shook her head. "No, though the lights in the lab weren't working, but the fridges and freezers were humming. But when I saw the fridge, I noticed that the door was open. That's why the temperature was rising."

"Why would a fridge door suddenly open in the middle of the night?"

That was more than just a little suspicious; it sounded like a setup. A trap for her to show up at the lab in the middle of the night —where nobody could protect her.

"I don't know. I thought maybe there was a little earthquake, and something moved inside the fridge and pushed against the door. But everything looked fine. So, I closed the door."

She swallowed hard.

"Go on," he murmured, keeping his voice calm while brushing his thumb over the back of her hand in reassurance. "What happened then?"

"I think somebody was there, in the lab."

His pulse kicked up a notch. "Who?"

Fallon shook her head, tears brimming in her eyes. "I don't know. I don't remember anything after closing the fridge door. I just have that feeling that somebody was there and hurt me." She rubbed her left shoulder, her hand visibly trembling. "My colleagues found me when they showed up for work at seven-thirty. One of the shelving units was lying across my body as if it had fallen on me. But I don't remember it falling."

Her breathing accelerated as if somebody was chasing her, and there was no doubt in his mind that Fallon was scared.

"Fallon," he said calmly, even though he wasn't calm inside, "take a breath."

He watched her forcing herself to inhale and exhale slowly.

"Tell me everything you can remember."

A tear freed itself from her eye and made its way down one cheek. He resisted the temptation to wipe it off with his finger. As a stranger, he had no right to touch her so intimately. He was already crossing the line by holding her hand.

"I just know that I used my cell phone light because the lights in the lab were off. I flicked the switch after letting myself in, but nothing happened. But when I regained consciousness when my colleagues showed up for work, the lights worked again."

Patrick absorbed the information. Any janitor or other employee could have tampered with the fuse box. It was a simple thing to do: flip a fuse to *off*, and then switch it back to *on* later. As long as somebody could pick the lock to the electrical closet in the building's corridor, it would be an easy thing to do. But why?

"You said you received an alert on your cell phone about the refrigerator's temperature rising. Who knows about this alert?"

She shrugged. "Anybody working in my lab for sure."

"So, they would know that you'd come running to check on it, if you got an alert, right?"

"Yes. I can't just let the tissue samples spoil. It would set my research back by months."

"Is it possible that you slipped in the dark? I mean, you only had your cell phone light."

"No!" A hurt expression spread over her face. She pointed her finger to the area beyond the curtain. "You believe them? That the shelving unit fell on me?"

Again, she rubbed her shoulder. Patrick's gaze was drawn to it, but before he could ask her about it, she continued, "You believe that I slipped? I didn't slip. Somebody attacked me."

"I believe you, Fallon," he assured her, and though she couldn't provide any more information about it, he sensed that her fear was real. "I'm just trying to figure out what happened." He already had a suspicion, and short of a staff member of her lab playing a cruel trick on her, there was only one other person who was capable of such a deed.

"Did Cameron know of the alert you'd get if a fridge door is left open?"

Fallon shivered visibly, nodding. "He was at my place one evening when I got an alert. And he was annoyed that I would interrupt our evening to rush to my lab to check on it." She met his eyes. "He knows I would come to the lab no matter what."

He'd suspected as much. But why attack Fallon? What would he gain by that? What would be the purpose of it? By attacking her, Cameron was all but assured that she'd never get back together with him.

"And the injuries?" Patrick asked, running his eyes over the exposed parts of Fallon's body, her face, neck, and arms. "Nothing major?"

"Cuts and bruises. There was broken glass on the floor when they found me. But I don't remember any glass breaking."

"Has somebody already cleaned up the area where it happened?"

"I don't know. I assume so. I mean they had to, or they'd be stepping on glass, hurting themselves."

That was to be expected, but maybe it was best to check it out anyway. "Alright. How's your head? Any pain? The nurse said it's possible that you have a concussion."

She shook her head but stopped immediately as if the motion was causing her pain. "No, she didn't say that. She said that the doctor wants to keep me here for observation—*in case* I have a concussion. But I don't wanna stay."

"Are you sure?"

Fallon sat up straight and leaned in, lowering her voice. "I don't feel safe here. If somebody got into my lab to attack me there, it's gonna be even easier in a hospital room. They're not locked. Anybody can just walk in there."

Patrick nodded quickly. He had expected as much. "Good, I'll take you home. But before that, I'd like to see your lab. You need to show me where it happened."

It took a few minutes until Fallon had signed all the paperwork, confirming that she was leaving the hospital against the doctor's orders. The nurse handed her antibiotics and painkillers, demanding that Fallon take the antibiotics because there was a chance that she could get an infection caused by whatever had fallen on her. After all, in any lab all kinds of bacteria could be present that could harm a human. Infections contracted in hospitals could become life-threatening. But Patrick already had a plan of how to prevent anything serious from developing. He just needed to execute his plan covertly so that Fallon didn't stumble on his secret.

Medications in hand, they made their way to her lab on the 9th floor of the Medical Sciences Building. As they entered, Fallon's colleagues greeted her with questions. They all appeared concerned about her well-being, and Patrick didn't notice anyone feigning their well-wishes.

"This is where they found me," Fallon said with her arm

stretched out toward one corner of the large space. "The refrigerators are back there."

Patrick walked to the area and looked around. There were plenty of supply closets and shelves where somebody could easily hide in order not to be seen immediately. Even though Fallon had had her cell phone light, the beam would have only illuminated a small part of the room as she crossed it to reach the refrigerator in question.

There wasn't much else to glean. "Alright. I've seen what I needed to see. I'll take you home."

She hesitated, and he half expected her to say that she wanted to stay and work, but it appeared that even Fallon knew that after being attacked in her own lab, it was best not to stay here. At least not today.

"Alright."

In the car during the ride to her flat, Fallon was quiet, and Patrick used the time to go over everything she'd told him about the attack. There was no doubt in his mind that somebody had set a trap for her to come to the lab where nobody would hear her and come to her aid. He was also pretty certain that Cameron was behind this. But the rest? The attack itself made no sense if Cameron was the one who'd attacked her. Tricking her to come to the lab in the middle of the night, yes, that looked like a desperate move by her ex to be able to talk to her face-to-face, knowing that she wouldn't invite him into her flat.

But why attack her? There had to be a good reason. Had they argued, and things had gotten out of hand? Or had Fallon tried to flee when she'd realized that Cameron was waiting for her, and had tripped during her escape? It would account for her injuries. But what didn't make sense was her memory loss. What had caused it?

Did she have a concussion, and that was the reason for her not remembering the event? It would explain her memory loss at least temporarily. But according to the nurse, the doctor hadn't specifically diagnosed her as having a concussion. So why didn't she remember the attack? Or did she simply not want to tell anybody about it? He hated himself for thinking this, but he didn't know Fallon well enough to know what was going on inside her. And he hadn't had sufficient time to make himself a good picture of Cameron Gallagher, and what he was capable of.

He would work on that shortly, but first, he had to make sure that Fallon would heal quickly. There was no need for her to feel any more pain than necessary. He already knew how to take care of that.

When they entered Fallon's flat, Patrick closed the door firmly behind them and flipped the deadbolt.

"You should take your medication," he suggested.

"You're right. I'll get something to swallow them with." She already made a step toward the kitchen, when he stopped her.

He pointed to the couch. "You sit and rest. I'll get you a glass of something so you can swallow the pills."

"You don't have to. I'm feeling fine," she protested.

"Let me just do this for you, okay?" he asked softly.

She relented and walked toward the sofa, while Patrick marched into the kitchen. It was small, and not difficult to navigate. Glasses sat on an open shelf over the sink. He took one and opened the refrigerator. Inside it, he perused the drinks. Since she couldn't very well down the pills with a glass of wine, he chose the next best option, a liquid that would hide what he had to put into it. He poured apple juice into the glass, while he kept the fridge door open so his next action was hidden from Fallon, should she look over her shoulder into the kitchen. He set the glass on a shelf, willed his fingers to turn into claws, and pricked the soft pad of his thumb with it. He held the bleeding thumb over the glass to allow the blood to mix with the apple juice. The juice became a tiny little bit darker from the blood, but Fallon wouldn't notice it. When he was done, he licked his thumb, closing the tiny wound with his saliva.

His vampire blood would help her heal much faster and eliminate the need for pain medication. It was the least he could do. The thought of Fallon drinking his blood excited him, but he tried to push that thought from his mind. Just as he ignored the next thought that emerged: in a human, vampire blood acted as an aphrodisiac.

12

Fallon popped the antibiotics capsule and the anti-inflammatory pill into her mouth and reached for the glass Patrick handed her. She watched him pull his cell phone from his pocket and start typing something. Not wanting to look curious, she swallowed the medications quickly and chased them down with a couple of large gulps of the apple juice. There was a strange taste in her mouth, and she stared at the glass. Had the juice spoiled? She sniffed at the glass, taking in its scent. There was something off about the juice. Its color looked a little darker too, not as pale as usual.

"Something wrong?" Patrick asked, concern in his voice just as a ping sounded, indicating that he was receiving a text message.

Not wanting to sound difficult, she lied, "I just don't like taking medications." She placed the nearly empty glass on the coffee table.

"You won't have to take them for long, I'm sure." He gestured to the cuts on her arms. "Luckily, they're not very deep. It could have been much worse."

He was right. She was lucky that she only had minor injuries.

Yet, she didn't feel lucky. She felt on edge. Her life was being upended. Nothing felt right anymore. She wasn't safe anywhere.

"I wish I could see it that way. But no matter how superficial the injuries are, they are proof of what a mess my life is." Right now, she couldn't see a way out of it.

Patrick sat down next to her on the sofa, turning his body sideways to face her. "I know it's a lot you have to deal with right now."

Tears threatened to well up in her eyes, but she forced them down. She didn't want to feel like a victim. She wanted to be strong. "I don't understand why he's doing this to me. How can somebody be so vicious? So cruel?" She lifted her hand to brush a lock of her hair behind her shoulder, and noticed that her hand was trembling. Her nerves were frayed. How much longer would she be able to keep a brave face, when all she wanted was to wallow in her pain and let the tears wash it away?

Patrick took her hand and squeezed it, making her jolt involuntarily.

"I'm sorry," he apologized quickly and released her hand. "I didn't mean to frighten you."

"You didn't; you don't," she replied, raising her gaze to his face. "I know you're doing so much for me already. I don't mean to be ungrateful, but I wish all this was over already." She sniffled. "But what if he'll never give up? What if he never goes away?"

She expelled a breath, and with it, a sob tore from her throat. She pressed her hand on her mouth, trying to stop herself from crying, but to no avail. Maybe she needed a good cry, but she didn't want to do this in front of Patrick. She didn't want him to see her as a weak woman who needed a man's shoulder to cry on.

"I'm sorry..." she whispered, trying to turn away.

Another breath, and she felt Patrick's arms around her, pulling her against his broad chest.

"Don't be. This is my fault," Patrick claimed. "If I'd followed up with Cameron last night, this might have never happened..."

She lifted her head from his chest, staring at him. "You can't know that..."

As if he'd done it many times before, he wiped a tear off her cheek, the tender touch awakening something in her. Something she shouldn't allow to rise to the surface. But she had no strength left, and simply let it happen.

"I could have done more yesterday, but—" He sighed. "I'm dealing with a big murder case... Time got away from me last night after I left your place."

In light of this revelation, she pulled back. "A murder case? Why would you even deal with my little problem when you have a much larger one to investigate?"

He pinned her with his eyes, his arms still around her, and had he been any other man, she would have felt imprisoned, trapped, but Patrick's arms around her made her feel cradled the way somebody cradled something precious.

"It's not a little problem," he said. "In a way, a case like yours is more important, because in your case I can still prevent something terrible from happening, whereas in a murder case, all I can do, is find the killer, but I can't bring back the victim."

She hung on his lips, hearing the passion he had for his job, and understood that he gave a hundred percent to everything he did. And she heard a promise echoing in his words, the promise to protect her.

"You're a good man, Patrick." There was no doubt about it. This man had integrity.

A half-hearted smile formed on his lips. "I wish it were true. But I'm just as selfish as everybody else."

She didn't understand what he meant by that. "Selfish?"

He leaned in closer, bringing his face to within inches of hers. Her breath hitched at the sudden nearness.

"Don't you remember what I did yesterday?"

She knew very well what he was referring to. "You mean when I kissed you?"

He shook his head. "No, when *I* kissed *you*." His eyes dilated, their green color shimmering seductively. "Just like I want to right now. And that makes me no better than your stalker."

For a moment, her mind went blank, and she just stared at him, her heart suddenly pounding out of control. She was fully aware of the need that had risen inside her earlier. The need that urged her to take action.

"You shouldn't have to deal with unwanted attention," he continued. "It's bad enough that Cameron is making your life hell. You don't need any added trouble from me."

She swallowed slowly, gathering all her courage. "You're right, Cameron is making my life hell, but you're no trouble..." She hesitated, not knowing how to proceed. "I enjoyed kissing you..."

The sunlight shining in through the windows made Patrick's eyes shimmer almost golden now.

"You shouldn't tell me that."

"Why not, when it's the truth?"

"Because you make it even harder for me to leave you in peace now." He reached for a strand of her hair, and swept it out of her face, his finger brushing over her cheek in the process.

She'd never been so aware of another person's touch.

"What if I don't want you to leave me in peace?" she murmured.

From where she took the courage to utter such an obvious come-on, she didn't know. Something inside her pushed her to go for what she wanted, what she craved. And she craved Patrick. Everything female in her was awakening fully for the first time in her life, and she'd never been so clear about what she needed. It was as if a veil had lifted from her eyes, allowing her to see the world with more clarity.

She inhaled Patrick's masculine scent, letting it draw her closer. When had she turned into a woman who acted with such directness and without shame or embarrassment? She'd never been the kind of woman who found it easy to show her sexual interest in a man. She'd always been too shy for such an act, too worried that it would turn into an embarrassment. But with Patrick, it seemed different. In his presence, she felt powerful and more aware of her female attributes than ever before. Last night, she'd felt it sizzling between them, but now it was even more pronounced.

"Fallon," he whispered, his breath ghosting over her face. "Please ask me to leave."

"I can't."

Who bridged the last few inches between them, she would never be able to recollect later, because all she suddenly felt was Patrick gently kissing her, while he tilted his head to the side. He shifted her in his arms until she was sitting on his lap, her legs spread to either side of his hips, her breasts pressed to his chest. She returned his kiss with the same tenderness he lavished on her. Her fear and her tears were forgotten. Instead, heat spread inside her as if somebody had lit a match to her, setting her on fire. Yet this fire wasn't destructive even though it engulfed her in its midst.

Patrick explored her with his tongue, stroking against hers, licking over her teeth, taking his time without rushing her. She heard his moans and felt the tender touch of his hands on her back, one sliding down to her bottom, the other cupping the back of her head. He held her there, while he deepened his kiss and nibbled on her lips. With every second, she became more aroused by his masterful kisses. And as her arousal rose, Patrick's kisses became more demanding—as if he could feel that she was ready for more. Because she was.

FALLON SUDDENLY SHIFTED in his lap, pressing her core to his groin. A gasp coming from her confirmed that she felt the massive erection he sported. However, she didn't withdraw, didn't stop responding to his kisses, nor did she push away his hand that he now slipped onto her ass to rock her against his hard-on. Despite the layers of clothing between them, he relished the contact and feared that if they continued like this, he would climax without her even touching him. Yeah, that's how badly he wanted her. That's how hot she got him.

It was all his own fault. Had he not poured a good number of drops of his blood into her glass, it was doubtful that she would have responded to his advances. But with his vampire blood inside her, she was easily aroused, turning into putty in his arms. Fuck! This was bad. He knew he should stop this madness now before it went even further. But how could he stop this embrace, when it felt so good? When it helped him forget the fear he'd felt when he'd gotten the call from the hospital?

Besides, he couldn't blame the vampire blood for everything: if Fallon wasn't attracted to him at all, it wouldn't have driven her into his arms. However, it definitely helped to lower or remove any inhibitions she might have otherwise had.

He tasted the salt of her tears on her lips, reminding him how vulnerable she was. But even that fact couldn't stop him from kissing her as if his life depended on it. He'd always loved kissing a woman thoroughly before engaging in full-blown sex, bathing in the anticipation of making love. Just like he felt the anticipation now. It charged through his body, leaving no cell untouched, as he tasted her lips and her tongue. She wasn't a shy wallflower in his arms, instead she urged him to deepen the kiss, to intensify the connection between them.

He'd hoped that she was the kind of woman who let her partner know what she expected from him. And he'd been right. Every action on her part told him what she needed: a man who allowed her to be the person she was, a man who accepted every fiber of her being, a man who didn't judge. A man who wanted to be seduced by her. He could be all that for her, and more. Because he could also be the man to protect her, the man who could help her forget all her troubles.

Patrick ripped his lips from hers, breathing hard. "You feel so good."

"Don't stop," she begged.

One look into her passion-drugged eyes, and he knew he couldn't deny her anything.

"I won't."

He sank his mouth back onto hers and lifted one hand to run it along her side, before reaching her breast and capturing it in his palm. A gasp and a moan filled the room. The moan was hers, the gasp his, because he could feel that she wasn't wearing a bra under her T-shirt, and her nipple was as hard as a pebble. Not wasting another second, he brought his hand to the hem of her shirt and slipped underneath it. Her skin was soft and warm. He trailed his hand up to her breasts, caressing them, squeezing them gently, rubbing his fingers over her nipples.

With every touch, another moan tore from her chest, and he swallowed it greedily. He loved the way she reacted to him, without inhibitions, without hesitation.

For a second, he let go of her lips. "Touch me, Fallon."

He didn't have to wait long for her to follow his command. Her hands went to the waistband of his pants, where she pulled his shirt free, then started to unbutton it. When she laid her palms onto his chest, intense desire shot through his entire body. He ripped his mouth from hers, and pulled on Fallon's T-shirt, yanking it over her head.

"Fuck!" he cursed as he stared at her perfect breasts.

They were firm and plump, topped with hard, dark nipples. Impatiently, he dipped his head to one breast and sucked the nipple into his mouth. Fallon's head fell back as she arched into his touch, pressing her breast deeper into his mouth. He licked and sucked the beautiful flesh, and inhaled her natural scent. Fallon's moans filled the room, and he noticed how she now gripped his arms for balance, her fingernails digging into his biceps. He welcomed the sensation, and had she been a vampire female, he would have asked her to bite him so they could connect on a deeper level.

"Yes," she cried out, her voice breathy. "So good."

As he brought his mouth to the other breast to caress it in the same manner, he could already smell the aroma of her arousal. Her pussy was weeping for him. Holding her with one hand, he shoved his other one into her loose-fitting jogging pants, and gasped instantly. It appeared that they'd taken all of Fallon's clothes and only given her the T-shirt and the jogging pants, no underwear.

His fingers connected with her naked sex. Her pussy was drenched in her juices, her female folds supple and welcoming.

"Oh, God, yes," she whispered on a breath.

He lifted his head from her breasts and met her gaze. "You wanna come for me?"

"Yes..."

Their eyes locked, and he rubbed his finger along her slit, gathering the moisture that seeped from her, before drawing his finger farther up to find her clitoris. Her mouth opened, and a gasp escaped.

"There it is," Patrick murmured, and began to rub his finger over the sensitive organ. "Kiss me, baby."

Fallon brought her lips to his and kissed him, first by gently nibbling on his lips, then by sweeping her tongue into his mouth and exploring him. She was taking charge, and he liked that— because he was busy with something else. He painted small circles on her center of pleasure, teasing her clit with every caress. He could feel how Fallon was surrendering to him, trusting him to take care of her, to give her the pleasure she craved, all the while following her body's subtle clues as to what gave her the most pleasure.

Again and again, he dipped his finger lower to gather more of her juices, thoroughly lubricating her clit while he fell into a faster tempo. His sensitive vampire hearing picked up her accelerated heartbeat, when she suddenly severed the kiss. A breathy gasp rolled over her lips, and he could feel her body tensing, while she closed her eyes.

Not wanting her to climax yet, he eased up on the pressure and slowed his tempo. She opened her eyes and stared at him.

"Not yet, baby," Patrick said softly. "It feels too good."

Before she could protest, he thrust one finger into her pussy. Fallon moaned, and her eyelashes fluttered. He followed it up with another thrust, just as deep and hard, before he withdrew his finger and swept upward to tease her clit again.

Fallon brought her face to his, her mouth to his ear. "I want your cock inside me."

Her words sent a thrill through his body, making his cock jerk in anticipation. He was harder than he could remember ever being. It was almost painful the way his erection pressed against the zipper of his pants. But he wanted to pleasure Fallon first, because he wasn't sure he would last long enough to make her climax once he was inside her.

"First you'll have to come for me."

To emphasize his words, he rubbed over her clit, back and forth, his tempo and pressure increasing. Fallon's eyes fell shut again, and her head tipped backward, while her breath became ragged, and her heartbeat thundered in his ears as if a thousand horses raced through the flat. This time, he didn't stop. Instead, he increased his tempo even more, recognizing the signs of Fallon's body that she was close. Another breath, another heartbeat, and she moaned, while she shuddered beneath his touch. Not wanting to miss out on anything, he plunged his finger into her pussy, feeling her interior muscles clench and release around his digit as she climaxed.

When the spasms subsided, Fallon rested her head in the crook of his neck, sighing contentedly. His finger was still inside her, and he gently moved it in and out.

"Oh." Fallon blew a breath against his neck.

"You feel amazing, baby," he murmured into her ear. "Your pussy is so soft."

"Mmm." She dropped one hand to his pants, trying to open his fly.

"Not yet," he said. "I'm not done with pleasuring you."

She lifted her head to look at him. "But you just made me..."

He smiled at her hesitation. "...climax? Yes." He locked eyes with her, while he moved his finger in her pussy in and out. "But I'm not done... see?" In a steady rhythm, he pumped in and out of her. When she relaxed in his arms, he added a second finger and slowly drove into her with both.

"Patrick! Oh..."

"See? I told you I wasn't done yet." He pressed a kiss to her lips. "I think I can make you come once more. Don't you?"

The shrill sound of the doorbell nearly pierced his eardrum, and they both jolted. His fingers slipped from her pussy, as she stared at the door in horror.

"Oh my God! Is it Cameron?"

She jumped off his lap, her entire body visibly tensing. As she snatched her T-shirt from the floor, Patrick put his hand on her forearm.

"It's probably Lydia," Patrick said, quickly glancing at his watch.

"Lydia?"

"My colleague." He'd texted her earlier to ask her to come to Fallon's flat. He walked to the door and pressed the intercom. "Who is it?"

"It's Lydia."

"Come on up."

When he walked back into the living room, Fallon was already fully dressed again. Her red cheeks were the only sign that she'd been in the throes of passion only moments earlier.

"Your shirt."

She pointed to him, and he realized that it was open. He began buttoning it.

"What is your colleague doing here?"

"She's going to protect you while I go back to the office to investigate Cameron."

For a moment, he thought she would protest, but then she nodded. "Okay."

There was a knock at the door. Patrick took Fallon's hand and looked into her eyes. "And what just happened..." He sighed. "I would like us to continue that... if that's what you want too."

"Patrick, open up already!" The voice came from Lydia on the other side of the door.

He walked to it to let her enter, aware that Fallon hadn't given him an answer yet. Maybe it was best to give her time to think things over. After all, he'd totally steamrolled her. And what was worse was that he didn't even feel guilty about it. Because he'd never felt anything so pure as giving Fallon pleasure while holding back his own need for release. In a few hours, whatever decision she would come to wouldn't be tainted by the effect of his blood.

13

Patrick walked into the command center, where Sebastian, the twenty-eight-year-old half-Asian son of Oliver and his blood-bonded mate Ursula, was on duty. But he wasn't alone. Thomas was already waiting, as were Buffy, Benjamin, and Nicholas.

"Sorry for the delay. My new client was attacked last night," he explained, even though he owed nobody an explanation. But he didn't want anybody to think that he was slacking off.

"Anything you need help with?" Sebastian asked. "Not that we have a lot of staff that's not already on other assignments."

"I've got it under control. Thanks, Sebastian," Patrick said and looked at the assembled. "So, what's the latest on the Presidio murder?"

Thomas motioned to a monitor on the wall. It showed a map of the Bay Area with several red dots on it.

"Eddie and I went through reports of suspected animal attacks, and found quite a few." With the mouse he indicated the area. "Almost all of them occurred in Marin County. Since that's not within Chief Donnelly's jurisdiction, we weren't made aware of them. But from the information in the Marin County police reports we were able to piece things together, and we determined that there were similarities with our murder case."

"Thomas is correct," Buffy confirmed. "I went through the autopsies, and in two of the three cases of supposed mountain lion attacks, the heart was missing in the victims."

"Fuck," Patrick cursed.

"I looked at the photos," Buffy continued. "And the bite marks look very similar to those our victim has. The coroner and the detectives on those cases in Marin County determined that these were mountain lion attacks and closed the cases."

Patrick rubbed his neck. "Did the coroner in the Marin County cases note that they found animal hair on the vics?"

Buffy nodded. "Yeah, that's why they determined that those were animal attacks. Though they didn't specify that the hair found was that of a mountain lion. Just that it was animal hair."

"And were other organs missing too? Or just the heart?"

"Just the heart."

Patrick exhaled, digesting the information, when he remembered something. He looked at Buffy again. "How about the hair you found under our vic's fingernails? Were you able to determine—"

Buffy's nod cut off his question. "It was from a wolf."

His heartbeat spiked. "A wolf? In the middle of San Francisco? That can't be."

"Has to," Buffy insisted. "I double-checked. At first, I didn't think I got it right, but I compared the hair I found with several different strands of wolf hair—or rather fur—and the result was always the same: it was a wolf. A black one. And a pretty big one. Standing on its hind legs, it's probably as tall as you."

"How did you determine that?" Patrick asked, surprised.

"By the size of the bitemarks, and—" She gestured to Nicholas. "Nicky?"

It looked like Nicholas wanted to protest at Buffy using his childhood nickname but seemed to think of it otherwise. "The pawprints I took around the crime scene. When Buffy told me that it was a wolf, I called a contact in Yellowstone who's working with the park service protecting the wolves there. She helped me calculate the size of the wolf using the pawprints and the bite marks."

"You trust her assessment?"

Nicholas nodded. "She was confident in the data, though she was surprised that a wolf had shown up in the city. They avoid people, and her best guess was that it wasn't a wild wolf, but one bred in captivity."

"Like in a zoo?" Patrick asked.

"That's possible," Nicholas said, then added, "but not necessarily in a public zoo. Some rich people like to keep their own little zoos, you know."

"Then we'd better check them all to see if anyone is missing a wolf," Patrick suggested. "Benjamin, Nicholas, the two of you can do that."

"How far out do you want us to check the zoos?" Benjamin asked.

Patrick turned to Thomas. "How long ago were the attacks in Marin County?"

"They both happened between eight to ten weeks ago. Nothing since then. So, we can assume that the wolf migrated from the north down into San Francisco."

Patrick furrowed his forehead. "Yes, and no. I don't see a wolf crossing the Golden Gate Bridge on foot, do you?" He looked at his four colleagues.

"You mean he hitched a ride?" Benjamin asked.

"Or was brought over," Patrick mused. "Because even if it was a wolf attacking those people in Marin County and our victim in the Presidio, I still think that somebody else was involved. Maybe an animal trainer who's using a trained wolf to kill people."

He addressed Nicholas, "Can you talk to your contact in Yellowstone again?"

"Sure."

"Ask her if it's possible to train a wolf to the point where a person could be directing a wolf to follow specific commands."

"It sounds a little far-fetched, don't you think?"

"It's the only thing that makes sense. Otherwise, a wolf wouldn't just rip out the heart, leaving the rest of the person untouched."

"Alright, I'll get right on it," Nicholas agreed.

"And ask your contact if they have a list of animal trainers that are working with wolves."

Nicholas nodded.

"Benjamin, you get started on checking on all the public zoos, if they're missing a wolf. Start in Marin County."

"I'll research who in the area might have a private zoo or animal sanctuary," Thomas offered. "Benjamin, I'll send you the details as soon as I have them."

"Do you need anything else from me?" Buffy asked.

"No, thanks. Good work."

Buffy nodded and left, Benjamin and Nicholas followed her.

"And update the command center as soon as you have any leads," he called after them.

His two colleagues looked over their shoulder, nodding in agreement, before leaving and shutting the door behind them.

"Sebastian, you're responsible for making sure everybody is kept up to date on this case. Once they call in with any news, send everything directly to me and Thomas. Alright?"

"No problem," Sebastian said firmly.

He was glad that Sebastian was on duty in the command center. He was detail-oriented, and super smart, as well as very practical.

"Okay, thanks guys," Patrick said. "I've got a few things to do. I'll be in my office for a while."

"I'll walk with you," Thomas suggested. "I need to go back to my office anyway."

As they left the command center, and walked to the elevators, Thomas let out a breath.

"So, who's the new client who got attacked?"

Patrick gave him a sideways glance, while he pressed the button for the elevator. "A young doctor who's being stalked by her ex."

"And we're involved why?"

The elevator doors opened, and they both entered.

"There's a chance that her ex is a vampire or rather a vampire hybrid."

And that was all he'd tell Thomas. While he liked Thomas and respected him immensely, he didn't feel comfortable telling him more about Fallon, worried that the more he spoke of her, the more likely it was that Thomas would discover that his interest in Fallon was more personal in nature than was appropriate. Thomas was far too perceptive to be fooled for very long.

"Need any help checking out the guy?" Thomas asked, his voice just as casual as before.

"You've got plenty on your plate. I have it under control."

If only he had his emotions under control as well. But having touched Fallon so intimately, having made her climax, was causing turmoil inside him. His vampire side was trying to emerge, and it was harder to keep it beneath the surface and pretend he was a civilized man, when he knew all too well that in Fallon's presence, he was anything but civilized. He was wild, untamed, without restraints. It was something he had to hide from Thomas, because above everything, Thomas was fiercely loyal to Samson. If he felt that Patrick was slipping up, he'd step in to intervene. He wouldn't even blame Thomas, because they all knew that his intent was to keep everybody at Scanguards safe.

They all had to look out for each other, because at any time, their vampire side could take over, making them act irrationally. It was more likely to happen to himself or one of his vampire hybrid brethren who hadn't found their mate yet. Once blood-bonded to their soulmate, a different side of the vampire emerged: that of the protector. While fierce, that side of their nature was more predictable.

It was as if the blood-bonded mate tamed the vampire. In a way, it was like that. He'd seen it in many of his friends, even in his own brother, Grayson, who'd turned into a rather love-struck man who treated others with more respect, was less aggressive, and less contentious. Monique, his blood-bonded mate, had truly tamed him, and it was rather sickening to watch the lovey-dovey looks they exchanged. Luckily, they lived in New Orleans now, running the Scanguards branch there.

"You coming?" Thomas suddenly asked.

Patrick blinked, and realized that the elevator doors stood open, and they'd arrived on the top floor, where all executive offices were located. It was the floor where only vampires, vampire hybrids, their blood-bonded mates, and other supernatural creatures were allowed—no humans. However, that rule had been broken more often than it had been adhered to. Why it still existed was anybody's guess.

He exited the elevator. "It's all good. I just have a lot of things on my mind." He walked toward his office. "Thanks for your help, Thomas. Keep me posted."

"Sure thing."

In his office, Patrick let himself fall into his chair. He logged into his computer. It was time to find out more about Cameron Gallagher.

14

Fallon stepped out of the tub and started drying off with a large, fluffy bath towel. She looked into the mirror, inspecting the bruises on her body. To her surprise, they looked like they were healing very quickly, almost as if the whole incident was just a nightmare. But it wasn't. She rubbed her left shoulder, and although it wasn't injured, she could feel something there. No pain, no, not really, but something else that made a shiver run down her spine into her tailbone. It was as if touching the spot unlocked something inside her: a memory.

She'd always known that perfume or other distinct smells could help recall memories, just like listening to music could remind a person of things from long ago. But a touch? So why did she feel that there was something there, so close to touch, yet still beyond her reach?

She tried to block it out, not wanting to destroy the relaxing state the bath had put her in. She'd relived the intimate moments she and Patrick had shared. She'd felt safe in his arms—and cherished. Patrick had been gentle, not demanding like Cameron had always been. At the thought of him, she felt pain in her left shoulder again. She rubbed the spot, wishing the feeling away, but it persisted.

She reached for the clean clothes she'd placed on the hamper. Slowly, she put on panties and a fresh pair of khakis. When she pulled the long-sleeved T-shirt over her head and the fabric connected with her left shoulder, a jolt of fear rushed through her. She shivered involuntarily.

Her heart beat like a jackhammer, and her throat went dry. She smoothed down her T-shirt, trying to calm herself, but realized that her hands were trembling. The fear she'd felt the previous night when she'd encountered her attacker, came back in all its facets.

And with the fear, a memory emerged. She closed her eyes, focusing on it, her pulse racing the way it had raced when she'd turned away from the refrigerator in her lab to face the intruder. At first, all she saw was darkness. It was suffocating. She gasped for a breath, but her body tensed, knowing what was coming. She saw the eyes then, but she didn't recognize them, because they glowed in the dark. Fear spiked inside her. Like a predator, he approached, leaving no doubt as to what he wanted. When he spoke, she recognized his voice. It was Cameron who'd attacked her.

"It's your fault, Fallon. You leave me no choice." The icy words felt like blades slicing into her skin, tearing her flesh.

When he gripped her shoulder, and his nails dug into her skin, she tried to free herself, but he was stronger. His face was only inches from hers. She felt paralyzed, unable to move, unable to escape.

"You'll be mine," he claimed.

Tears stung in her eyes, making her vision blurry. She felt excruciating pain in her shoulder, as if he was slicing her open. She couldn't tell what was happening, whether it was Cameron's hand that was hurting her, or whether he was biting her, ripping her flesh. All she knew was that she wished she was dead so she wouldn't have to endure the pain and fear any longer.

"Nooooo!" she begged, trying to appeal to his mercy. *"Please, let me go!"*

But he had no mercy to give. No heart to appeal to. No compassion for her pain. He was evil to the core. Bad through and through.

"Fallon!?"

A female voice pulled her back into the present. Lydia, Patrick's blonde colleague, rushed into the bathroom.

"What's wrong?" she asked, concern in her voice.

Fallon felt her body shake and recognized that tears were streaming down her face. Lydia pulled her into a sisterly embrace, and she welcomed the comfort her arms provided.

"It'll be alright, Fallon," she murmured, comforting her as if she were a child, and right now that was what she needed: to feel safe, to know that somebody was there for her, to protect her, to care for her. And right now, she was glad that it wasn't Patrick who was holding her. In this moment, she didn't want to feel Patrick's sensual embrace. It would only confuse things. Right now, she needed to remember what Cameron had done, no matter how much it hurt to relive it.

"I remember some of it now," Fallon said, lifting her head and wiping away the tears.

Lydia released her from her arms. "About the attack?"

She nodded. "I saw him. It was Cameron." She rubbed the spot on her shoulder that still ached. "I could feel him. He hurt me."

"Tell me how."

Fallon shook her head, still not understanding what exactly Cameron had done. "I'm not sure. I saw him. He grabbed me. Here." She pointed to her shoulder. "I can still feel the pain."

"May I?" Lydia pointed toward her shoulder.

Fallon nodded.

Lydia pushed the T-shirt aside to look at the shoulder. "I can't see a bruise or an abrasion."

"I know." She felt like crying again. She wasn't lying. "But I felt it. It was as if his fingernails were claws. As if—"

"Claws?" Lydia interrupted, her eyes widening.

"Yes, it felt like it, or like his teeth. As if he bit me. I know it doesn't make any sense, but I know what I felt. I remember it. I can still feel his touch."

"I get it, I do," Lydia said, nodding. "I'm not discounting what you're saying, but you should tell Patrick what you remember. He needs to know what Cameron is capable of."

"But it makes no sense." Patrick would think that she was making it up. "I can barely believe it myself. I mean, why would he bite me? If that's what he did. No, he couldn't have. It must have been his fingernails." She furrowed her forehead and looked at Lydia. "I'm a doctor. I know what happens when a person bites someone. There's always an infection. And it would heal really slowly, but I can't see a wound…"

The more she talked, and the more she thought about it, the more confused she was getting. Something was seriously wrong.

"I know Cameron hurt me. I know it was him. I recognized him. But the rest? I don't know for sure what he did to me. Only that he did something. And that it was my fault."

"Your fault?"

"Yes, he said it. I remember it clearly."

"Let's call Patrick. He needs to know." Lydia pulled out her cell phone and tapped on a contact. "Hey. Fallon is starting to remember things." There was a short pause. "I'll let you talk to her."

Lydia handed the phone to her, and she took it hesitantly. "Hi, Patrick."

"Hey," he said softly. "You're remembering the attack?"

"Only parts of it. And I'm not even sure about some of it, other than that I recognized Cameron. It was him, and he attacked me."

"What else do you remember about the attack?"

"Tell him about the bite and the claws," Lydia urged her.

"What was that?" Patrick asked as if he'd heard Lydia's words.

Fallon cleared her throat. "I think—and I'm not a hundred percent sure—that he either bit me in the shoulder or dug his claws into me."

"His claws? You saw claws?"

She shook her head. "I didn't see them. I felt them. As if his fingernails were two inches long and sharp like blades."

Patrick cursed under his breath, but she heard it nevertheless.

"You don't believe me. I knew it. I shouldn't have told you."

"No, Fallon. I do believe you. There are men who're capable of anything."

A sob traveled up from her chest, and she suppressed it. "I don't even believe myself. But I can still feel the pain. But there isn't even a bruise there."

"Don't think about that right now. At least you can be sure now that Cameron did this. We'll get him for it. I promise you that."

She didn't know what to say, but she felt grateful. Lydia took her hand and squeezed it in reassurance.

"I've been looking into Cameron a little more. Can you tell me, have you ever been to his flat, stayed overnight there?"

"No. He lives all the way out in Marin County, so he always just stayed with me when we were going out."

"Marin County?" he asked, a quizzical tone in his voice. "His driver's license shows an address in the city."

"That can't be," she insisted. "He told me he lives out somewhere near San Rafael. That's why he always suggested that he stay over at my place. He said it would be better for me, since I go to work early, and if he had to drive me all the way from San Rafael to UCSF in the morning, we'd be stuck in traffic." He'd made it sound like he was concerned for her wellbeing. "Why would he lie about that? Are you sure he has a flat in the city?"

"I'm gonna find out. One other thing: I couldn't find anything on where he works. Do you know?"

"He said he works for his family. They have, I don't know, some businesses. And it sounded like he was managing some of them. But I didn't ask what it was exactly. The corporate world doesn't really interest me." Maybe her lack of interest about what Cameron did for a living should have made her realize earlier that she didn't really want a future with him.

"Alright, not to worry. I'll go to the flat and check it out now."

"What are you gonna tell him, when you find him?" Her hand trembled again at the thought that Patrick would confront Cameron, and that Cameron would lash out at him, hurt him like he'd hurt her.

"That depends on what I find. I'll first have to confirm that he still lives at the address on his driver's license."

"Be careful, please," she said, turning away from Lydia, and lowering her voice. "I don't want you getting hurt."

A soft chuckle came through the line. "You won't have to worry about me. Just promise to stay with Lydia no matter what. She'll protect you. I'll talk to you soon, okay?"

"Okay."

She disconnected the call and turned back to Lydia, handing the phone back to her. Lydia gave her a warm smile.

"He can take care of himself," Lydia said. "We had the same training. He is one of the best."

Fallon forced a smile. She hoped that Lydia was right, because her memory of the attack had made her realize one thing: Cameron was stronger and more dangerous than he looked.

15

The address on Cameron's driver's license was a third-floor walkup in a large Victorian home in the Marina district of San Francisco that had been converted into three units. The doorbell didn't show a name but only the flat's number, which wasn't unusual. Lots of people didn't want their name on the door.

Patrick stepped back from the entrance door and looked up at the building. There was no light in the top unit, indicating that Cameron wasn't home. It was way too early for him to be asleep already—or still, if he was a vampire. The sun had set a short while ago. If he wasn't home, this was a good occasion to check out his place. But he had to be prepared just in case Cameron was in his flat.

Patrick returned to his car, retrieved a clipboard, and took a padded envelope from his trunk. Quickly, he used a Sharpie to write Cameron's address on it and put a fake name as the recipient, before returning to the entrance door. He was ready to pretend he had a package that needed a signature so he could draw Cameron out, and see for himself if he was a vampire or not. His aura would give him away. It was the way supernatural creatures recognized each other. However, it was invisible to humans.

Patrick rang the doorbell and waited. He heard no sounds from upstairs, and after thirty seconds, he rang the doorbell again. But there was no reply. Looking over his shoulder, he quickly assessed his surroundings. It was a quiet street, and only a few cars drove by. There were no pedestrians. He took his lockpicks from the inside pocket of his windbreaker and went to work.

Everybody who trained at Scanguards learned essential skills, and picking a lock was one of them. He had no trouble opening the entrance door that led into the short hallway with a door to the first-floor apartment. Stairs led to the other floors. He hurried up to the third floor and listened at the door. But no sounds came from the flat. Again, he used his lockpicks and made short work of the lock.

He eased the door open quietly and squeezed inside. The place was comfortably furnished, definitely not on the cheap side. The touch was decidedly masculine with clean lines and dark tones. He kept his eye open for any mail, but found none lying around. There were several houseplants in the living room. Patrick pressed his finger into the soil and noticed that it was moist. Somebody definitely lived here and had recently watered the plants.

He marched into the kitchen. A glance into the trash bin revealed an empty wine bottle and wrappers of junk food. He opened the refrigerator, and found it relatively bare, except for a couple of steaks in the meat drawer, several beers, white wine, and a few condiments. No bottled blood. This ruled out Cameron being a pure-blooded vampire. But he could still be a vampire hybrid, since hybrids could eat human food in addition to blood. The lack of bottled blood in Cameron's fridge could mean that he preferred to hunt for blood and drank directly from a live human.

Patrick opened the kitchen drawers and looked through them for anything confirming that Cameron still lived here, but found nothing in the kitchen. The living room proved to be more fruitful. Underneath a manual for a speaker system, he found a packing slip showing Cameron's full name. The packing slip was recent. He'd received the speaker system only a week earlier. This confirmed that this was indeed Cameron's flat. So why had he told Fallon that he lived in Marin County?

What did he have to hide? Was he living with somebody? Patrick went into the bedroom and found only clothes for a man. There were no toiletries or makeup for a woman, and only one toothbrush. Cameron lived alone.

Patrick glanced at his watch. He'd already spent enough time here. It was best to leave, before Cameron caught him snooping around. As he left the flat and made his way down, he heard voices from downstairs. Doors were opened and closed; footsteps echoed in the hallway. His pulse hitched, but he forced himself to remain calm, while holding on to the clipboard and the padded envelope. He had his excuse ready. If Cameron had just entered the building, he was ready to pretend that he had an urgent delivery, which required a signature.

The sound of the footfalls came closer, then stopped suddenly. He heard the sound of a key being inserted into a lock. Moments later, a door was opened, then closed a few seconds later. The resident on the second floor had come home. Relieved, Patrick rushed downstairs and left the house unseen.

Outside, he looked at the trash cans that were lined up to one side of the house. He grabbed two of them and rolled them in front of the garage. Done with this task, he got back into his car. It was parked on the other side of the street with a clear view of the entrance door to the three-unit Victorian.

The first step was done. He'd confirmed that Cameron lived here. But it didn't tell him whether he was a supernatural creature or not. To determine that, he would need to see the man with his own eyes. Therefore, he had to wait for him to come home. However, there was no guarantee when and if he would return home tonight.

Patrick pulled a burner phone from his glove box and typed in

Cameron's cell number that Fallon had provided him with. He let it ring. On the second ring, it was answered.

"Hello?"

"Mr. Gallagher?" Patrick said, changing his voice a little to sound older and less polished. "I'm George, the plumber for your neighbor, you know, the one below you. Sorry to disturb you, but…"

"Yeah, what is it?" Cameron asked impatiently.

"Well, there's water coming down from your flat. I knocked on your door… well, you need to do something… the water, it's still running. The damage is getting worse…"

"Fuck!" Cameron cursed.

"I'm sorry, Mr. Gallagher, but if you can't turn it off, it'll cause structural damage. The condo insurance won't cover it, if we don't stop it. We'll have to break down the door—"

"Don't you dare break down my door," Cameron thundered. "I'll be there in fifteen minutes."

Cameron disconnected the call, and Patrick removed the SIM card from the phone, broke it in half, and tossed it in the cup holder to be disposed of later. The dark Scanguards SUV he was driving tonight had tinted windows, making it impossible to see inside. He could wait for Cameron here without being seen. Patrick cast a last look at Cameron's driver's license photo that he'd sent to his cell phone earlier to make sure he'd recognize him. After a long look at the jerk, he put it back in his pocket and waited.

He'd never liked waiting much. Stakeouts definitely weren't high on his list of favorite things about his job, because they felt so passive. And he didn't like being passive. He loved being proactive. Therefore, he was glad that his ruse had worked on Cameron. Nobody thought too long about it when getting a phone call about water damage in their home. He'd counted on it, because had Cameron thought about it for a few moments, he would have realized that if it had really been a plumber who'd called him, said plumber could easily have shut off the water to the entire building, thus stopping any further damage. There would be no need for Cameron to rush home.

Patrick leaned back and kept a close eye on every car that passed and the few pedestrians that walked down the sidewalk when his cell phone rang. He looked at the caller ID and answered the call.

"Nicholas?"

"Got some news about the wolf."

"Shoot!" he said, while keeping his eyes peeled on the street so he wouldn't miss Cameron.

"I spoke to my contact at Yellowstone Park. She laughed when I asked her if a wolf could be trained like a dog. My ear is still ringing."

"So that's a no?"

"A hard no. Of all the species that humans have tried to train, the wolves have turned out to be the least capable of submitting to any commands. So, there's no way that a wolf was used by a human to attack our vic."

Patrick rubbed his neck. "Guess that theory was too good to be true. Thanks for checking it out anyway. I'll check in with Sebastian shortly to see if any of the other leads panned out."

"I can save you that call. I'm in the command center, and Sebastian just filled me in. Thomas and Eddie are still working on the traffic cams and the security cams of the houses around the entrance to the Presidio."

"And?"

"No matches in our database of known vampires so far. But Ethan and Damian checked in."

"They spoke to the jewelers who're attending the convention?"

"Apparently our dead guy was popular. No enemies, nothing suspicious. That's a dead end. And none of the other jewelers was staying at the Drisco Hotel. He was the only one. Supposedly, he chose the hotel because it has a great view over the bay."

"Thanks, Nicholas. I'll be at HQ soon. Just gotta check something out."

"See you, bro."

Patrick disconnected the call and put his phone back into the cup holder, when a swanky sportscar shot around the corner. As the car slowed when it reached the three-unit Victorian, the gate to the garage was already lifting. The sportscar screeched to a halt. The driver had realized that the trash cans were preventing him from driving into the garage—exactly as they were meant to do.

The engine of the sportscar was still running, when the driver's side door was opened, and a tall man exited the car. He rushed to the trashcans and pushed them aside just enough so his path was clear. When he turned back to his car, Patrick could finally see his face.

This was Cameron Gallagher. No doubt about it.

But that wasn't the only thing he realized instantly. He identified his aura, and it sent a shockwave through his entire body. He felt ice coursing through his veins, chilling him to the bone. Fallon had been right about being afraid of Cameron. Seeing him now confirmed his greatest fears. Cameron was dangerous, more dangerous than he'd feared.

While Cameron drove into his garage, the gate closing behind his car, Patrick tapped on Lydia's number and put the call on handsfree. He maneuvered out of his parking spot, and drove off, not waiting for Cameron to come back out of the house, most likely utterly pissed off, when he found out that there was no water running, no plumber, and no water damage. There was no time to be lost now to get Fallon to a safe place.

"Hey," Lydia said, answering the phone.

"Lydia, can you talk without Fallon hearing what I'm saying?"

"Yeah, sure. What's up?"

"Have Fallon pack a bag for a few days. She needs to move out of her place. We have to bring her to a safe house. Now." His heart was thundering in his chest, and he felt perspiration collecting on his nape.

"What happened?"

"I saw Cameron Gallagher. He's not a vampire or a vampire hybrid."

"Well, then why are you concerned?"

"Lydia, don't react to what I'm telling you now, or Fallon will become worried. She can't know about this."

"Alright. I'll listen."

"Cameron Gallagher is a werewolf."

There was silence on the other end of the line. Only the sharp intake of a breath reached his ears. A few seconds passed, before Lydia answered, "I'll get her packing. What's your ETA?"

"I'm fifteen minutes out."

"We'll be ready."

16

Fallon watched Lydia disconnect the call and shove her cell phone back into her pants pocket.

"What's wrong?"

"You need to pack a bag."

Nervous energy pulsed through Fallon. "Why? What did Patrick say? That was Patrick, wasn't it?"

"Yes. Let's get you packed," Lydia said evasively. "He'll be here in fifteen minutes. We need to be ready to leave by then."

Her hackles went up. What was Lydia keeping from her? Whatever Patrick had told her had spooked her. She'd seen it in Lydia's face. She'd been unable to hide her shock.

"It's about Cameron, isn't it? Did Patrick confront him?" she pressed. "I have a right to know!"

"Please, Fallon. Patrick will explain everything to you, but for now, for your own safety, you need to get ready to leave. You can't stay here. It's not safe anymore."

Lydia's words sent a chill through her bones. *Not safe anymore.* What did she mean by it? What had happened since Patrick had told her he'd check out where Cameron lived? What had he found?

Realizing that Lydia wouldn't tell her anything and that she would have to wait until Patrick showed up, she capitulated, "Fine, I'll pack."

She marched into her bedroom and pulled a travel bag from underneath her bed.

"For how long do I need to pack?"

From the door, Lydia said, "A few days. Just make sure you have everything with you that you can't buy readily: any meds you're on, your computer and other electronics, your phone, credit cards, ID."

Fallon threw a few items of clothing into the bag, added socks and underwear, then went into her bathroom to collect her essential toiletries.

"Where is Patrick taking me?" she asked while she stuffed toiletries into a plastic bag, before putting them into her travel bag.

"To a safe house."

A safe house. The words conjured up images of spies and witness protection. Of running for her life. Of constant danger. Of a life that wasn't hers anymore. None of these images did anything to make her feel better. She shouldn't need a safe house just because she'd broken up with a man who couldn't take no for an answer.

She looked at Lydia and noticed how tense she had become since Patrick's call. Earlier, she'd been friendly and chatty, easy to talk to. But now, something was stressing her out. She appeared more alert, her head turning toward the apartment door, whenever there were sounds coming from the stairwell.

She now recognized the bodyguard in her, the woman who didn't get distracted from her duty. It was odd to see her change like that in a matter of seconds. She ran her eyes over Lydia, noticing for the first time how well-developed her biceps looked under the tight-fitting long-sleeved T-shirt. Her long legs were encased in form-fitting khakis, and she could easily picture her in hand-to-hand guerilla-style combat. She looked strong and determined, fierce even. Yet from what she could see, Lydia didn't carry a weapon. She might be a trained bodyguard, but would Lydia be able to protect her from Cameron, who was much taller and stronger than the beautiful blonde?

Fallon looked at her watch. Still a few minutes until Patrick was supposed to be back. She walked back into the living room and collected her computer and her handbag with her phone, making sure she had the chargers for both. Then she let her gaze roam, wondering what else she needed to pack. She couldn't think of anything. She hated packing last minute. The few times she'd gone on vacation, she'd laid out everything she wanted to bring well in advance so she wouldn't forget anything. But without even knowing where she was going, she felt panicked.

Did she need to bring towels? Bottled water? Snacks? She walked into the kitchen and opened the fridge. There was nothing in it that qualified as finger food easy to take along on a trip.

"What are you looking for?"

Fallon whirled around and saw Lydia standing in the doorframe. She hadn't even heard any footsteps. She took a steadying breath.

"Do I need to bring food?"

Lydia shook her blonde locks and approached, putting a calming hand on her forearm. "No matter which safe house he's taking you to, everything you need will be there. You won't have to worry about those details. Just make sure you have your personal items with you."

She nodded quickly, wishing her nervousness would subside with Lydia's reassuring words, but it didn't. "I wish I knew what's going on."

"Patrick will be here any moment now."

Lydia walked to the window and peered outside. Fallon followed her to see what she was looking at. Even though it was night—with the streetlights and the headlights of passing cars illuminating the night—it was brighter than usual. She looked up. The moon was almost full and appeared to hang lower in the sky than normal. It seemed bigger and closer, so close that she felt she could reach for it and touch it.

"He's here," Lydia finally announced and pointed to an SUV that was double-parked in front of the apartment building's entrance door. "Let's go."

Lydia ushered her outside. Fallon locked the door before walking downstairs. By the time she reached the entrance door to the building, Patrick had already gotten out of the car and was waiting at the door. She opened it and walked outside, Lydia on her heels.

Fallon was glad to see Patrick, but he too, looked more worried than earlier in the day.

"Patrick, what's going on?" she asked, while he reached for her travel bag.

"I'll explain everything in a minute, but right now we have to get off the street and get you to safety." He looked past her at Lydia. "Follow and make sure nobody is tailing us."

Patrick opened the trunk of the SUV and lifted her bag inside, then closed it.

"No problem," Lydia said, and headed to a dark blue BMW.

"You think Cameron is going to follow us?" Fallon glanced around nervously.

"I don't think so. At least not if we leave right away."

A few seconds later, they were sitting in Patrick's SUV, and drove off.

Fallon fidgeted. "Did you see him?"

Patrick nodded, turning his face to her for just a second. "Yes."

The monosyllabic answer didn't sit well with her. What was he not telling her? "Did you confront him?"

"No. Don't worry, he never saw me."

"So why a safe house? Something must have happened."

"I discovered more things about him. Had I known earlier, I would have brought you to a safe house yesterday."

His words made her shiver. "What did you find?"

Patrick hated lying to Fallon, but he had no choice. He couldn't very well tell her that her ex was a werewolf, one of the most dangerous, most uncivilized of supernatural creatures.

"He comes from a crime family, and from what I could find out, he's in his family's employ. When they don't get what they want, they'll just take it, no matter the law. They don't care about collateral damage."

"Cameron's in the Mafia?"

He looked at her from the side, placing one hand on hers, and noticed that she trembled. He wished he could be entirely truthful with her, but it was better that she thought they were a crime family rather than having to reveal that the Gallaghers were werewolves. She wouldn't believe him anyway, think he was crazy, and stop cooperating. He couldn't risk that.

"In a way, though they don't call themselves Mafiosos. But don't underestimate them: they will do whatever it takes to get what they want. Including killing someone who's in their way."

Tears shot to her eyes, and he felt the urge to wipe them away, but he held back.

"Oh my God. Why did I date him? I should have never dated him. If I'd known that... if only I'd had a clue." She sniffled. "He really did beat up Hank, didn't he? Just because he was jealous."

Even though he hadn't been able to confirm this independently, he replied, "It's very likely. That's their modus operandi: intimidating and coercing others."

"And you think he'll come after me because I rejected him?"

"I believe so."

He knew it for a fact. The few things he knew about werewolves made it very likely. When werewolves found the person they wanted to mate with, they didn't stop at anything until they got what they wanted, even if that person resisted them. In fact, by breaking up with Cameron and refusing to even speak to him, Fallon had activated Cameron's hunting instinct. Now more than ever, he would pursue her.

"What am I gonna do? I can't just hide from him forever."

"I'll figure something out, but right now, the most important thing is that he doesn't know where you are."

Patrick cast her a sideways glance and noticed how tightly she clenched her jaw as if trying to steel herself for whatever bad things were going to happen. But she didn't know the half of what she was facing: a werewolf who wanted her and would never give up. It would be easier to deal with a member of the Mafia. But a werewolf was another level of danger, and an entire pack spelled disaster. This wasn't something he could handle on his own. He needed the full force of Scanguards behind him. And that would throw up all kinds of complications. Confronting a pack of werewolves meant outright war between their two species. And there was no guarantee that Scanguards would emerge as the winner.

17

Fallon shivered. The shock that Cameron was part of a Mafia family still sat deep in her bones, when Patrick slowed the car and drove into the garage of a large Victorian home. Was this the safe house he'd spoken of? If this was it, then the house had most likely been split up into several flats like so many old Victorian mansions in San Francisco. Several cars were parked here, and when she glanced to her right, she noticed that the garage seemed to extend beneath the neighboring house, providing space for at least eight cars.

"Let's get you settled," Patrick said and exited the car.

Fallon got out on the passenger side, and by the time she reached the back of the car, Patrick had already lifted her travel bag out of the trunk and closed it.

"This way." He pointed to a staircase.

As she followed him, she asked, "How many flats are in this house? It looks pretty big."

"It's one residence."

Surprised, she followed him. At the top of the stairs, he pressed his hand to a scanner. A soft beeping sound drifted to her ears before Patrick pushed the door open and walked into the house. Moments later, Fallon entered the foyer, and Patrick pulled the door shut behind her. Another beep sounded, and she assumed that it was the alarm resetting itself.

As she took in the rich wood-paneled foyer, disbelief flooded her. "This is a safe house?"

He smiled at her, already tapping on a contact on his cell phone. "It's my parent's house. Make yourself at home."

Walking a few steps away from her, he brought the cell phone to his ear and listened for a moment, before he said something so quietly that she couldn't hear it. The conversation only lasted a few seconds, before he shoved his cell phone back into his pocket and turned back to her.

"Nobody followed us. You're safe here."

"Why did you bring me here? I mean, I don't want to inconvenience your family."

"My parents are on vacation in Alaska, so you're not inconveniencing anybody. Besides, the house is so big that you wouldn't even hear them if they were home." He cast her a reassuring smile.

She took a breath, still feeling awkward about being in somebody's home without their knowledge and perhaps even without their consent. "You can't possibly be bringing every client who's in danger to your parent's house."

"You're right." He lifted her travel bag, which he'd placed on the floor earlier, and pointed to the stairs. "But your case is special, and you'll be safest here. My parent's house has the best security system, and you won't be alone here. I live here too."

At his words, a breath of air rolled over her lips, and her pulse quickened, her eyes meeting his in stunned silence. She would be staying here with Patrick?

He lifted one hand to prevent her from replying. "And before you get worried, let me assure you that you'll have your own room and bathroom, and I won't intrude on your privacy."

Heat shot into her cheeks at the thought of what he meant by privacy. He wouldn't touch her again. "Oh."

For a long moment, their eyes met, and she wasn't sure what to think or say. Or do.

"I'll protect you no matter what. I don't expect anything from you. In spite of what happened between us earlier today, I don't want you to think that I expect you to... uhm... what I'm trying to say is that I didn't bring you here to seduce you, even though we're going to be alone here."

Her chest lifted with her next breath. "Patrick, about earlier..." She was trying to find the right words to tell him what she felt. But she'd never been good at saying the right things at the right moment.

"You don't have to say anything right now. Just know that all I want is to keep you safe."

He motioned to the stairs. "Let me show you to your room, and then I'll be out of your hair."

As she followed him silently, she contemplated his words. He'd sounded almost nervous, and even though she believed him when he'd indicated that he wasn't expecting any sexual favors, she also recognized that he wouldn't turn her down if she made the first step. She'd felt it earlier in the day when he'd touched her, and she felt it now: Patrick desired her.

Automatically, she compared what she saw in Patrick with Cameron. Cameron's desire for her had always been different, insistent, demanding, without an option on her part to reject him. But Patrick seemed different. He was considerate. He was giving her a choice, assuring her that he would still keep her safe, even if she rejected his advances. He went even further: Patrick wouldn't even put her in a situation where she would have to make a choice.

Patrick opened the door to a room on the second floor and ushered her inside. She looked around. The room was rather large for a Victorian home, with high ceilings, cozy furnishings, a fireplace, and wainscoting inviting her warmly. There was a closet with sliding doors and an ensuite bathroom. The window looked out over a tiny backyard.

Patrick set the travel bag onto a chair. "Make yourself at home. There are fresh towels in the bathroom, and if you want something to eat, the kitchen is downstairs. The fridge is a little bare, but I've already sent Lydia to the grocery store. I'll wait downstairs for her until she's back. She'll protect you here at the house while I'll go back to the office."

"You're leaving again? But it's night."

He gave her a kind smile. "Crime never sleeps." He looked at his watch. "Lydia should be back in about forty-five minutes." He turned toward the door.

The thought of him leaving with this unspoken thing between them didn't feel right. She reached for his arm. "Patrick."

He turned back to her, seemingly surprised. "Yes?"

"It's about what happened earlier," she started, collecting all her courage, her eyes dropping to his parted lips, before her gaze shifted to his neck, where his carotid artery pulsed visibly. Oddly enough, she could almost hear his pulse drumming against his skin, and the sound drew her to him.

Pushing the odd sensation away, she ripped her eyes from his neck and met his gaze. He simply stood there, waiting patiently, giving her the time to collect her thoughts without interrupting her.

"I don't regret what we did." She took a step closer to him, suddenly feeling her body growing warmer. Damn, she wasn't used to making the first step, although this wasn't technically the first step. But in a way it was. "This isn't as easy as it looks."

"What's not easy?"

"Telling a man that I want to have sex with him." The words were out, and there was no taking them back now. All she could hope was that she'd been right in her assessment of Patrick, in her belief that he wanted more.

For a moment, only silence surrounded them. They both stood there as if frozen in time. And maybe time had just stopped, because she wasn't even breathing. It was only when she felt Patrick's warm hand on her face, stepping closer that she realized that she was breathing again.

"You made it look pretty easy," he murmured with a smile on his lips. "And what man with a pulse could ever say no to such an offer?"

His words infused her with confidence, and she brought her body flush to his, feeling his heat join hers. "Is that a *yes*?"

He chuckled softly. "Let me show you what a *yes* feels like."

An instant later, Patrick's lips were on hers, and he was kissing her tenderly. It was different than when they'd kissed before. This kiss was slow and gentle. Their breaths mingled, and their tongues danced, exploring each other. Patrick put one arm around her waist, holding her tightly to him, while he slid his free hand to her nape, caressing her sensitive skin, igniting her cells as if she were a furnace and he was the match to ignite the fire. She let herself go in his embrace, molding her body to his, her hands clinging to his shoulders, not wanting him to change his mind and stop. Maybe she was only dreaming this, because everything she felt seemed more intense. It was as if her senses were sharper, and she was able to absorb his scent and taste to merge with her own.

Patrick was taking his time, not rushing anything, even though she could feel from where their bodies touched that he was aroused. His hard-on was impossible to miss, particularly since he rubbed himself against her sex. But even in that particular movement lay no rush, no hurry, because he wasn't seducing her so she would sleep with him. No, that hurdle had already been eliminated: she'd already told him what she wanted from him. No persuasion, no coaxing was necessary on his part. Instead, every movement, every touch was meant to pleasure each other.

Instinctively, she thought of Cameron, and how he'd been

during sex. While he'd certainly pleasured her, she'd always felt his impatience, as if all he wanted was her submission and his own pleasure. At the thought, she stiffened.

Cool air wafted against her lips, and she realized that Patrick had severed the kiss.

"Is something wrong?" he asked, meeting her gaze. "If you've changed your mind, it's okay."

She shook her head quickly, surprised that he'd noticed the subtle change in her body. "Nothing is wrong. And I haven't changed my mind."

He smiled, and his eyes seemed to sparkle, a golden hue reflecting in them. "I'm glad. But if you want me to go slower, I will. You just have to tell me."

She looked into his eyes. Was this affection that shone from them? She'd never seen it in Cameron before. It had always been lust and desire. Maybe even love. But never affection and kindness. Patrick was different. Warm and gentle. Understanding and patient.

"Make love to me," she whispered, realizing too late what she was saying. Earlier, she'd asked him to have sex with her, but now she wanted him to make love to her. Would he realize the distinction her subconscious had made for her? Did it even matter what she called it?

He brought his face closer to hers, his lips now hovering over her mouth. "Tell me what you like."

"Can we get undressed?"

He kissed her deeply before severing the kiss again. His hands were on the hem of her top, and he shoved it up and over her head, freeing her from it quickly. Beneath it, she wore only a thin silk camisole but no bra. She noticed him roam his eyes over her torso, and at that, her nipples turned hard like little pebbles. When he cupped both breasts with his hands and squeezed them ever so lightly, she gasped at the spear of heat his action sent through her body.

"You're not wearing a bra," he murmured, while he dipped his face to her breasts.

"I only wear one when I'm at work."

Patrick licked his hot tongue over one nipple, making the silk wet and transparent, then did the same with the other breast. Her pulse raced. Wanting to feel him on her skin, she yanked the camisole out of her pants. He helped her pull it over her head. She had no idea where it landed, because an instant later, Patrick's hands were back on her breasts, and he was squeezing them again.

"You have gorgeous tits," he said, lifting his gaze to meet hers, while he continued kneading her flesh, driving her insane with the need for more. "Would you like me to suck them?"

Air rushed from her lungs. "Yes."

Before she knew what was happening, she found herself with her back on the bed, Patrick braced over her, sucking her left nipple deep into his mouth. When she felt his tongue swirl around her hard nipple, she gasped at the pleasure his touch sent through her core and straight to her sex. When he released her nipple, the cool air blowing against her wet nipple made it even harder. Already, Patrick was unleashing the same treatment on her right nipple, and she could feel her clit pulsing with need. She couldn't wait much longer. She needed him inside her.

"Patrick," she said, tilting his head up with her hand under his chin. "What happened with getting undressed?"

He smiled mischievously and winked at her.

"I got sidetracked. Can't blame a guy."

Touching Fallon's beautiful breasts, kneading her firm flesh, and feeling her react to him, had shut down his brain in less than a second. It had been a while since he'd been with a woman. He'd let his responsibilities to his work and his family take priority over his life in the last few months, and if he was honest with himself, he hadn't encountered anybody who he'd been drawn to. Until now. Maybe that was the reason why Fallon had such an effect on him—because he'd been abstinent for too long.

With efficient movements, without giving away that he could undress himself at vampire speed if he wanted, he took off his clothes. From beneath half-lowered lids, Fallon watched him, and he had to admit, he liked that. When he pulled his boxer briefs down and freed his rock-hard cock, Fallon's lips parted, and an appreciative sound rolled over them.

Her eyes on his erection made him even harder. She wasn't shy about what she wanted, and he liked that in a woman.

Finally naked, he stepped closer to the bed again and began to free Fallon of her clothes. Her shoes and socks went first, then her khaki pants, leaving her with only her bikini panties. They were of the same silky material as her camisole. He hooked his fingers into the waistband, and pulled them down her long, toned legs, until he could free her of them completely.

Taking his time, he let his gaze roam over her body. She was perfect. Her breasts were firm and the perfect size for his palms. Her skin was pale like that of so many San Franciscans who rarely ever saw the sun.

"Uhm, Patrick?"

At the sound of his name, he lifted his eyes to meet her gaze. "Hmm?"

"Getting sidetracked again?"

"It's hard not to."

"I can see that." She gave a pointed look in the direction of his cock.

He smirked. He liked that she was direct. "Give me a sec. I've got condoms in my room." He pointed to the wall that separated this room from his own.

"I'm on the pill."

He hesitated. As a vampire hybrid he was born sterile, and he couldn't contract or spread any illnesses, but it wasn't something he could tell the women he slept with. So, he'd always used condoms to guard his secret. But to sleep with Fallon without a condom was tempting.

She lifted herself onto her elbows, her chest thrust in his direction. "If you want to wear one, that's fine, but I'm okay if you don't."

That sealed it for him. With Fallon he wanted the most intimate contact without any barriers between them. He crossed the remaining distance between him and the bed with one large step. Sliding one knee onto the mattress, he leaned over Fallon, bracing his hands on either side of her torso.

"So, uhm, tell me what you like." He ran one hand over her flat stomach and slid it between her legs. Damp heat met his hand, but he didn't move any farther down, and instead waited for her answer.

She reached up and placed her hand on his nape, pulling his head closer to hers. "Your cock inside me. I don't care how, as long as you do it now, before I burn up."

Happy to hear that she was as eager as he, he used his knee to spread her legs wider, so he could slide in the space. "No foreplay?"

"I think you did that already earlier today." She put her hands on his hips and pulled him closer.

"I remember." He touched her nether lips and rubbed his fingers along her cleft. She was drenched in her own juices, and he couldn't help himself and groaned with pleasure. "Damn, how did you get so wet?"

"Watching you undress does something to me," she whispered.

"Good to know." For next time. Because there would definitely be a next time.

"Are you gonna talk the entire time?" she teased.

Without replying, he brought the tip of his cock to her sex and plunged inside, seating himself to the hilt. Despite her plentiful juices, she was tighter than he'd expected. The way her interior muscles squeezed him felt better than anything he'd felt in a very long time—if ever. He stopped moving, remaining lodged deep inside her welcoming pussy, allowing the pleasurable sensation to spread to every cell in his body, while Fallon wrapped her thighs around him, opening up even wider, imprisoning him inside her tantalizing flesh.

He locked eyes with her, gazing deep into her grey irises. Desire blazed from them, and he realized now that she could make any man fall in love with her just by looking at him like this. As if she was a siren, or a witch who'd cast a spell on him. He wasn't sure how long they'd been staring into each other's eyes, before he sank his lips on hers, and kissed her as if his life depended on it.

As he began to thrust in and out of her sweet pussy, he angled his head, seeking a deeper connection, kissing her with abandon. He'd always loved kissing a woman while making love rather than simply thrusting in and out because a kiss intensified the intimacy between them. Just like it did now. He could feel their bodies move in sync with each other, separating and coming back together in perfect harmony, a sensual dance where the chemistry that was sparking between them was dictating the tempo.

His vampire senses, which allowed him to hear her heartbeat and feel the blood rushing through her veins, helped him anticipate what she needed from him. He let his senses guide him to give her the pleasure she wanted and deserved, without focusing on his own needs. They would be fulfilled soon enough. He knew he would be able to climax within seconds if only he allowed himself to surrender to the beautiful woman who was guiding his body as if she were its mistress.

Every sigh and every moan that drifted to his ears filled him with joy, because pleasuring the woman in his arms was all he wanted. With every hot breath, every stroke of her tongue against his, he felt his movements become faster. Despite the increasing tempo of his thrusts, they continued to move in sync with each other.

Fallon's hands were roaming his body, exploring him, pulling him closer, forcing him deeper into her by digging her fingers into his ass. Every time she yanked him closer, he wished for her fingernails to draw blood, and the more often that thought repeated, the more his vampire side battled him for supremacy. The vampire in him wanted to break to the surface and sink his fangs into her alabaster skin, taking her blood inside him to experience the intimacy that only a vampire's bite could create.

His hips moved frantically now, his cock sliding in and out of her pussy. They were both perspiring. It made every slide of skin on skin smooth and sensual like an erotic massage. When he suddenly felt Fallon's tongue swipe against his fang, he felt it lengthen, ready to descend. Panicked, he severed the kiss, and willed his fang to retract, before she could notice it.

Fallon's face glistened, her cheeks were rosy, her lips looked bruised. He could hear the thundering of her heartbeat reverberate against his chest and her breath rush over her lips.

"I love how you take me," she whispered.

"I've never felt anything so good," he confessed. "I don't wanna stop."

"Then don't."

She slid one hand to his nape and caressed him there, sending a shudder down his spine. He pressed his eyes shut and clamped his jaw tightly together to stave off an immediate climax.

"Fuck!" he managed to let out and opened his eyes again. "Just a little warning: you do that again, and I'll come in an instant."

A mischievous glint shimmered in her eyes. "Really?"

"Seductress." He pulled out of her, and sat back on his haunches, but before she could voice a protest, he'd already rolled her onto her stomach.

Her surprised gasp was muffled by a pillow. She turned her head sideways. "I wasn't done."

"I know." He chuckled and pulled her onto her knees, then positioned her so that she could brace her hands on the headboard of the bed. When she was in the position he wanted her in, he kneeled behind her, grabbed her hips, and sank his cock back into her.

A relieved sigh came from Fallon.

"That way I know where your hands are," he teased, then he slipped his right hand around her hip and cupped her pussy. "And I have my hand free to make you come."

When he gathered some of her juices with his finger and rubbed them over her clitoris, she sighed. "Oh."

"Now hold onto the headboard and let me take care of you." He brought his mouth to her ear. "And if there's anything I'm doing wrong, you'll let me know, because we're not leaving this bed until you're completely satisfied."

"How about yourself?" she asked with a look over her shoulder.

He smirked. "I could come by just looking at you. You're so damn hot. So, don't worry about me."

He continued thrusting in a steady but slow pace, while he caressed her clit, painting little circles around the engorged organ. Beneath his fingers, he felt Fallon surrender to his touch, moving with him. Her breaths became irregular, her long hair fell over her shoulders, swinging back and forth, from side to side.

With his free hand, he brushed her hair to one side to expose the graceful column of her neck, where her carotid artery pulsed in rhythm with her heartbeat. Like a beacon, it called out to him, tempting him to throw caution to the wind and bite her, but the man in him pulled back the beast. Fallon needed to be wooed, not conquered. It had to be her decision, not his demand. Her experience with Cameron had left her cautious when it came to relationships, and if he revealed now that he was a vampire, she would flee in horror.

He had to give her time.

And give her pleasure without putting any demands on her. Just like he did now. From earlier in the day, he knew already how to caress her center of pleasure so she could let herself go. Patiently, he touched her, rubbing back and forth over her clit, every so often gathering more of her juices to make his touch smooth.

"Oh, yes," she murmured, panting now.

With his mouth at her neck, he whispered endearments. "You're beautiful. So sexy." With his free hand, he cupped one breast, squeezing it in the same rhythm as he thrust into her from behind while caressing her clit.

He pressed open-mouthed kisses to her heated skin. "You make me so hot. I'm gonna burst any moment now."

Fallon let out a yelp, and her body stiffened.

"Oh, fuck, baby! You feel so good," he ground out, barely holding on to his control now.

Then he felt it. Fallon's muscles contracted around his cock, squeezing him again and again as she climaxed. Relieved, he let out a breath. With it, his orgasm washed over him, shaking him to the core. He pressed one hand against the headboard, bracing himself, while he felt his knees wobble, the impact of his climax more intense than he'd felt in a long time.

Fallon sighed contentedly, blowing out audible breaths. Patrick released her clit and wrapped his arm around her waist, pressing her to him, while nuzzling his face in the crook of her neck.

"Wow!" she said in a breathy voice. "That was... wow."

He chuckled and lifted his head a little. "Better than wow for me." He kissed her neck. "Damn, you feel so good in my arms. I don't want to let go."

A soft chuckle came over her lips, and she turned her face to him. "You're amazing."

He smiled. "I simply followed your lead." He drew his hips back a little, before slowly driving his still-hard cock back in to the hilt.

"Mmm."

"You like that, hmm?" he asked.

"I do. How about seconds?"

Surprised, he met her gaze. Most women didn't immediately want to go another round, unless they hadn't reached their climax. And Fallon had definitely climaxed.

"I'd love to. But—" He'd already heard the garage door opening a moment earlier, and now it was closing again, which meant that Lydia was back. He pointed to the floor, indicating the first floor. "Lydia is back. I need to get back to Scanguards."

"Oh." Fallon moved, and his cock slipped from her.

He could sense her disappointment. When she turned, he put his arms around her and pressed his forehead to hers. "I can't think of anything I'd love more than to spend the rest of the night in bed with you as your love slave."

"You're not just saying that?"

"I'm not just saying that." He pressed a kiss to her lips. "But to keep you safe, my colleagues and I have to come up with a plan for how to remove Cameron from your life permanently. And then there is that murder case I'm working."

She nodded. "I know. I totally understand." She gave him a sweet smile. "You'd better go then."

"Alright. Just promise to stay in the house with Lydia. She'll protect you. And I'll be back as soon as I can. Get some sleep." He climbed off the bed and gathered his clothes.

"I'll take a quick shower before I leave." He couldn't very well have his vampire colleagues make comments about him smelling of sex.

At the door, he looked over his shoulder. "And if you want me to join you in bed when I'm back, go to my room and sleep there. First door to the right. But if you want a good night's sleep alone, just stay in this room, and I won't intrude."

He raked a hungry look over her. She smiled at him, and the sparkle was back in her eyes. He could guess from the look in her eyes where he would find her when he returned home.

18

Patrick parked the car in his assigned spot in the parking garage underneath Scanguards' headquarters building and got out. At the elevator, Benjamin was already waiting.

"Hey, got Lydia's call to come to HQ right away. What's so important?" Benjamin said, just as the elevator doors opened.

Patrick entered just behind him. "I'll catch you up when everybody is here."

"Fair enough. By the way, I just got back from talking to somebody who has a not-so-legal private zoo down on the Peninsula, but the wolf they keep there is a big white one. Beautiful actually, but Buffy said that the hair she found was black. And anyway, their wolf is accounted for."

Patrick nodded. "Any other zoos that you still need to check out?"

"Nope. No leads there."

"Not surprising," Patrick said with a shrug. "I spoke to Nicholas earlier, and he said it's impossible to train a wolf. Our theory that somebody could have trained a wolf to kill that jogger and rip his heart out is dead in the water."

The elevator doors opened, and he and Benjamin headed for the command center. When they entered, several of his colleagues were already assembled. Their conversations quieted, and they turned their heads to look at him and Benjamin.

"Hey, guys, thanks for coming," Patrick said, greeting them.

"We've been here a while," Eddie said with a look at his watch.

"I know. Apologies, but when you hear what I've found out, you'll understand."

That he'd had sex with Fallon, and that was the reason why he was late, was something he'd keep to himself. It would only distract from the problem at hand.

He cast a long look at his colleagues. There weren't as many assembled as he'd hoped, but it would have to do—for now. Besides the hybrids Sebastian, Benjamin, Nicholas, and Ryder, several pure-blooded vampires were present: Eddie, Amaury, and John. It appeared that everybody else was out on assignments.

Patrick took a deep breath. There was no way to break the news any other way than coming right out with it.

"We have a situation. There's a werewolf roaming San Francisco and its surrounding counties."

For a fraction of a second, it was completely silent in the command center, and apart from the humming of the computers, nothing made a sound, not even his own heartbeat. Maybe because his and his colleagues' hearts had all just skipped a beat.

Amaury was the first to find his voice. "Are you shitting us?"

"I wish I were. But I've not only seen him, I know who he is, and where he lives. And I have reason to believe that he attacked and killed our vic."

He caught Nicholas nodding to himself. "That would track with the size of the pawprints I found around the body, and the black wolf hair Buffy found under his fingernails."

"How about you fill us in on the whole story," John said calmly, his southern accent just as pronounced as always. "I have the feeling that you didn't just run into a werewolf by accident. And trust me, you don't wanna get involved in anything to do with werewolves. They are ruthless, uncivilized, brutal creatures. And where there's one werewolf, the pack isn't far."

Amaury jerked his thumb at John, grunting, "What he said."

The vampire who was as massive as a linebacker crossed his arms over his chest as if he was a bouncer standing in front of a club, intent on letting nobody enter.

Patrick nodded. "I get it. Trust me, I'm aware of the danger werewolves represent. I've heard the stories from all you old-timers."

Amaury narrowed his eyes and grunted. He was one of the old-timers, a vampire who was over three hundred years old.

Patrick lifted one hand as an apology. "And that's exactly why we have to get involved. We don't want a pack of uncontrollable werewolves roaming our city. Can you imagine the bloodshed?"

He shifted his gaze from Amaury to John and then to the rest of the assembled. Nobody replied.

"That's what I thought. We've gotta deal with this before it gets worse. So, hear me out. Anita brought me a case of a young doctor who's being stalked and threatened by her ex-boyfriend. At first, I wanted to reject it, but Anita is very persistent, as you all know."

A few grunts bounced against the walls.

"After Fa—uhm Dr. Doyle was attacked by someone or something two nights ago, I looked into her ex. I saw him tonight, and I recognized his aura as that of a werewolf. I researched his background. His family is wealthy and owns properties all over the Bay Area, mostly in Marin County. But there isn't much information about them anywhere."

He looked at Eddie. "Maybe you can dig around a bit, see what you find? Their last name is Gallagher."

Eddie nodded. "I can do that."

"So far I don't see any evidence," John chimed in. "At best, it's circumstantial. I hate seeing a werewolf in San Francisco as much as the next vampire, but we can't just pin any crime on him, no matter how much we'd like him gone."

"No, there isn't a lot of evidence, not yet. That's why I called this meeting. What we do have is what the autopsy tells us: our victim was killed by a wolf, who ripped the heart clean out, and most likely ate it, since we couldn't find any trace of it. And since Nicholas confirmed with his contact at Yellowstone National Park that wolves cannot be trained like dogs, the attack couldn't have been perpetrated by a regular wolf. That leaves us with the only possible suspect: a werewolf. Now, I'm not saying that Cameron Gallagher is the werewolf who did this—" Though he really wanted him to be the killer, because it meant that he could justify eliminating him. "—but as you pointed out, John, where there's one werewolf, the pack isn't far. My guess is that the pack lives in Marin County."

"That's all well and good," Amaury said, nodding, "but that's still not gonna tie him to the Presidio murder."

"No, it doesn't, but—" An idea sparked. "—we might be able to place him at the Presidio if we compare his photo to the security footage that we pulled from the neighbors in the area. Eddie?"

"Yeah, we can totally do that. We just finished checking if any vampire in our database was in the area that morning, but we came up empty. I can do facial recognition using that guy's photo. What's his name?"

"Cameron Gallagher. He's got a California driver's license, but it's expired."

Eddie tapped something on the computer console, clicked on a few links, and moments later, Cameron's driver's license appeared on the large monitor on the wall.

"Handsome guy. That him?" Eddie asked.

"Yeah."

"I'll get on it."

Patrick nodded and turned back to the others in the room. "I also need somebody to talk to Hank Corcoran. He used to work at

Dr. Doyle's lab at UCSF. He was beaten up by Cameron, but he denies it, and he never pressed charges."

"Why would he beat up a lab assistant?" Ryder asked.

"Because that lab assistant hugged Fa—Dr. Doyle to congratulate her on the grant she got, and Cameron saw it. He considers her his property."

"Wow," Ryder said shaking his head. "If that's true, he's a piece of shit. I mean I get jealousy, I do, but there's a line you just do not cross. Women don't like to be treated like property."

"Is that why she broke it off with him?" Benjamin asked.

"Yep. She confronted him after she saw what he did to Hank."

"Yet, Hank denies it happened?" Ryder asked.

"Who knows what Cameron threatened him with," Patrick replied. "I questioned him, but he stuck to his guns and said that he fell down the stairs."

"That might well be—if Cameron pushed him," Ryder said dryly. "I'll go speak to this Hank guy."

"Thanks, bro. Use mind control if he still denies it."

Ryder tilted his head to the side. "Why didn't you use mind control to make him tell you the truth?"

Patrick shrugged. "The situation didn't warrant it. When I spoke to him, I didn't know that Cameron was a werewolf, and it was also before the attack on Fal, uhm—"

"Patrick," Amaury interrupted. "A word outside."

Patrick stared at Amaury. "What the—"

"Now!" Amaury bellowed and marched toward the door.

He had no choice but to follow him, while his colleagues stared at them in confusion. Once in the hallway, he closed the door and turned to Amaury.

"What is it?" Patrick asked, taking the offensive. He wouldn't let Amaury steamroll him, whatever this was about.

Amaury narrowed his eyes and took a step closer, going nose-to-nose with him. "Are you fucking suicidal?"

"What the fuck are you talking about?" Patrick grunted. "Are you challenging my authority? 'Cause I don't remember my father putting you in charge during his absence! Or have you forgotten that?"

Amaury made a dismissive movement with his head, before jabbing his index finger into Patrick's chest. "You think I don't know what's going on here? You're sleeping with this werewolf's ex!"

Shock made him take a step back. "How the—"

But he didn't even get a chance to finish his sentence.

"Oh please! Every time you speak of Dr. Doyle, you wanna call her by her first name, which wouldn't be suspicious at all if you weren't trying to correct yourself every time. And you'd only do that because you're trying to hide that you're fucking her." He paused for a moment. "Besides, you reek of sex."

Apparently, taking a shower after leaving Fallon's bed hadn't been sufficient.

"It's none of your business!" Patrick ground out.

"It is when you're painting a target on yourself and on Scanguards. The moment Cameron figures out that you're sleeping with his girlfriend—"

"Ex-girlfriend!" he corrected his colleague.

Amaury scoffed. "As if that'll make a difference. He'll come after you. He'll come after all of us. And I don't particularly want a pack of werewolves gunning for our necks. You don't know what I know. Trust me, werewolves are uncontrollable, and a jilted lover is just like a wounded animal: more dangerous than anybody else."

"That's exactly why we have to nail Cameron for what he's done. As long as he's out there, he'll kill other innocents." And the next one might be Fallon. But he wasn't going to voice his concern in Amaury's presence.

"Well, then you'd better find some evidence!"

"I intend to." And he wouldn't rest until Cameron had been dealt with and was out of Fallon's life. Out of all their lives.

19

Fallon tossed and turned, unable to find a comfortable position. After the very satisfying sex with Patrick, she should have fallen into a deep sleep, yet sleep eluded her. Maybe it was the unfamiliar house, or the strange bed—Patrick's, not the one in the guestroom—but something wouldn't let her find the rest she craved. There were so many different sounds that drifted to her: the cars passing by the street in front of the house, as well as the creaking of wooden floorboards in the house itself. They had to be coming from Lydia, who was on the first floor, awake, watching over her.

After Patrick had left the house, Fallon had dressed in jogging pants and a T-shirt and quickly gone downstairs to get some water and a yogurt. She'd thanked Lydia for having gone food shopping, before going back upstairs and following Patrick's invitation to sleep in his room.

The thought that he'd join her in bed when he was done with work pleased her, although she didn't understand why she was jumping head over heels into a new relationship. After her experience with Cameron, it would be smarter not to date anyone for a while, but there was something so comforting and right about being with Patrick. He was gentle and considerate, despite the confidence with which he carried himself, and the responsibilities on his shoulders. Men in his position—and with his good looks—often displayed a certain amount of arrogance and entitlement, yet both personality traits seemed to be absent in him. Or was he just better at hiding them?

Her head was spinning now, not just from the thoughts going through her mind, but also from the sounds that seemed to get louder with every minute. She was getting a headache, and perspiration started to engulf her, drenching her to the point where the T-shirt she slept in clung to her breasts and back.

She tossed the thin duvet off her body, trying to find relief from the heat, but she found none. She felt feverish. It was as if her body was burning up from inside. Was she coming down with something?

She sat up and swung her legs out of bed, setting her bare feet on the cool wooden floor. For a moment, she felt a semblance of relief, but it didn't last long. Her entire body began to ache now, not just her head, but everything: her skin itched as if she'd fallen into poison ivy. She switched on the bedside lamp, and the light fairly blinded her despite the dark lampshade that should have only thrown a soft glow on her surroundings. Instead, the small light source illuminated the room as if she were in a lab with harsh industrial lights. For a moment, she had to close her eyes to stop them from hurting. When she opened them again and started to get used to the light, she examined her skin, but despite her skin itching, she found no hives, no red patches. The little hairs on her arms rose, adding to the prickling sensation. Something was wrong.

Had she come into contact with chemicals during the attack in her lab to which she now showed an allergic reaction? Or worse, had she been infected with anything in the hospital? She knew—better than anybody—that hospitals were breeding grounds for superbugs, and any of those bacteria could have entered her bloodstream via the cuts and abrasions she'd sustained during the attack.

She remembered the antibiotics she'd started right after returning home from the hospital. They should help, but what if whatever she'd caught was resistant to antibiotics?

Knowing she had to do something, she stood up, wrapped herself in her bathrobe, and left the room. When the door shut behind her, it made a deafening noise as if she'd slammed it, even though she hadn't. Downstairs, she found Lydia sitting in the living room, reading. She looked up.

"Can't sleep?"

The sound of Lydia's voice sent a ringing through her ears, startling her. Instinctively, she put her hands over her ears, drowning out the noise.

"Something is wrong." Her own voice sounded different, too shrill and too loud.

Lydia shot up from the sofa, and the sound of her shoes tapping on the wooden floor reminded her of a loud knocking on a door.

"You don't look too good," Lydia said, approaching.

"My head hurts, everything is so loud... I'm hot...I think I got infected with something..." She felt her heart pounding in her chest, and her Apple Watch beeped, indicating that her heart rate was spiking.

She glanced at it and had trouble focusing her eyes on the display, until she was finally able to read the numbers: 156bpm. She rarely ever reached that heart rate even when sprinting on the treadmill or running up the stairs.

Trying to calm herself, she pressed her hand to her chest and felt the reverberations of her heart drumming against her palm.

Was she having a heart attack?

"I need a doctor..." she pressed out.

But the thought of returning to the hospital, where she didn't feel safe, scared her. "Not UCSF."

Lydia was already tapping something on her phone, before pressing it to her ear. "Patrick? Fallon isn't well. I'm bringing her in."

Fallon felt Lydia take her by the arm, and picked up a few more words from her conversation.

"Get Buffy to meet us at HQ."

Moments later, she sat in the passenger seat of Lydia's dark blue BMW. As the engine roared, the loud noise intensified the pain in her head and drove her heart rate even higher. The beeping of her Apple Watch warning her of her high heart rate was unbearable by now, and she tugged at the watch strap and ripped it off her wrist, tossing it between her feet. Finally, the beeping stopped, and she leaned back in the seat, while the engine sound turned into a dull humming noise. The lights of other cars coming toward them blinded her, and she pressed her eyes shut.

She wasn't sure how long she'd kept her eyes shut, until it got quieter around her. The sounds of other cars dissipated, and she finally only heard the humming of the BMW wrapping around her like a cocoon. Isolated from other sounds, it became bearable, and she let out a sigh of relief.

A moment later, the car came to a stop and silence surrounded her.

"We're here," Lydia announced, her voice much softer now, almost soothing as if she spoke to a child.

She appreciated it and opened her eyes. As she glanced around, she recognized that they were in an underground parking garage.

"This isn't San Francisco General," she murmured.

"I brought you to Scanguards' medical center. We can help you here."

Before she could ask why a security company operated a medical center, the passenger side door opened, and a hand reached for her.

Startled, she gasped, and spun her head to see who it was, but even before her eyes could perceive the person, she recognized him by the scent that drifted to her nose.

"Patrick," she whispered.

He helped her out of the car, and put his arm around her, supporting her weight.

"Baby, you're burning up," he said, deep concern in his voice.

The sound of the car doors closing echoed in the vast space, sending another shockwave through her body, making her flinch.

With Patrick on one side of her, and Lydia on the other, they led her to an elevator. The doors already stood open with a gurney ready to receive her.

She didn't protest when Patrick lifted her onto it, feeling relief spread in her aching limbs. She took a deep breath, squinting when she looked straight into the lights on the ceiling of the elevator. Patrick leaned over her, blocking out the light.

"Better?" he asked.

She was surprised that he'd realized without asking her that the light was causing her discomfort.

"Yeah." Her reply was more breath than word.

She felt the movement of the elevator as it descended. In her addled mind she briefly wondered why a medical center would be below ground. She let her eyes drift closed for a while. At some point the elevator stopped, and the doors opened. She heard footsteps as Lydia and Patrick wheeled her along a corridor.

After a turn, a set of doors opened, and there were voices. The humming and beeping of machines, the familiar sounds of a hospital drifted to her ears.

"In here," a female voice said with authority.

A warm hand touched her forearm, and she knew it wasn't Patrick's. She would have recognized his touch.

"I'm Buffy. I'll take care of you, alright, Fallon?"

She wanted to nod, but the mere thought of moving her head sent another wave of pain through her body.

"Thank you, doctor," she said instead.

"Just Buffy," she corrected. "Tell me your symptoms."

"Headache, it's so loud..." She took a breath. "So bright... everything hurts. I'm so hot. A fever maybe."

"Alright, Fallon, just rest now. I'll examine you. You'll feel better soon, I promise you."

Even though she didn't believe Buffy's statement, Fallon was grateful for the positive attitude.

Another hand squeezed hers ever so lightly. "You can trust Buffy," Patrick confirmed. "I'm right here with you."

She hummed her approval and surrendered to the care of the people around her. She felt safe now.

20

Patrick watched closely as Buffy began to examine Fallon. He was concerned. It was evident that Fallon was sick, and he could only guess that it had something to do with the attack from the previous night. Had the doctors at UCSF missed something? Or was she reacting to the medications they'd prescribed her?

"Are you taking any meds right now?" Buffy asked.

Patrick answered in her stead, "They gave her painkillers and antibiotics. Anything else, Fallon?"

Fallon took a breath. "Just oral contraceptives."

"Are you allergic to penicillin?" Buffy asked.

"No."

"Okay. I don't think you're reacting to any of the meds you're on. I need to run a few tests," Buffy explained. "I'll draw some blood. You're okay with that?"

"Yes."

While Buffy prepared the tools for drawing blood, Patrick remained standing next to the gurney, stroking Fallon's arm gently. He caught Lydia's gaze on him. There was no surprise in Lydia's eyes at seeing the tender gesture. He was certain that Lydia had already recognized his scent on Fallon, realizing that they'd been intimate. He didn't care that she knew. He didn't need to justify his actions to anybody. Besides, Lydia was no stranger to instant hook-ups and one-night stands. Not that what he and Fallon had was a one-night stand. At least he hoped it wasn't. He felt something more than just sexual attraction. He was genuinely concerned about her well-being, and not just because she was a client. He couldn't bear the thought of Fallon being in pain.

When Buffy began drawing Fallon's blood from the vein inside her elbow, Patrick could smell her blood more intensely and felt his throat tighten at the thought of tasting her blood. He pushed his need down, knowing he couldn't allow exposing himself for what he was. He couldn't afford to frighten her. Despite the fact that they'd had sex, he was still a stranger to her, and he had no reason to believe that she trusted him sufficiently to accept his vampire side.

When Buffy pressed gauze over the puncture wound the needle had left, and bandaged it, he caught her eye.

"Fallon, I'll give you something that'll make you feel better," she said, and motioned to Patrick. "Patrick, give me a hand with it, will you?"

He recognized that Buffy wanted to talk privately and nodded. "Fallon, I'll be right back. Lydia will be by your side for a minute, okay?"

"Okay," Fallon said.

He and Buffy walked to one of the private examination rooms and entered. He shut the door behind them.

"Do you know what's wrong with her?" Patrick asked instantly.

"No idea. All her vitals are fine. Actually, not just fine, but excellent. I need to run some tests on her blood, but that'll take time. But she's clearly in pain. You need to give her your blood."

He nodded. He'd expected as much. Vampire blood was a cure-all for humans. In fact, years earlier, the staff at Scanguards' medical center had cured a stage four cancer patient with infusions of vampire blood.

"How do you want me to give it to her? She can't know what it is."

"I'll disguise it in cough syrup. It's sweet enough so she won't taste that it's blood."

"Alright."

It took only a few moments for Buffy to pour cough medicine into a small cup and for Patrick to drip an almost equal amount of blood from his finger into it. Buffy stirred it and nodded.

"Ready."

Fallon still lay on the gurney, Lydia by her side. When he and Buffy approached, Lydia cast a knowing look at the little plastic cup in Buffy's hand. She knew why he'd disappeared with Buffy: so that Fallon wouldn't know that she was being given vampire blood to help her heal.

"Fallon, let me help you sit up." Patrick reached around her and pulled her up to a sitting position.

In his arms, she still felt feverish.

"This is a tonic that'll help you feel better in a few minutes," Buffy said, and put the cup to her lips.

Fallon's eyes were open now. They looked bloodshot, and for a second, Patrick wished he'd put even more of his blood into the cup to eradicate whatever was causing this.

Without a word, Fallon drank the liquid and swallowed it, gagging and scrunching up her face in disgust.

"Yuck, that's sweet," she commented.

Good. That meant she hadn't picked up on the metallic taste of the blood.

"It should work pretty fast," Buffy commented. "I suggest you rest now."

She lifted her head to look at Buffy. "Do you know what's wrong with me?"

"Not yet, but I'm running blood tests. In the next 12 to 24 hours, we should know what's happening with you. In the meantime, this tonic will temporarily dull the symptoms you described. All you can do now is rest and wait." Buffy turned to him. "Patrick, you can take her home. I'll call you when I've got the results."

"Alright," Patrick said. "Thank you, Buffy."

"Yes, thank you, doctor," Fallon added.

"I'll take you home myself," Patrick said, then looked at Lydia. "Take the rest of the night off. I'll stay with Fallon at the house. I'll need you to take over mid-morning."

"No problem," Lydia replied. "Just text me when you want me back at the house."

"Will do."

When Fallon tried to get off the gurney, Patrick stopped her.

"You're not wearing any shoes. Stay on the bed until I get you to my car."

By the time he reached the parking garage and his designated spot close to the elevators, Fallon's face had taken on a more natural color, and the feverish look was waning. His blood was doing its job, healing her from the inside and getting her body's functions back to an even keel. When they sat in the car, he could hear her heart beat at a slower tempo than when she'd arrived with Lydia.

As he merged into light after-midnight traffic, he reached for Fallon's hand and squeezed it. He gave her a sideways look, and it appeared that she finally took in her surroundings again. In fact, it almost looked like she only now realized that she was wearing only a bathrobe over a T-shirt, no shoes, no shorts, her shapely legs exposed under the short robe.

He navigated the car through almost deserted side streets until they reached his parents' home in Nob Hill, where he parked the car in the garage. He wasn't going to return to the office tonight. His colleagues were following any leads they could during the remainder of the night, and he would take care of other issues in the morning. But for now, even he needed a few hours of sleep. It had been a long and eventful day.

"You must be tired," he said to Fallon as he led her into the house.

"I was. I guess I am. I feel better... But my T-shirt is soaked with sweat."

"Let's go upstairs. I'll give you one of mine to sleep in so you'll be comfortable."

"Thank you."

Fallon looked stable enough to walk up the stairs without his assistance, and he was happy to see that she was feeling better. He opened the door to his room, and entered, intent on fetching a T-shirt for Fallon, when his gaze fell onto the bed.

It was unmade—somebody had slept in it.

He looked over his shoulder at Fallon.

"You slept here?"

She cast him a slow smile. "You said I could if I wanted to..."

"I'm glad you did." He reached for her hand, and she stepped closer. "Do you want to sleep here, with me, or would you rather stay in the guestroom so you can rest?"

"Can't I stay here?" She smiled at him now.

He slung his arm around her waist and pulled her closer. "Of course you can, though Buffy said you need rest." And he wasn't sure how much rest she would get if they slept in the same bed.

"This doctor, Buffy, she works for Scanguards?"

He nodded.

"So, technically, she works for you, right?"

"Yes, why?" He had no idea where she was going with this.

"So, you could override her orders, can't you?"

When he realized what she meant, he chuckled. "I could, but she's the doctor."

"Does that mean you won't let me sleep here?"

He pressed his forehead to hers and noticed that the temperature of her skin was back to normal. "Do you really think I can say no to you?"

"Oh God, I hope not."

Unable to resist the temptation, he captured her lips with his and kissed her tenderly, while he undid the belt of her bathrobe and tunneled underneath it to explore her luscious curves. When he touched the damp T-shirt, he released her slowly.

"Let me get you a clean T-shirt first, and then we both need to sleep." He met her gaze. "Together, in my bed." With a smirk, he added, "Doctor's orders."

21

Dressed in a large white T-shirt, and wearing only her bikini panties, Fallon snuggled against Patrick's chest. Except for his boxer briefs, he was naked, his arm wrapped around her shoulder, the other hand on her hip. She could hear his heart beating rapidly, almost as if he'd done a sprint before coming to bed.

"I don't know what Buffy gave me, but I'm feeling so much better," Fallon said. "She's a good doctor. I'm surprised, because she looks so young."

"She has a lot of experience in Emergency Medicine. That's really all that Scanguards' medical center deals with."

"I don't understand why a security company needs a med center. Why not send people to the ER at San Francisco General?"

A soft breath blew against her temple before Patrick spoke again.

"With our kind of work, we get into tons of scrapes every day, and we don't want to overwhelm the ERs in the city when we can treat our own people more efficiently ourselves. It's actually cheaper for us to maintain our own medical center than to pay health insurance for our employees. And of course, any client who gets injured on our watch is treated there too."

Surprised, she lifted her head to look at him. "About that. I mean... I'm your client, right, but I haven't even signed a contract or paid you a retainer..."

He stroked his finger along her jawline. "Don't worry about that."

"But I have to pay Scanguards for all the work you're doing for me. Or—" She hesitated.

He tipped her face up to look directly at her. "I hope you don't think that you have to sleep with me so that I help you. You don't."

He dipped his face to hers. "You can change your mind any time you want. It won't change anything about my commitment to keep you safe."

She brushed her lips over his and kissed him gently. He responded to her in the same way but didn't deepen the kiss. However, his hand on her hip slid lower and he cupped her ass, pressing her more tightly against his body.

He severed the kiss. "I suppose that means you won't change your mind."

"You probably think I'm easy, I mean because I've hopped into bed with you so quickly... Especially after what happened with Cameron. But I just feel safe with you. I don't know why, because I don't even know you..." And maybe she was making a mistake. She hoped not, but her judgment hadn't exactly been stellar in the last few months.

"By the same token you must find me easy too," he said, "because I made love to you within twenty-four hours of meeting you."

She chuckled softly, appreciating his words. "If you put it that way."

He hummed softly. "Tell me a little about yourself. What's your research about?"

Surprised that he asked about her work, which Cameron had never shown any interest in, she said, "Aging. I'm trying to find the genes that make our cells age, to figure out how to switch them off to stall or slow aging."

"So you think there might be a way for humans to stop aging?"

"I hope so. I mean, isn't that what everybody wants? A fountain of youth?"

"What made you go into that field?"

"It was actually my grandmother who gave me that idea. As far back as I can remember she used to say *If they don't find something soon, then we'll all die*. When I asked her what she meant by that she told me that if the doctors can't find anything to stop a person from aging, eventually we'll die. And she didn't want to die. She was such a fun-loving woman. She was the one who told me that even though her body was that of an old woman, inside it, she was still the young woman who loved adventures."

She sighed at the memories of her grandmother. "She died a few years ago. When I saw her a few days before her passing, she told me to continue my research so that maybe for my generation, it wouldn't be too late. I think she knew she was dying."

"I'm sorry," Patrick whispered and pressed a kiss to her temple. "My grandparents are long gone too. I actually never met them."

"That's sad. Having grandparents was such an important part of my childhood. I can't imagine never having met them."

"And the rest of your family? Where are they?"

"My parents live in Boston. Mom is still working for a charity, and my dad is an accountant for a big firm."

"Do you have siblings?"

She shook her head. "No. You?"

Patrick laughed softly. "Yep, two. Both older than me. My brother is married and runs the Scanguards branch in New Orleans, and my sister is married too, and has a toddler. She works at Scanguards too, and her husband owns a nightclub, the Mezzanine. You might have heard of it?"

"Heard of it? It's just about the hardest club to get into. That bouncer is totally intimidating!"

Patrick laughed a deep roaring laugh. "That bouncer is my brother-in-law, Orlando."

"But I thought you said he owns the club."

"He does. But he loves to control who gets into his club and who doesn't. It's a sport for him. I can put you on the permanent guest list for the club, and he'll wave you right through."

"Thank you, but I doubt I'll be going to any clubs anytime soon. I've never liked to go to clubs on my own."

Patrick slid his fingers under her chin to tilt her face up. "Then maybe I should accompany you."

"I'd like that." Her gaze dropped to his parted lips, and she inched closer until their lips touched.

When she kissed him this time, she felt her hunger for him reemerge. Her body felt normal again, the strange aches and pains from earlier completely gone. What remained was the sensation of awareness that spread to every cell of her body.

She caressed his chest while she shifted in his arms, intensifying the kiss. Patrick's response was passionate, and she felt his heartbeat accelerate under her palm. It felt as if his body was awakening too. Sexual arousal charged through her body, and she slid her hand lower to his flat stomach, where her fingertips bumped against the waistband of his boxer briefs. She let her hand slide over the fabric until she encountered the hard outline of his cock. Before she could squeeze his erection, Patrick wrapped his hand around her wrist, stopping her.

He ripped his lips from hers, panting. "Fuck, Fallon. What happened to getting some rest?"

There was no anger in his words. Instead, he sounded like a man on the verge of surrender.

"We can rest later," she murmured, ready to seduce him with all her feminine wiles to get what she wanted. And what she wanted was Patrick—his cock inside her, his arms around her, his lips devouring her.

His grip on her wrist loosened, and she squeezed his cock, wringing a strangled moan from his throat.

WHEN HE FELT Fallon's hand squeeze his cock, he gave up all resistance. Fuck, Fallon wanted him, and if she didn't feel she needed rest, who was he to force her to sleep?

He tugged on her T-shirt, and pulled it over her head, an action that made her release his cock for a moment. When he tossed her T-shirt behind her, she was already freeing him of his boxer briefs. But before he could do the same with her bikini panties, she was lowering her head to his groin.

The realization of what she was about to do sent a spear of lust into his balls, tightening them, while his cock jerked, eager for her touch.

Fallon licked over the tip of his erection, causing a loud moan to rip from his throat.

"Fuck, baby!"

She gripped the base of his shaft with one hand, before she placed her lips around his cock and took him inside her warm and wet mouth. Her saliva turned the descent into a drive into pure paradise. She took him deep, her lips closing tightly around his sensitive flesh, sucking him like he was a popsicle about to melt in the hot sun. But he didn't melt, didn't shrink like an ice cream cone in the heat. Instead, he grew harder, his arousal reaching the stratosphere.

He reached for her, one hand on her nape, the other cupping one cheek, not to force her to take him deeper, but to be able to pull out of her mouth should the pleasure become too intense. His entire body felt as if he were floating, softness surrounding him, Fallon cradling him. Her touch was tender and all-consuming. His brain had long ago shut down, and he was now guided by his vampire instincts. His gums itched with the need to extend his fangs and drive them into the woman who made love to him, claiming her. But he pushed that particular desire away, focusing only on his sexual desire and the lust that was coursing through his veins now.

Fallon slid up and down on him, her tongue caressing the sensitive underside of his cock, her hand around his base adding to the intensity of her motions. When she suddenly touched his balls, cradling them in her other hand, he used both hands to push her back, making her release his erection.

"Stop!" he cried out and sat up.

With a sly glance, she looked at him. "Didn't like it?"

Her smile told him that she knew full well what effect she had on him.

"Take off your panties, or I'll rip them to shreds," he ground out, barely able to hold on to his control now.

Fallon heeded his command and removed her last item of clothing, while he raked a hungry look over her body. Her breasts were firm with hard, dark nipples that were proof of her arousal. He pulled her onto him, her legs falling open to either side of his hips, her sex lining up with his groin. Without a word, he lifted her hips just high enough so he could adjust his cock to touch her nether lips. Warm wetness greeted him, and without losing a second, he thrust upwards, seating himself in her welcoming pussy.

Fallon gasped, staring at him in surprise. "Oh, God, you're even bigger than earlier."

"That's 'cause you sucked me," he replied. "Damn, woman, you drive me insane with need."

She put her arms around him and tilted her head to the side. He welcomed her invitation and took her lips with his, kissing her as she began to ride him. Not wanting her to tire too soon, he placed his hands on her hips to support her weight while she continued to set the rhythm.

The tempo of their lovemaking remained slow, and he appreciated it because he didn't want it to end, despite his body craving to shoot his seed into her as if she was his and his alone. He knew he couldn't make such a claim, not yet anyway. Fallon was still vulnerable, not ready to make a commitment, even though he was. He realized this with a start: he wanted her as his mate, the only woman he wanted to touch for the rest of his life. It hit him broadside, though he shouldn't be surprised. After all, his vampire instinct had known it all along—from the very moment he'd first seen her—that she was destined to be his partner, his mate for life.

He understood so much now, understood what his siblings and his friends had gone through when they'd met their mate. He'd always wondered how they could know with such certainty who they were meant to be with. He knew it now, even though he was unable to describe the feeling, just like his siblings and friends had never been able to describe what happened in that moment.

Patrick ripped his lips from hers, severing the kiss. His eyes found hers, and he recognized the passion in them.

"Oh, baby," he whispered, lifting one hand to brush his fingers over her cheek. He wanted to tell her about the feelings that he carried in his heart, the love that was growing there for her, but he knew he couldn't. It would only frighten her and make her withdraw, because she would feel pressured to respond. And he didn't want her to feel pressured.

"I love how you ride me," he said instead. "Tell me what you need from me."

Her lips parted with a sigh, her lids halfway closed. "You're already giving me all I need. I'm so close."

He dropped his hand to where their bodies were joined and found her clit.

"Oh, yes," she whispered, her head tilting back.

The movement thrust her breasts toward him. He began to caress her clit with his finger, while he brought his face to her breasts, pulled one nipple into his mouth, and sucked her.

Fallon gasped and murmured something incomprehensible. Encouraged by her reaction, he scraped his teeth along the sensitive skin of her breast. His fangs extended involuntarily, and his cock spasmed, the lust too great to contain. Despite his efforts to suppress his vampire side, he couldn't. Knowing there was no way back now, he licked her tit, coating it with his saliva, before he drove his fangs into her flesh.

Fallon cried out, her tight channel contracting around his cock as she climaxed. He tasted her blood in his mouth and swallowed the rich liquid, letting it coat his throat, while he shot his seed into her. Her blood tasted different from any human blood he'd ever had, and he'd tried all blood groups in his life. But Fallon's was special, richer, with a flavor that made the vampire inside him roar like a beast. More waves of pleasure hit his cock as Fallon continued to climax. His bite was prolonging her orgasm, and he knew that she didn't feel any pain, and wasn't even aware that his fangs were lodged in her breast, the pleasure he was bestowing on her with his bite drowning out everything else.

As his orgasm subsided, he slowly retracted his fangs, and licked over the tiny incisions, making sure no blood remained on her skin. His saliva mended it to leave no evidence of his bite, before he lifted his head and looked at her.

Fallon's lips were parted, her eyes half closed, her breath ragged, her body relaxing against him.

It took a few moments before she found her voice. "Oh, Patrick, that was... that was..." She blew out a breath.

"Good?" he asked with a grin.

She shook her head, a smile forming on her lips. "Not good. Not good at all. Just... wow... just amazing."

His chest swelled with pride. She'd enjoyed his bite, even though she wasn't even aware of it.

"You were amazing," Patrick said. "And your lips on my cock. Damn it, just thinking about it makes me hard again."

But he knew they both needed rest.

"We should sleep," he said, lifting her off him gently.

As they slipped under the covers together, Patrick molded his front to her back, tucking her ass into the curve of his groin. His cock was rock-hard again, a result of Fallon's blood. Unable to resist, he adjusted himself behind her, and drove his erection back inside her still wet pussy.

She gasped in surprise, but pressed herself closer to him, taking him deep inside. "I thought you wanted us to sleep."

"I want you to sleep," he corrected her. "You need it. Just ignore my hard-on. There's nothing I can do right now to get it to relax."

She giggled. "I know what'll get it to relax."

"Apart from THAT!" he said, chuckling. "You should sleep. I promise not to disturb you. Well, at least not much, unless you insist on me pulling out of you."

She reached back to put her hand on his hip, drawing him toward her. "Stay inside me. It feels good."

He moved back less than an inch and forward again, and Fallon sighed contentedly.

He would remain hard for hours, and it would only take a few shallow thrusts for him to find release again. He wrapped one arm around her, cupping her breast, caressing the spot where he'd bitten her. This wouldn't be the last time he drank her blood. But next time, he wanted her to be fully aware of what he was doing, and still want it, want him.

22

"So, you and Fallon," Anita said into the silence.

Patrick cast her a quick sideways glance. They were in his car, driving on the 101 Freeway through Marin County just north of the Golden Gate Bridge. It was late morning, and traffic was light.

"What makes you think that?" he finally deflected.

"Everybody knows. Amaury isn't the only one who smelled her on you. Besides, Lydia isn't blind either."

He wasn't surprised about that. He and Fallon hadn't exactly been very discreet. "So Lydia told her brother, and Cooper told you."

She shrugged. "Cooper is concerned about you."

"Cooper should mind his own business, no offense."

"Actually, it is his business. It's all of Scanguards' business. You can't just hook up with the girlfriend of a werewolf and think nothing bad's gonna happen."

"Ex-girlfriend," he corrected, irritated. And he wouldn't exactly call it a hookup either. What he and Fallon had was more than a fling. At least for him.

"Hey, I'm just saying. And occasionally you could thank me for having brought you this case. My gut feeling was right again. I told you there was more to it than an obsessed ex-boyfriend."

Patrick inhaled a long breath, then turned his head to look at Anita. "Thank you for bringing me this case. Happy now?"

"I'll be happy when the threat this werewolf represents is eliminated. Frankly, I had no idea werewolves existed."

"Yeah, well, we knew, though nobody at Scanguards was aware that there's a pack so close to San Francisco."

"Cooper said werewolves are more dangerous than vampires. Is that true?"

"Yes and no. They are definitely more animal than vampires. I mean, fuck, they can shift into a wolf, and you wouldn't know that they have a humanoid body. Whereas we still retain our bodies even in vampire form. They're wild, living by different rules than ours. We blend in. They don't."

"How would you know that? I mean, look at it: there's a pack in Marin County, and you didn't know about them until a day ago. Doesn't that mean that they can blend in too?"

Patrick shrugged and contemplated her words for a moment. "If they can blend in, it makes them even more dangerous. They are inherently violent creatures."

Anita let out a chuckle. "Look who's calling the kettle black!"

"Vampires aren't violent!"

"Yeah, the ones working for Scanguards aren't, because you all live by a code of ethics, but don't pretend you don't know that most other vampires continue to exhibit their violent nature unchecked."

"Just because you're blood-bonded to a vampire hybrid doesn't make you an expert on vampires."

She rolled her eyes. "Yeah, well, I'm just trying to make the point that anybody can be violent, werewolf, vampire, human. We all have it in us."

At her last words, he realized that only a few days ago he'd mused about the same thing, about the fact that given the right motivation, anybody was capable of violence.

Slowly, he nodded. "I guess." He stared through the windshield, reading the signs, before making a turn. "We're almost there."

Anita looked at the car's navigation system. "Seems to be a pretty large property." She pointed to the outline on the map. "About 10,000 acres, mostly forested, with a large house and several stables and other buildings on the side of a hill."

"That's about a third of the size of San Francisco," Patrick commented. "Must be worth a shitload of money."

"Not necessarily," Anita said. "Most of that land can't be built on. I checked the assessor's records, and the zoning doesn't allow for any additional homes. There are no water or sewer lines going to the property. Water comes from a well."

"Sounds pretty… uhm, what do you call those people? Doomsday preppers?"

"Yeah, looks like they're pretty self-sufficient."

Patrick brought the car to a stop along a fence. "And not exactly welcoming." He pointed to the barbed wire sitting on top of the nine-foot stone fence.

"Somebody likes their privacy," Anita added.

A few hundred yards in the distance, Patrick could make out a large gate. Farther down, the stone fence turned into a wire mesh fence. The terrain there was more rugged, and it appeared that the access road stopped abruptly.

"Cameras?" Anita asked.

Patrick let his eyes roam, using his superior vampire vision to search for electronic surveillance. He found it. The cameras mounted on the gate were hard to miss, but there were more, and they were harder to make out. A human would miss them entirely.

"Cameras on the gate, and more in the trees just inside the property line," he reported.

"You sure?" Anita squinted. "I can't see any."

"Trust me, they're there." He put his hand on the gearshift and turned the car around. "We'll come back another time." When they were more prepared. This was only a reconnaissance mission to get as much information on the Gallaghers as possible.

"Okay," Anita agreed, nodding. "Let's go see the sheriff then."

The Sheriff's Department was located a twenty-minute drive from the Gallagher property. Patrick parked the car in the parking lot adjacent to the building, and they got out.

"Like we discussed," Anita reminded him, "I'll take the lead. You're a civilian."

Patrick gave her a sideways glance. "And you're making it blatantly obvious that you like being the one with the badge. I don't know how Cooper can stand it."

She smirked, a mischievous glint in her eyes. "He totally loves me in a badge."

Cooper rolled his eyes, instantly catching on to her meaning: just the badge, and nothing else. "Of course, he does. He probably enjoys the handcuffs too."

A giggle was Anita's reply, before she opened the door to the building, and they entered.

All business now, she approached the reception area, flashed her badge, and asked to see the sheriff.

"He's expecting you," the young officer replied, and pointed to a door to her left. "Right through here."

Anita headed for the door, and Patrick followed.

"Excuse me, sir," the officer addressed him. "May I help you?"

Patrick looked over his shoulder, while pointing to Anita. "I'm with her."

Anita stopped and pivoted. "A consultant working with the SFPD."

The officer smiled. "Alright, go ahead."

With a nod, they continued down the short hallway, until they reached the door with Sheriff Berry's name on it.

Anita knocked, and something sounding like a growl came from the other side of the door. She opened the door, and together they entered.

Behind a massive oak desk, a heavy-set man in his sixties rose to his feet, while placing the receiver of his phone onto the cradle.

"Officer Diaz-Montgomery?" he asked, his hand extended in greeting.

"Sheriff Berry, nice to make your acquaintance," Anita said and shook his hand.

When his gaze fell on Patrick, Anita stepped aside to introduce him. "This is Patrick Woodford, a consultant with the SFPD. We're working on this case together."

As they exchanged greetings, Patrick quickly assessed the man. He was human, and appeared to be an open, friendly man with a pleasant demeanor.

"So, what can I help the SFPD with?" he finally asked, after Anita and Patrick sat down in the chairs in front of his desk.

"It's about the mountain lion attacks in the past four months, where two hikers were killed in separate incidents."

A frown line formed on the sheriff's forehead. "Hmm. Those cases are closed. Tragic, but there wasn't much to it. I'm surprised San Francisco is interested in them."

Patrick cleared his throat. "Well, it looks like we're dealing with the same kind of attack in the Presidio that left a jogger dead a few days ago."

"Oh? Are you saying you're dealing with mountain lions in the city? That's unusual," he claimed. "Golden Gate Bridge is kind of a natural border, stopping them from migrating south." He shrugged.

"We're aware of that," Anita said quickly, smiling sweetly. "That's why we're here. We're wondering if it's possible that the two attacks you had here, specifically the ones where the victims' hearts were missing, could have been perpetrated by a human."

Instantly, Sheriff Berry became defensive, his smile wiped from his face. "You think we don't know how to do our job here in the country? I know in the eyes of a big city cop we probably look like country bumpkins to you, but—"

"No, that's not what we meant, Sheriff," Anita interrupted quickly. "I worked in the sheriff's office of Elko County in Nevada for most of my career, and I know first-hand how hard and how diligently the staff at sheriff's departments are working. We're not here to criticize your work but rather to ask you for help." She cast him a gentle smile, and the sheriff's anger seemed to dissipate. "You see, we're stumped."

Patrick suppressed a grin. Anita really knew how to butter up a guy with her innocent-looking smile and her gorgeous eyes. The guy didn't stand a chance.

"Oh, I see."

"Sheriff," Patrick added, "we've been having trouble wrapping our heads around who or what could have killed the man we found in the Presidio. We'd love to close this case as fast as we can, but our boss just doesn't buy that it was a mountain lion. I mean, only the victim's heart was missing. Nothing else. It's just strange."

Sheriff Berry grunted. "Yeah, we had the same issue: two of the three victims had their heart missing too. But when forensics found animal hair in the victims' wounds, our hands were tied, and we had to rule those cases were animal attacks. Sorry, but we couldn't find any evidence of human involvement. Sure, it was odd that only the hearts were missing, but the bite wounds and claw wounds were definitely from an animal."

"Hmm." Patrick nodded slowly, getting ready for the questions he really wanted to ask, but which would have sounded out of place earlier.

"Were there no witnesses to the attacks?" Patrick asked. "I mean, my understanding is that two of the three attacks took place on land owned by the Gallagher family. Were they questioned?"

"What are you insinuating?" Sheriff Berry pinned him with his brown eyes. "The Gallaghers are upstanding citizens. Yes, they own a lot of land around here, but that doesn't mean that they know what's happening in the woods they own. Besides, they've been more than cooperative during the investigations, giving us access to their land and their security footage. That was more than we expected, particularly after the tragedy with their oldest son."

"Tragedy?" Patrick echoed.

Sheriff Berry nodded. "Yeah, real shame what happened."

23

It was early afternoon when Patrick entered his home accompanied by Anita. He found Fallon in the dining room, a half-empty plate in front of her. Lydia sat across from her, with only a glass of water in front of her.

"You're back," Fallon said, a relieved expression washing over her face. "Oh, hi Anita."

"Hey, Fallon," Anita replied.

Patrick pulled the chair next to Fallon out from under the table and sat down on the edge of it, his body turned toward Fallon. He took a breath, not knowing how to start. Anita remained silent, and Lydia cast them a worrying look. She knew him well, and clearly sensed that he had important news to share.

"What's wrong?" Fallon said into the silence, dropping her fork onto the plate, where it made a clanging noise.

"It's about Cameron," Patrick started.

He noticed Fallon holding her breath.

"The Marin County Sheriff's Office told us that he died in a car crash about two months ago."

A loud gasp tore from Fallon's throat, and her eyes widened in disbelief. "That can't be! It's impossible. I saw him, I spoke to him."

Patrick put his hand on hers, noticing how it trembled.

"They're lying," Fallon insisted. "Why would they lie about that?" Her gaze shifted to Anita.

Anita stepped closer to the table. "We don't know why."

"First, we have to confirm that we're talking about the same person, or whether the man you know is an imposter," Patrick said, although he didn't believe it, but he needed to be thorough before they could move on to the next steps. He pulled his cell phone from his pocket and tapped on the driver's license he'd downloaded earlier.

"What do you mean?" Fallon asked.

He turned the display of his cell phone toward her so she could see the photo. "Is that the Cameron Gallagher you were dating?"

Fallon stared at the photo and instantly nodded. "Yes, that's him." She lifted her eyes to meet his. "What is going on?"

Patrick glanced at his two colleagues, then looked back at Fallon. "We don't know yet, but according to the sheriff, Cameron died in a car crash about eight weeks ago. His body was so badly burned that the only way he could be identified was by dental records."

"They must be wrong!" Fallon cried out. "He's alive. He attacked me in my lab only two nights ago. And you said you saw him." The more she spoke, the more agitated she sounded.

Patrick took her hand in his. "Fallon, please, take a breath. I saw Cameron, too. Somebody faked his death, either he himself or his family. I don't know yet."

"But why? Why would he fake his own death?"

"There could be many reasons. And we'll find out why." He exchanged a look with Lydia. "I've gotta go back to the office. I need you to stay with Fallon."

"No problem," Lydia replied.

"What are you gonna do?" Fallon asked, anxiety visibly wrapping around her.

"We need to figure out what he was trying to hide that made him feel it was necessary to fake his own death." And he knew it had something to do with the fact that Cameron was a werewolf. But he couldn't tell Fallon that. She would freak out.

He had his suspicions as to why Cameron saw the need to fake his own death, but he needed to speak to his colleagues to confirm he was on the right track.

"Once we know," Patrick added, "we can take him down, and you'll never have to see him again."

Fallon nodded, her jaw locked, her expression grim.

Patrick reluctantly let go of Fallon's hand and rose. He wanted to take her into his arms to reassure her that everything would turn out alright, but he couldn't do it for two reasons: he didn't want to openly show his feelings for Fallon, and he wasn't entirely sure that everything would be alright. After all, they were dealing with werewolves. Any number of things could go wrong. And a werewolf like Cameron, who'd most likely killed before, was unpredictable.

"Anita, let's go. They're waiting for us at HQ."

24

The sun was almost down when Fallon felt her skin prickle, just like the night before. Whatever Buffy had given her the previous night, which had alleviated her symptoms, was waning. It felt as if she was coming down with something. The ache in her limbs was back, this time even more pronounced. Her neck itched, and she rubbed it furiously, yet felt no relief. It was as if she was wearing a woolen sweater that scratched her naked skin, even though she wore a soft cotton T-shirt that should have felt good on her skin.

After the news Patrick had shared with her, she'd lost her appetite and threw the rest of her lunch into the garbage. The thought of eating anything made her feel nauseated, yet her stomach grumbled as if she was hungry and needed nourishment.

She'd never felt so many conflicting sensations in her body. In fact, it felt almost foreign to her, as if she'd taken over somebody else's body, and it didn't quite fit. Like an ill-fitting costume.

She'd taken a bath, hoping it would make her feel more relaxed, but it had done the opposite. The warm water had made her feel too hot as if she'd jumped into a boiling pot.

Now all she could do was sit curled up on the massive couch in Patrick's living room, while her mind was doing cartwheels, trying to make sense of what Patrick had told her. Why had Cameron faked his own death? Or was it possible that it was just a case of mistaken identity, and Cameron didn't even know that somebody had died in a car crash and been mistakenly identified as him? No, no, that would make no sense. Surely, the police would have been able to identify his car, which would have led them to speak to the Gallagher family and, hence, to a dentist who would have provided Cameron's dental records.

Was it possible that Cameron was hiding something from his Mafia family? Had he tried to leave them to get out of their criminal enterprise, and had therefore faked his death, so he could disappear? But then why stay in San Francisco, so close to where his family lived?

Wouldn't he have gone far away so there was no possibility of a chance encounter?

Her head was spinning. The more she thought about it, the more she was confused. In any case, it didn't matter why he'd faked his own death, he was still a dangerous man, and he'd hurt her. Nothing could ever change that. There was no excuse for what he'd done.

Her phone vibrated, and she pulled it from the pocket of her yoga pants. The number was a San Francisco number, but she didn't recognize it. Maybe it was somebody from Scanguards. Perhaps Buffy had gotten the results of her blood test back. She didn't want to miss the call and pressed answer.

"Yes?"

"Fallon."

The male voice sent a shockwave through her; fear and anxiety collided inside her, making her shoot up from her position as if to ready herself for a quick escape.

A breath rushed from her lungs. "Cameron."

Her hand holding the phone to her ear trembled.

"You've disappointed me, Fallon," he said, his voice seemingly calm, though she could hear the dangerous undertone in it that indicated that he was angry, furious in fact.

Her lips trembled as she tried to find her voice, but he was faster.

"But I'll forgive you. After all, you'll need me. And I'm not one to hold a grudge."

She wanted to scoff, but her throat was as dry as the Sahara, and no sound came over her lips.

"I'll take care of you. I'll teach you everything you need to know. After tonight, you'll understand. You'll be mine."

Finally, she found her voice again. "I'll never be yours! Leave me alone! There's nothing left between us."

"On the contrary. You and I, we belong together. We will be one. You'll accept it soon enough."

"Never!" she ground out. "You really think I'd wanna be involved with you again? You're cruel and brutal, and dangerous. No, I don't wanna have any ties to you or your Mafia family."

"Mafia? You think we're the Mafia?"

He let out a cold laugh, and the sound penetrated every cell in her body.

"Stop denying it!"

"You're so wrong. No matter. Tonight, you'll find out the truth. Wait and—"

"Fuck you, Cameron!" She pressed the *end call* button, cutting him off, then silenced her phone and tossed it on the couch, away from her, as if that would remove the threats Cameron had issued.

25

"He confirmed it?" Patrick asked, looking at Ryder. They were in the command center at HQ, where several of his colleagues were working on digging up more about Cameron to find evidence that he was responsible for the Presidio murder, and the two supposed animal attacks in Marin County.

Ryder nodded. "I used a little persuasion, but, yes, Hank confirmed that the night they all went out for drinks to celebrate the NIH grant, Cameron came to his place and beat the living daylights out of him."

"Alright, that establishes that he's violent." Not that he really needed that confirmation. But then, he was biased. He believed Fallon and knew that her fear of Cameron was fully justified.

From behind him, Eddie called out, "Hey, I've got a positive ID from one of the security cameras on Broadway."

Patrick turned on his heel and bridged the distance with two large steps. He looked past Eddie's shoulder to the monitor in front of him.

"That's clearly Cameron walking past this house. The street

leads directly to the Presidio. The time tracks with when we think the jogger was attacked and killed."

Patrick looked at the grainy image. "Can you zoom in a little?"

Eddie shook his head. "The more I zoom in, the grainier the picture will get. But facial recognition gives me an 87% chance that this is Cameron. Might not stand up in court, but it's good enough for us. It's not like that guy is ever gonna see the inside of a court, right?"

"Not if I can help it," Patrick replied. "Good work, Eddie. That means we can tie him to the Presidio murder."

He turned around and looked at Sebastian. "Anything on the dental records that supposedly identified the charred body from the car crash as Cameron?"

"Still working on that. I'm close," Sebastian said. "But as we all know, dental records are easy to manipulate. Somebody only needed to change out some of the X-rays on the dentist's database, and boom, the dead body is Cameron."

"Okay, keep working on that."

He looked around the room, where several others were on the phone: Nicholas, Benjamin, and Anita. Nicholas suddenly lifted his hand, as he finished his call and put down the receiver.

"Got something," he said.

Eagerly, Patrick approached. "Yes?"

"I went through the reports of the two animal attacks in Marin County. There was a witness in one of them, who supposedly saw something on the day the hiker died, but the witness report is incomplete, and it looks like it was never followed up on after forensics established that the fatal injuries were inflicted by an animal."

"I need to speak to that witness."

Nicholas scribbled something on a piece of paper. "That's Walter Banks, his property borders on that of the Gallagher family."

Patrick took the piece of paper. "I'll go and see him."

"I'll come with you," Nicholas offered.

Patrick nodded. "Let's go."

Traffic was heavy on the 101 North, with rush hour starting in the mid-afternoon and not letting up until past seven o'clock. But crossing the Golden Gate Bridge was still the shortest way to get to Marin County, even though it took them almost an hour to reach Walter Banks' residence, a ranch-style home on a lot of about four acres.

The building was old but looked well-maintained.

Patrick stopped the car and turned off the engine. He exited, while Nicholas did the same on the passenger side. He'd barely made two steps away from the car, when he perceived a movement on the front porch of the house. A shadowy figure stepped forward, though the person's face still lay in the shadow. A human wouldn't have been able to make out the man's face, but Patrick's vampire vision allowed him to see whom he was dealing with.

The man was in his 70s, his skin leathery, his remaining hair gray and scraggly. He wore casual work pants and a flannel shirt.

"Mr. Banks?" Patrick asked.

"Who wants to know?"

"I'm Patrick Woodford. I'm a private investigator, and this is my colleague, Nicholas Eisenberg. We're here to ask you about what you witnessed a little over two months ago when a jogger was found dead in these woods."

Faster than he expected, the old man turned and reached for something near the door, before pivoting and aiming a shotgun at him and Nicholas.

"I suggest you leave," he warned them. "I'm a pretty good shot."

Patrick showed his hands in surrender and saw from the corner of his eye that Nicholas did the same.

"We don't mean you any harm. We only want to talk to you about what you saw."

"You think you can intimidate me?" He spat on the floor. "Tell

Gallagher I'm not gonna change my statement. I saw what I saw no matter how many goons he's sending."

Patrick exchanged a quick glance with Nicholas. The man's hostile behavior and statement that he believed the Gallaghers had sent them to intimidate him, could only mean one thing: the Gallaghers didn't want whatever Banks had seen to come to light.

"I can assure you that we're not working for the Gallagher family," Patrick stated calmly. "We're here because we believe that these so-called animal attacks on the Gallaghers' property weren't mountain lion attacks. We suspect that the Gallaghers are involved somehow."

He noticed the old man relax a little, though he still kept his shotgun pointed at them.

Banks tipped his chin toward him.

"Alright. So what do you want to know?"

"You made a statement to the sheriff's department, but the file we saw was incomplete, and didn't tell us what you actually saw."

"Why am I not surprised?" Banks grunted. "They didn't like what I had to say, so they just kept it out of the report. Corrupt bastards!"

"You're talking about the sheriff?"

"Yeah, him and everybody else." He scoffed. "I told them what I saw, and they didn't like it."

"What did you see?"

"Hmm." Another grunt, then he continued, "The day that hiker was found dead, I was up early, and I saw Cameron Gallagher, the oldest son, run past my fence." He pointed toward the area where his property bordered on the Gallaghers'. "He was stark-naked, and I swear he had blood all over himself."

Patrick's heart beat faster. Finally, they were getting somewhere. They had an eyewitness who had identified Cameron close to the crime scene.

"But when I reported it, Gallagher... you know, the old man... his father, claimed I must have been drunk. Fucking asshole. I wasn't drunk. I saw what I saw."

"And what did the sheriff's department say when you gave your statement?" Patrick asked.

"They believed Gallagher. And a couple of days later, they dismissed the whole inquiry, 'cause suddenly Cameron had a car accident. It was a huge explosion. But just because he died, doesn't mean that I didn't see what I saw."

"We believe you, Mr. Banks. You've been a huge help. May I ask you one more thing?"

"Sure. Go ahead."

"I'd like to show you a picture of Cameron Gallagher so we know we're talking about the same person."

Banks nodded slowly, but remained on his porch, holding the shotgun in a more relaxed way now.

Patrick pulled his cell phone from his pocket, navigated to Cameron's picture, and walked closer to Banks to show it to him. A few feet away, he held the phone out to him.

Banks looked at it, then nodded. "That's Cameron. That's who I saw."

"Thank you, Mr. Banks. One more thing: have you seen Cameron since the car accident?"

He furrowed his brow and stared at him, looking perplexed. "'Course not. He died in the accident."

"Of course." Though Patrick now knew with certainty that Cameron had faked his death, because now he knew the reason why: so he wouldn't be arrested for the murder of a hiker in Marin County. Had his family helped him stage the accident?

Back in the car, Nicholas turned to him. "We've got him."

"Yes and no. We know he's good for all three murders, the two in Marin, and the one in the Presidio, but we don't know where he is right now."

"Guess then we'd better start looking for him," Nicholas mused.

Before Patrick could answer, his cell phone rang. The caller ID identified Lydia.

"What's up?"

"Fallon has locked herself in the bathroom. Something is wrong."

Instantly worried, he replied, "I'm on my way."

26

Fallon took a deep breath.

Something was wrong with her, seriously wrong. No, not just something, everything.

She'd never felt so out of place in her own body. Her mind was racing, trying to explain what was happening to her, but she found herself in an endless closed loop that was maddening.

Her conversation with Cameron had riled her up, igniting an unspeakable fury in her that made her want to kill somebody, preferably Cameron. Hate and pain collided inside her at the mere thought of him. She'd never thought that she would be capable of such deep negative emotions. That she was capable of hurting somebody. That she was capable of violence. Yet she knew instinctively that she was.

She'd always seen herself as a good person, a gentle soul who wanted to help others. That's why she'd chosen to become a doctor, to do research to find something that might slow down the process that time exerted on a human body, ravaging it until all there was left was death. She'd seen herself as benevolent, when now, all she could feel inside her heart was hate and pain.

She was ready to lash out at anyone who came too close. That's why she'd locked herself in the bathroom, to avoid antagonizing Lydia, who was there to protect her, and surely only had her best interest in mind. But it didn't matter that Lydia wasn't her enemy. Her feelings were still the same: she wanted to hurt somebody to drown out the pain that she felt take over her body.

As if she was on drugs that were altering her personality. As if she was descending into madness. As if her entire past was gone, no longer influencing her decisions, her morals, and her principles. She felt as if only her base instincts were guiding her now. Her needs were unbridled, which made her feel uncivilized. In the mood she was in, she couldn't trust herself, because she had no idea what she was about to do. She felt a new sensation grow inside her: power. Physical power that was foreign to her. And with it came the need to use that power to make it clear to everybody that she wouldn't allow anybody to hurt her ever again.

"Fallon, please come out," Lydia coaxed her from the other side of the bathroom door.

"Go away!"

In her ear, her voice sounded strange. The pitch was lower, and the volume much louder than before.

She was losing control. Trying to calm herself, she braced herself on the vanity and stared into the mirror above the sink.

Her reflection made her rear back in shock.

Bloodshot eyes stared back at her. Her eyebrows were bushier, her cheekbones more pronounced, her lips peeling back from her teeth, revealing white teeth that looked as if they couldn't all fit into her mouth. She felt a tension in her jaw as if she sat on a dentist's chair, clamps in her mouth to widen it, so a tooth could be extracted. She tried to close her mouth, but her body didn't follow her brain's command. Instead, her teeth seemed to grow, to lengthen as she watched helplessly.

She pressed her hands to her cheeks, trying to exert pressure to close her mouth, only to gape at her hands. They weren't the gentle hands that handled delicate materials in the lab all day. No, these hands looked calloused and rough, with dark hair on their backs, and sharp fingernails. She'd had a manicure only a week earlier, but none of that was evident right now, because her fingernails were like sharp little barbs that looked capable of slicing through flesh like the sharpest surgeon's scalpel.

Panic elevated her heart rate. With it, more of her body seemed to change in front of her eyes. She fought it, but she knew instinctively that she didn't have a chance. Everything became clear in that moment. She knew what had happened to her the night she'd gone to her lab to check on the refrigerator. Every single second of that incident came back in vivid colors, and she realized that she'd pushed it out of her mind, too afraid of what it meant. But there was no denying it any longer. She knew what would happen. She knew what Cameron had done. And with all her might, she hated him for it. Hated herself for letting it happen, for being too naive not to see it coming. She felt like the stupid heroine in a B-movie: too stupid to live. Too bone-headed to recognize the signs, while everybody else could probably already see it.

Now, she saw it too. With that realization, her entire world collapsed around her, sending her reeling. She wanted to scream, to cry, to bemoan her fate, but what was the point?

"Fallon!"

The voice was Patrick's, and it came from the other side of the door.

She clamped her hand over her mouth, choking back a cry. She couldn't let him see her like this. He would recoil from her. And what would she do? Hurt him for rejecting her?

"Please, Fallon, come out," he begged, his voice beseeching.

"No!" The word burst from her lips without her doing.

"Fallon, baby, please, talk to me."

She shook her head to herself, when she heard Lydia addressing him.

"Patrick, it's Buffy. She needs to talk to you."

"Not now!"

"It's important."

"Fuck!" Patrick cursed, but then she heard his impatient next words, "Yeah, Buffy, what's so important? I'm in the middle of something."

To Fallon's utter surprise, she could hear Buffy's reply. Had Patrick put the call on speaker mode?

"I got the results from Fallon's blood test back. There's a problem."

"What problem?' Patrick asked.

"The blood must have been contaminated."

"Why?"

"Because it came back as animal blood, specifically as canine."

PATRICK'S HEART stopped for a moment, shock coursing through his body, paralyzing him before he could utter a single word.

"Canine?"

"Yes, like a dog," Buffy elaborated.

His head was spinning, and in the silence that followed, his gaze drifted from Lydia, who gaped at him with an open mouth, to the bathroom door that now swung open, making a creaking noise that echoed against the bedroom walls.

Fallon appeared in the open door, hesitating, her eyes seeking his.

All air rushed from his lungs, and his lips formed the next words involuntarily, "Or like a wolf."

He barely heard Buffy's reply and mumbled something that he

couldn't remember a second later, before disconnecting the call and tossing his phone onto a nearby armchair.

"Run," Fallon ground out from a clenched jaw, the cords in her neck bulging, attesting to the strength with which she tried to keep control over her body.

Not taking his eyes off her, he gave an order. "Lydia, leave us."

"Are you fucking crazy? She'll kill you!"

"She won't hurt me. Leave! Now!" he urged.

"It's your funeral," she grunted, but he heard her retreat and leave the room nevertheless.

Not that he thought that this would be the last he'd see of Lydia tonight. Knowing her, she was already calling for reinforcements to eliminate the threat. He knew he only had a short time until this whole situation would get out of hand, and somebody would really get hurt.

He was determined to defuse this situation by himself because what he saw in Fallon's eyes was fear. She needed him now to deal with what was happening to her.

"You have to leave," Fallon pressed out, tears shimmering in her eyes, eyes that were changing with every second that passed to look more and more like those of a wolf.

A werewolf.

"I won't leave you, baby," he assured her, making a small step toward her.

She growled, sounding like the beast that was trying to take over her body. But she was still in there, still fighting the change.

"I don't want to hurt you," she said, a single tear running down her cheek. She sniffled. "He did this to me, Cameron did this..."

Patrick nodded. Everything made sense now. Cameron had bitten or scratched her during the attack in the lab. He should have considered this possibility after seeing her defensive wounds in the hospital. He should have realized what Cameron had done, and that the full moon tonight would force the change in her.

Fuck! He was an idiot! But he hadn't wanted to see it. His subconscious mind had suppressed this possibility, fearing that this would make their relationship impossible. But even now, he denied his head to override his heart. Even as he saw her aura change to that of a supernatural being, confirming that she was truly a werewolf now, he remained steadfast in his determination to stand by her. To stand by the woman he loved. Consequences be damned!

"I'm not leaving your side," he vowed.

"You don't understand," she cried, "I'm turning into a werewolf. I remember everything now. Cameron bit me." More tears streamed down her face now. "He's a werewolf. And now, I'm one too…" She lifted her arms, showing him her fingers that had turned into sharp claws, the claws of a wolf. "I can't fight it. Please, Patrick, leave. I don't want to hurt you… But I can't control this. I don't know how."

Desperation shimmered in her eyes. He noticed how close she was to losing it, to giving in to the wolf inside her, to let it out of its cage.

"You can't hurt me, baby."

From where he took the confidence to make such a statement, he wasn't sure, but somewhere in the back of his mind, a faint memory pushed through: vampires and vampire hybrids couldn't be turned into different supernatural creatures. They were immune to the bite or scratch of a werewolf that would otherwise transform a human. He hoped that what he remembered from the many stories of his childhood was indeed true and not just fairy tales meant to lull a vampire child into sleep.

"But I can't suppress it any longer… I have the urge to… to… bite you." There was a deep rumble in her voice, something akin to a suppressed howl. "You'll turn into a werewolf… like me… I can't do that to you. I love you too much." A sob tore from her throat, and with it, her claws lengthened, and the bones in her face seemed to shift and crack.

He wished he could have savored her declaration of love, but there was no time for it now.

"Your bite won't turn me. It can't. I'm a vampire, Fallon. And I love you."

27

A vampire!

Fallon's heart began to race out of control, even more out of control than it had the moment she'd realized that she was turning into a werewolf. Everything she'd ever known as the truth, as natural laws and science were being turned on its head.

She shook her head, as if by doing so she could make it all undone. As if she could simply wish away the fact that her ex-boyfriend was a werewolf, and her current boyfriend—if she could call him that—was a vampire.

An instinct emerged with her new body that told her that she should be afraid of Patrick, see him as a natural enemy. Where this thought came from, she wasn't sure, but she felt it in her bones as if it was a law written into her DNA. Fight or flight were her choices. But she remained frozen as if her feet were glued to the floor.

Yet something moved inside her: the beast, the wolf she could hear howling inside her, wanted to be unleashed and defend itself. But why? And how?

Her human side fought against it, but she knew she was losing the battle that raged inside her. She would attack him.

"I love you, Fallon, with all my heart."

His words sank deep into her and lashed against the wolf.

Words formed in her head, and she spoke them without having made a conscious decision to speak. "You're a vampire..."

"Yes," he said calmly.

She watched him take another step toward her. She should run now, but her body didn't follow her mind's order, even though she knew that if she didn't flee now, she would do horrible things to him. Things that the wolf inside her wanted. To bite, to tear into his flesh, to make him submit to her.

With more effort than it should take, she lifted her arm to stop him from coming closer. "I don't want to hurt you."

"You won't."

Her eyes were filled with unshed tears making her vision blurry. "You don't understand: I want to bite you... And I can't hold the urge back any longer."

A growl coming from deep inside her followed her last word, and she knew she only had seconds left before she'd transform completely and lose control. She felt her skin stretch, her bones break and readjust, and stared at her arms, noticing the chestnut-colored hair growing thicker—no, not hair: fur! Fur started to cover her skin. Her tight T-shirt suddenly began to rip at the seams, making space for her new body. There was no suppressing it any longer.

"Fallon, look at me!" Patrick demanded.

She jerked her head in his direction and realized that he stood right in front of her now. The urge to dig her claws into him was more than she could bear.

"Bite me now, Fallon, do it!"

Had he really spoken, or was she projecting her own wishes onto him to justify what she was about to do?

"Run," she whispered, though she didn't know whether the command was directed at Patrick or meant for herself.

The word had barely left her lips when she pounced. With her front paws, she slammed Patrick backward, making him lose his balance. He landed with his back on the bed, and she was on top of him, her extremities in wolf form, the rest of her body still human, except for her mouth, from which sharp fangs protruded. She went for his neck, plunging her sharp canines into his flesh, lodging them deep so he couldn't escape. He was her prey now, she the predator. As she bit him, and his blood filled her mouth, she was surprised that Patrick made no attempt to fight her. Instead, she felt his arms around her torso, pressing her to him, holding her so tightly that she felt as if she were *his* prey.

Oddly enough, that feeling forced her to relax, to let go of the tension. Suddenly, new sensations flooded her consciousness, sensations that were foreign. With them, she felt arousal charging through her. Patrick's blood tasted sweet, not metallic like human blood. She couldn't get enough of his taste, of the rich viscous liquid that he seemed to share so willingly.

"I love you, baby," Patrick cooed, tearing the ripped T-shirt off her.

She let it happen, in fact, she welcomed it. She wanted this, wanted him. With her sharp claws, she began slicing his clothes into rags, tearing them impatiently, yanking them off until she could feel his naked skin. The moment her bare skin connected with his, she dislodged her fangs from his neck and lifted her head, rearing back.

She stared at the deep wound she'd caused and recoiled. Panic rose inside her, but before she could voice her regret and concern for his wellbeing, Patrick pushed against her and rolled her so she found herself on her back.

He braced himself above her, a few remaining shreds of his clothes hanging off his body, while he ripped her panties off her. She noticed that his hands were claws now too, and while that revelation would have frightened her in any other situation, she realized that she had nothing to fear. She wrapped her legs around his thighs, and drew him to her center. His hard-on connected with her skin, and an instant later, he plunged into her with such force that she was surprised that she felt no pain.

"Patrick!" she cried out. "Yes!"

"Fuck, you feel good, babe," he responded, riding her as if somebody was chasing him.

He was wild and untamed, his cock relentless in its powerful thrusts, his tempo increasing with every second, his pelvis grinding against her center of pleasure, igniting her, arousing her, pleasuring her.

She dug her claws into his butt, forcing him deeper into her, demanding he ride her harder. In his eyes, eyes that had turned golden, she saw his desire, and the lust that was driving him.

"Kiss me," he demanded, dipping his face to hers.

She wanted to push him back, afraid she might cut his face with her canines, when she realized that her fangs had retreated and turned back into normal teeth. She touched her lips, confirming that the wolf was gone.

"How?" she asked, staring at Patrick.

Continuing to thrust in and out of her, he brushed his lips over hers. "You're in control now." Not giving her a chance to reply, he captured her lips and kissed her.

PATRICK DELVED deep into Fallon's mouth, exploring her, tasting her, relieved that her transformation into her wolf form had reversed itself, and he was now able to kiss her. Not that he wouldn't have made love to her if it hadn't. Damn, he loved this woman with every fiber of his being, and nothing would stop him from showing her his love and devotion, even if it killed him. He trusted her, and his trust in her had been rewarded. And his vampire blood had done what he'd hoped it would do: spike her libido to subdue the wolf eager to come out on the first night of the full moon.

His neck wound was still bleeding, but it would mend on its own soon. If she were still human, he would have bitten her and taken her blood into him, and it would have healed him almost instantly. But he had no idea what werewolf blood would do to him, so he couldn't risk it. For now, it sufficed to make love to her and show her that he wasn't afraid of what she had become. Just like he had to show her that she could trust him, a vampire.

Her skin was soft and hairless again, her claws had turned back into fingers, and her pussy was welcoming him with its plentiful juices that made every slide into her like being cradled in a cocoon of silk.

Despite her inner wolf having retreated for now, he could feel it under the surface, ready to reemerge at any time. The full moon tonight made her volatile and unpredictable. He should heed the warning, yet he couldn't. Fallon was full of fire, of passion, desire, of unbridled lust, and he wanted to bathe in that passion and fulfill her every desire.

Her body molded to his with such perfection that it felt as if they were one. They moved in sync as if they'd made love to each other hundreds of times. New lovers rarely found satisfaction together so easily. But between them, it was all instinct. Their bodies understood each other without words, as if they communicated on a different level that nobody else could perceive.

With every touch, every sigh, every movement, he felt his body fill with more pleasure than he'd ever thought was possible. Fallon's skin was glowing, and he recognized that the glow was caused by the supernatural aura that engulfed her. He'd had sex with other supernatural women before, namely with vampires, but during sex, he'd never noticed their aura, maybe because it was like his own. But Fallon's aura was different from his. While they made love, it seemed to change, to grow warmer, changing colors from a blue tone to a golden hue.

Her eyes seemed to shimmer in the same golden hue. Fascinated, he slowed his thrusts and locked eyes with her. He wanted to say something, wanted to tell her how close he felt to her. But he had no words to share his feelings, only his body to express what was in his heart.

"I know," she murmured, replying to him as if she knew what he wanted to say.

Before he could wonder how this was possible, he felt her interior muscles squeeze his cock, trying to imprison him inside her. A moment later, the waves of her orgasm crashed into him out of nowhere, igniting his own climax. His cock spasmed, taking on a life of its own.

A groan tumbled over his lips, and he gave himself over to the intense pleasure that washed over him. He pumped his seed into her, and for a moment he wished that seed would take root. He continued moving in and out of her, riding out the waves of his orgasm. He was still aroused as if he'd been the one drinking her blood and not the opposite. He didn't care why he felt like this. All that mattered was that being inside of Fallon filled him with certainty about his feelings for her despite the short time they'd known each other, and the obstacles that lay in front of them. Nevertheless, he was already hers, his heart irrevocably in her hand. And he hoped soon, she would be his. He would do everything in his power to reach his goal.

"Fuck! Get her away from him!" The menacing male voice came from the door and shattered his bliss. He recognized the voice, but despite that—or maybe because of it—he jumped into protector mode and prepared himself for a fight—a physical one if necessary.

Nobody would separate him from the woman he loved. Even if that meant he had to go against everything Scanguards represented. His loyalty was to Fallon now. And that wouldn't change.

28

In the blink of an eye, Patrick rolled off Fallon and pulled on the duvet to shield her naked body from the eyes of his colleagues: Amaury, Zane, and Wesley. Amaury and Zane rushed toward the bed, their eyes blinking red, their fangs fully extended, intent on attacking Fallon, while Wesley made only one step into the room, raising his arms in a gesture Patrick was only too familiar with.

"Wes, you cast a spell, I'll rip your throat out!" he growled, his vision now tinted red, indicating that his own vampire side was emerging.

Wesley, Scanguards' resident witch, had the good judgment to lower his arms and shut his mouth.

Patrick glared at Amaury and Zane. "Another step toward her, and the same happens to you too."

Both vampires growled and flashed their fangs, but stopped a step away from the bed.

"She'll kill you," Zane claimed, pointing toward Patrick's neck wound. "She's already bitten you."

"We came just in time," Amaury added.

"Leave us."

"Don't be stupid," Amaury hissed.

"Fallon won't hurt me."

"You don't know that!" Zane's eyes were trained on Fallon, pure hatred spewing from them. The bald vampire was one of the most intimidating he'd ever met. He was known for violence, both for inflicting it, and for being able to endure it. Encountering him in the dark would make anybody cross the street quickly to avoid him.

"She loves me!" Patrick hadn't wanted to say that, but it was the only thing he could think of that would make them retreat.

Zane scoffed. "She's gonna have you for breakfast. She's a wild animal."

Patrick felt movement coming from behind him and glanced over his shoulder. Sharp fangs and silver eyes were the first things he noticed. Then, second by second, Fallon changed. He froze, and from the absence of sounds coming from his three colleagues, it was clear that they too were paralyzed by the sight before them. The only sounds in the room were those of bones breaking and readjusting as Fallon's body changed in what looked like a painful way. Her face pushed outward to turn into a wolf's snout, the mouth filled with the sharp teeth of a predator. Her spine elongated and bent, while her limbs changed, her hands transforming into paws, her legs into the hindlegs of an animal. Thick chestnut-colored fur covered her naked body. A menacing growl ripped from her throat, her eyes pinning the three intruders.

"Fuck!" Amaury cursed, while the other two let out similar curses.

"Leave," Patrick ordered.

"Not without you," Amaury insisted. "Your father would never forgive me."

Despite the unsettling feeling of Fallon being close enough to touch him with her new body, he replied, "She won't hurt me." At least he hoped that the transformation into a wolf hadn't changed her feelings for him. "But you're a threat to her."

He sensed it automatically, as if Fallon had told him so.

Zane didn't heed the warning and pulled his gun. Fallon growled at him. Even though he knew that the gun was loaded with silver bullets—bullets that could hurt him or even kill him—, Patrick shifted his position at lightning speed, blocking Fallon with his body. He felt the wolf's hot breath on his nape, and reached back with one hand, petting Fallon's fur to try to calm her. It was an odd sensation, to say the least. Mere moments before he'd felt smooth skin under his fingers, and now it was fur. It felt soft too, not the coarse fur he was used to from a German shepherd or a similar breed. This wolf's fur was just as soft as Fallon's skin had been.

"I won't let them hurt you, baby," he murmured.

A soft howl was her reply, before he felt her tongue on his skin. The contact jolted him for a second, but he forced himself to relax and let go of the initial fear that had gripped him. This was still Fallon, even though she was in wolf form. He had to trust her that she wouldn't hurt him.

"It's alright, baby."

Again, she licked over his skin, and he finally realized what she was doing.

"She's licking your wound," Amaury said with disbelief in his voice.

"To heal it?" Wesley asked, taking a step closer.

"Looks that way," Amaury replied.

"Fuck!" Zane hissed under his breath. "Now I've seen it all."

Fallon's tongue on his neck wound felt soothing as she licked him with long, smooth strokes that felt like a sensual caress. For a moment, he closed his eyes, allowing the pleasure of her touch to travel through his body, reaching every cell.

"I'm not watching that!" Zane ground out in disgust. "Fuck it!"

Patrick ripped his eyes open, and saw Zane turn on his heel and hurry outside.

Wesley pointed to Patrick's groin, before averting his eyes. "Might wanna cover that up."

So what if Fallon licking his wound was getting him hard again? It was none of their fucking business. But to him, it proved that he wasn't disgusted by what she'd become. It didn't matter to him in what form she came.

Amaury grunted, visibly displeased and equally embarrassed. "Get dressed. We'll wait downstairs."

Then he too, left the room.

Wesley hung back for another few seconds. "Uhm, yeah." He pointed to where Amaury had disappeared. "What he said." Then he shook his head, his gaze running over Fallon in her wolf form. "Fascinating. Absolutely fascinating." He left, having the decency to pull the door shut behind him.

They were alone again.

Fallon lifted her head, and he stared into her silver eyes. They sparkled like a million stars in the night, more vibrant than her grey human eyes, yet just as familiar.

"You're safe now, Fallon. They won't hurt you."

He put his arms around her gently, making sure she had every opportunity to free herself from his embrace if she needed to. But she didn't withdraw. Instead, she rested her head on his shoulder and let out a soft whimper. He sensed her frustration and her fear. He knew too little about werewolves to know if the shift had been painful, but he assumed it was. But he couldn't communicate with her this way, and there was too much to discuss, too much to clarify. He needed her to turn back into her human form.

Stroking her back gently, he spoke in a soothing tone. "Can you try to push the wolf back?"

Another whimper echoed in the room.

"I know it hurts," he whispered. "I know it's hard to control. But you did it once. You did it when you drank my blood." As if his blood had given her the strength to subdue the wolf in her so her human side could gain the upper hand.

She lifted her head and looked at him.

"You're so beautiful."

He knew she needed reassurance now. This entire ordeal had to be frightening for her. To suddenly discover that she'd turned into a supernatural creature with instincts she didn't know how to control, could throw anyone for a loop. He wished that Maya were here right now. She would know the right things to say because she'd been in a similar situation: she'd been turned into a vampire against her will. Awakening in a new body was scary. And it had to be even scarier for Fallon because her entire body had truly changed. A vampire looked rather human except for the fangs, the claws, and the eyes, but Fallon's body was that of an animal now. And she had neither the knowledge nor the guidance to control the shift.

In that instant, he understood what Cameron's words to her had meant: she needed him because only a werewolf could teach her to control the shift, if that was even possible. His heart bled for her. Would she always be helpless against the beast that the full moon brought out in her? How would she handle this? And how could he help her when he knew next to nothing about werewolves?

In that moment, he hated Cameron more than he'd ever hated anybody in his entire life. But he had to push that feeling back now because Fallon needed him. And it wouldn't help her if he showed his hate and anger. She needed him to be gentle and understanding, so he could prove to the wolf that he was no danger to her, and she could trust him.

A faint purring sound drifted to his ears, and he rubbed his thumb over Fallon's snout. In a show of trust, her eyes closed for a moment.

"We'll get through this," he said. "I'll stay by your side. You won't have to do this alone."

Whatever she needed, he would provide it.

Under his palms, he suddenly felt Fallon's muscles flex and shift, and then he heard it: the sound of bones cracking and rearranging themselves to create a different body, a human body. He let go of her and watched in fascination how the wolf transformed, the fur receded, and the face turned into that of the beautiful woman he loved.

"Fallon," he murmured.

She threw her arms around him, sobbing. "I'm so scared."

"My colleagues won't hurt you..."

"But I saw it... I felt it... They wanted to kill me..." A big sob tore from her chest, and she drew back to look into his face. "And I wanted to kill them... even though I don't know why."

He nodded and wiped her tears off her cheek. "It's your instinct. All supernatural creatures have it. It's a survival instinct."

"But what if I hurt somebody? I don't want to hurt anybody. I don't want to hurt you." Desperation shone from her eyes.

"I'll make sure you won't. I promise you that."

"Patrick, I can't control this. I don't even know how I managed to turn back into... into me."

She looked toward the window. The curtains were drawn.

"Even now I can feel the moon calling to me," she said, rubbing her neck.

"We'll find a way." Then he glanced around the room. Shreds of their clothes lay strewn about the floor, evidence of the intensity of their lovemaking. "Let's get dressed. We need to talk to my colleagues."

A visible shiver went through her, and Patrick placed his hand on hers, squeezing it in reassurance. "They only wanted to protect me. Now that they know that you won't hurt me, they won't attack you."

Doubt was still written on her face, but she nodded.

In silence, Patrick pulled fresh clothes from his closet, while

Fallon dug into the drawer where she'd placed the few things she'd brought from her flat, and they got dressed. He was done before her, and waited near the door, when she finally pulled her sweater straight and faced him.

She hesitated. "One of the men, he's not a vampire. I felt something different when I looked at him."

"Wesley is a witch. A good one. He works with us. And the other two are pure-blooded vampires. Amaury is the massive guy, Zane is the bald one."

"I don't like Zane."

Patrick let out a chuckle. "Few people do. He's somewhat of an acquired taste."

"And the other, Amaury. He looks very strong."

"He is. But he's really a total teddy bear when he's not trying to defend those he loves. He's my father's best and oldest friend." He took her hand. "Come. No more stalling."

"You think I'm stalling?"

He smiled. "That's what I would do if I were in your situation."

He opened the door and led her to the stairs. Intertwining his fingers with hers, he cast her a reassuring glance, before they walked down the large mahogany staircase. They were halfway down already, when he heard the front door slam.

"Patrick!"

29

The sound of the front door closing was followed by a cold wind gust reaching her as she walked down the stairs with Patrick. A beautiful young woman rushed toward them, her long dark hair flying in all directions, making Fallon freeze on the final step. As if the woman hadn't even seen her, she threw herself into Patrick's arms, pressing her body to his, imprisoning him in her embrace.

At the sight, rage charged through her, and she could feel her jaw tightening. Pain shot into her fingers, a sign she recognized from when she'd shifted into her wolf form. She was about to do the same now, because of this woman who embraced Patrick. In the same moment, she realized that the feeling that was urging her to shift wasn't rage but jealousy. How dare this woman touch the man she loved?

Mine.

With that thought, a growl dislodged from her throat, and her skin began to prickle, making her aware that fur was starting to cover her arms, growing thicker with every second.

"Oh my God, you're hurt!" the woman cried out.

"I'm fine, Isa," Patrick replied, but didn't step out of the embrace.

Fallon issued another warning growl, and finally, the woman met her gaze. She was a vampire with the same kind of aura that Patrick had, different from the other two vampires. Was she his girlfriend, or why else would she be so concerned for his wellbeing, and hugging him so tightly?

"Take your hands off him!" Fallon ground out and glared at her.

The woman glared back. "You hurt him!"

Finally, Patrick freed himself from her arms and turned. "Fallon, meet my sister, Isabelle."

Despite the relief she felt at that revelation, the wolf inside her was still demanding to be released, because Isabelle displayed anger that was directed at her. Before she could make a step toward her, Patrick stopped her with an outstretched arm.

"Easy, both of you. And Isa, no, Fallon didn't hurt me."

"That neck wound says otherwise," Isabelle pointed out.

"It's no worse than a vampire's bite."

Fallon caught his smile as he looked back at her.

"And just as enjoyable."

At his tender words, she felt the pressure in her jaw release and her human side take over again, pushing back the wolf for now. But she knew it couldn't be suppressed for long. Her shift had been painful and involuntary. The moon was ruling her. She could feel it in her bones, her cells, every inch of her body. It made her aware of the dangers around her and the need to protect herself. It was hard to suppress the instinct she felt when faced with a vampire, the instinct to fight for her life. She'd never felt so out of control, so uncivilized, so animalistic.

Patrick's voice pulled her from her thoughts. "Baby, everything's alright." He took her hand again. "Let's talk."

Hesitantly, she allowed him to lead her to the living room, Isabelle following them. There, the men who'd intruded on their lovemaking were waiting for them, all three pacing impatiently.

When they entered through the open archway, three sets of eyes landed on her. They were sizing her up, assessing whether she posed a threat right now, and she knew she was doing the same, her eyes roaming their bodies, looking for weapons or any sign of aggression toward her. The bald one, Zane, had the most hostile look of the three. Amaury and Wesley looked almost calm, but she knew that underneath it, they were both ready to spring into action if they believed they were in danger.

It was odd how she was looking at everything now, at the other doors in the room that could provide an easy escape, and at items like candlesticks and bookends that would lend themselves as weapons to defend herself with. She felt hypervigilant and more alert than ever before. As if she was on speed or some other drug that raised her level of awareness. She realized now that her complaints from the previous night were all precursors to the enhanced senses that being a werewolf had gifted her with. Not that she would call them gifts.

"Why don't we sit down?" Patrick suggested.

Amidst a few grunts and some grumbling, Patrick pulled her next to him on a two-seater couch, while Amaury and Wesley sat on the large sectional, and Isabelle took a seat in an armchair. Only Zane remained standing, and somehow, she had guessed that he wouldn't want to give up his superior position, which allowed him to react faster than those seated. Smart. She had to give him that.

"Let me first bring Fallon up to speed," Patrick said with a quick look at his colleagues, before looking back at her. "I found out last night that Cameron is a werewolf. That's why I brought you here and had you protected twenty-four-seven."

Her eyes widened, and her chin dropped, while her heart beat into her throat. "And you didn't tell me? You could have warned me."

He reached for her hand. "It was too late by then. He'd already attacked you at the hospital, and what would you have said if I'd told you then that he's a werewolf?"

"I would—" She stopped herself. She would have thought he was crazy.

He sighed. "Exactly. You wouldn't have believed me. You had no reason to." He took a visible breath. "I'm sorry, Fallon, it's my fault that I didn't figure this out earlier. And had I known that he'd bitten or scratched you in order to turn you into a werewolf, I would have..." Again, he hesitated.

She shook her head. "You wouldn't have been able to do anything, would you?" She shifted her gaze to the other people in the room. "This is irreversible, isn't it? I'll be a werewolf from now on, won't I?"

She didn't know from where she took the strength to even utter those words. She sounded so calm in her own ears, when everything inside her was whirling around like her insides were in a blender, and somebody had flicked the switch.

When only silent stares came as answers, she shook her head again as if she could shake the truth off like a nightmare.

"I can't do this. I can't *be* this." She slapped her hands against her chest. "This... this animal inside me... I don't *want* to be this."

She felt fresh tears rise, but pushed them down, not wanting to cry in front of these strangers. She wanted to retain as much dignity as she could. If she had any left. After all, the three men had seen her naked in bed with Patrick. It couldn't get any more embarrassing than that. Oh, yes, it could: they had seen her shift into her wolf form, and she was certain that sight was anything but pretty. A mass of flesh, bones, skin, and hair all being jumbled up and rearranged couldn't be something anybody would want to watch. She felt disgusted at the thought. It had been the moment where she'd felt the most out of control. As if somebody else was controlling her body. Because somebody was: the wolf.

"We don't know yet whether there's anything that can be done," Patrick said, his voice soothing. "Wes?"

The male witch sat up a little straighter. "I'm not sure. But

Charles and I can definitely do some research. See if there's a spell or something."

She watched him, but they all knew it: Wesley didn't have much hope of finding anything to turn her back into a human.

She let out a cry. "Why? Why did he do that to me? Why did Cameron do this?"

She felt Patrick's hand on hers again. "Because he wanted you as his mate. And deep down he knew that you wouldn't accept him. But as a new werewolf, you need the protection of his pack and the guidance that only another werewolf can provide you with. By turning you, he wanted to make sure you needed him."

She swallowed hard. "That's what he said. *You'll need me.* He said it that night, and he said it again later. It was always his plan, wasn't it?"

"I believe so. At least after you broke up with him. It made him desperate."

"He would have done it anyway," Amaury added, drawing her attention to him.

"What do you mean?" she asked.

"From the little I know about werewolves, I know how they mate. The male bites the female during sex. So, if they mate with a human, it would turn the human into one of them—if she survives it."

The words hung there in the silence that followed. Her gaze ping-ponged back from Amaury to the others. "But you must know more. I mean, none of you is human. You must know more."

"Vampires and werewolves have never been on a great footing," Amaury said. "We're natural enemies, and—"

"Amaury!" Patrick interrupted.

"Well, it's the truth," he said defensively, before casting an apologetic glance back at her. "I'm sorry, but that's just how it is. Of course, *we* won't hurt you, because... well, because we can see you don't want to harm Patrick. But not every vampire out there is gonna feel the same."

She nodded. She understood what he was trying to tell her. "So, because you're natural enemies, you don't know anything else about werewolves?"

"Other than a silver bullet to the head kills 'em for sure?" Zane interjected, his voice as cold as ice.

A cold shiver ran down her spine, chilling her to the core.

"Shut up, Zane!" Patrick snapped. "There's no need for that."

The bald vampire shrugged as if the reprimand hadn't even touched him. "Just saying."

"We need to find out more about werewolves, do some research," Patrick suggested.

"I'll contact Samson," Amaury said.

"No!" Patrick's protest came as if fired from a gun. "That's not necessary. He can't do anything we can't do ourselves. Everybody who's been working on the Presidio murder case will work on this now."

Her forehead furrowed, and she looked at him from the side. "But that's a murder case you need to solve..."

Patrick shook his head. "It's already solved. Cameron killed the jogger in the Presidio. He ripped his heart out, and we have to assume that he ate it."

Her stomach flipped, and nausea overcame her all of a sudden. Cameron had killed somebody? And eaten his victim's heart? There was only so much she could handle, and this went far beyond the threshold she believed she had. She jumped up, holding her hand to her stomach, trying to hold down the little that she had in it. She saw no other choice but to hurry out of the room. Relieved that she knew where the powder room was, she almost kicked the door in and bent over the toilet bowl. Just in time.

Somebody followed her, reaching her just as she began to retch.

"I've got you."

It was Isabelle who reached for her hair now and held it back. Fallon threw up the little food she had in her stomach, while fear and disgust gripped her. She was a monster now, a monster that killed people and ate their hearts. How long would she be able to fight against what she was now? When would she start killing innocent people?

She couldn't live like that. No, she would rather die than be a killer.

30

Patrick had run after Fallon, concerned about her wellbeing, but Isabelle who'd been sitting closer to the hallway, had been faster and reached the powder room before him. She blocked Fallon from his view, but he could hear her throwing up.

"I'll take care of her," Isabelle said with a look over her shoulder and shooed him away.

He retreated to the living room.

"Is she alright?" Wesley asked.

Patrick ran a hand through his thick hair. "No. You heard her. How can she be? It's all my fault. I shouldn't have told her about Cameron eating his victim's heart. No wonder she's throwing up." He looked at his colleagues. "If only I'd taken her seriously when Anita brought her to me and put her in a safe house right away, Cameron would have never had the chance to—"

"Don't!" Amaury interrupted. "You couldn't have known then that he's a werewolf. Nobody could have known. So don't do this to yourself. It's not gonna help us figure out how to proceed."

Slowly, Patrick nodded. Amaury was right. Nothing would be

gained by him wallowing in his guilt. He needed to find a solution to Fallon's predicament.

"Wesley, hit the books," he ordered. "There must be something about werewolves in your spell books. Charles can help you." Charles was the other witch working for Scanguards. And he'd been a witch much longer than Wesley and had much more experience and knowledge.

"Alright," Wesley replied. "But don't get your hopes up. As you know, most spells are only temporary and will eventually go poof." He made a dramatic gesture with both hands to indicate an explosion.

"I know. Still, we have to do something."

"You do know that we can't harbor a werewolf," Zane suddenly interjected.

Patrick snapped his gaze to him, challenging him. "Yeah, and why is that?"

Zane narrowed his eyes. "It'll be perceived as us holding a werewolf prisoner. Her pack's not gonna like it. They'll fight us and claim her as theirs."

"Her pack?" Patrick went nose-to-nose with his much older colleague. "You're suggesting that the Gallaghers are her pack?" He stabbed his index finger into Zane's chest. "You listen to me: Fallon was turned against her will. She didn't choose this. She deserves our protection. And I'll be damned if I let the Gallaghers take her. They're not her pack."

"But they are, aren't they?"

Patrick spun around to look at Fallon who'd spoken. She stood in the archway to the foyer, looking dejected. There was silence in the room, and he swallowed hard, not sure how to respond, because there was a kernel of truth in Zane's words.

"So, it's true," Fallon said into the silence, standing there as if frozen in place. She tipped her chin up, determination sweeping over her face. "I'll never be one of them."

He crossed the distance between them with several steps and took her hands into his. "You'll always be under my protection."

With a sad smile, she shook her head. "That's not enough, is it? Like Zane said, they'll come for me." She swallowed, pressing her lips together in a clear effort not to cry.

"They might try, but they won't succeed," Patrick said with a firm voice. "We have to confront the Gallaghers about Cameron."

"What will that accomplish?" she asked, doubt in her voice.

"That depends on whether they know that Cameron has faked his own death or not."

"I'm not following," Amaury interrupted.

Patrick turned to look at his colleagues. "If the Gallaghers don't know that Cameron is still alive and hasn't only killed three people recently but also turned Fallon into a werewolf, they might help us find him and take him down. And they won't claim Fallon as one of theirs."

At least he hoped that the Gallaghers had some sense of honor that would make them respect Fallon's wishes not to join their pack and punish one of their own for his evil deeds. The vampires at Scanguards had done this many times: punished a vampire for killing innocents, and for turning humans against their will. He hoped that this werewolf pack lived by the same kind of code.

"And if the Gallaghers are complicit?" Amaury asked.

"Then we know that we can't expect any help from them and have to find Cameron ourselves and be prepared for resistance."

"Resistance?" Zane huffed. "You mean war. And it doesn't matter if they were complicit or not. They'll never go against one of their own. They'll protect Cameron no matter what."

"You can't know that!" Patrick replied.

"Neither can you!" Zane countered.

Patrick made an impatient hand movement to shut him up, not wanting Zane's doubts to intensify his own. "In any case, Cameron has to pay for what he did. He's a killer. And as long as he's out there, nobody's safe, least of all Fallon."

"I agree," Amaury said. "How do you suggest we confront the Gallaghers?"

"We'll pay them a visit."

"I need to come with you," Fallon said.

He stared at her. "No. You can't. You're too volatile during the full moon."

"I'm not," she protested.

But her body betrayed her immediately. With her protest, her eyes began to change in color, becoming larger, while hair began to grow on the backs of her hands. She was on the verge of shifting again. He had to calm her down to help her fight it.

"Fallon, baby. Look at me," he said calmly, pinning her with his eyes.

A tear loosened from her eye and ran over her cheek. "Patrick, I have no control... But I have to do this. I have to tell his family..."

All the while, he recognized that her body was readying itself to shift. All he could do was give in to her demand.

"Alright, you'll come with us, but not tonight."

Her response was a growl.

"Fallon, please listen. You're about to shift again. You can't control it. We can't risk you going there at night."

He took a step closer and noticed all of a sudden how the moonlight shone into the room hitting her as if it was a spotlight.

Below his breath, he instructed his colleagues, "Guys, very slowly, close the curtains."

"What's that gonna do?" Zane asked.

"Just do it."

Fallon's eyes reacted to the movement in the room. They narrowed, zooming in on his colleagues, who were quickly drawing the curtains shut.

"Fallon, baby, please look at me."

She turned her head back to him.

"We're going tomorrow during the daytime. You're coming with us."

Fallon seemed to relax a little. "Thank you," she pressed out as if speaking caused her pain.

The curtains were finally closed. Fallon glanced in their direction. "It won't help for long." Then she met his gaze. "You have to lock me up. Do it now, while I can still fight the wolf. Once I shift, I can't guarantee anything. And I will shift. I have no choice."

Realizing that Fallon was holding on to her human form with all her strength, and would lose the battle soon, he gave an order. "Zane, get the van. We'll have to lock her in a cell at HQ."

"Hurry," Fallon pleaded.

31

Fallon woke in a bleak white room with concrete furniture fused to the floor. The bare walls reminded her of depictions of the interior of an insane asylum—or a morgue. Though a morgue at least had steel tables and refrigeration units as well as other equipment. This room was devoid of them.

She shivered and looked down at herself. She was naked. She didn't remember having been brought to this room, but she knew what it was: an underground cell at Scanguards' HQ. Patrick had told her that he would bring her here, but she'd shifted at some point during the transport. However, she wasn't sure if it had happened in the van or in the building.

She let her gaze roam the room, searching for her clothes. There were none. But she noticed a monitor next to the door. It displayed a message.

Fallon, now that you're awake, please enter the code 8095 into the keypad below. It will open a door behind you. Behind it, you'll find a small bathroom with toiletries and clothes. Take your time. You had a rough night. I'll come to get you when you're ready. Love, Patrick.

Fallon glanced around. Only now, she noticed claw marks on the walls and deep scratches on the door. It appeared that she'd tried to get out when she was in wolf form. But her temporary prison had held. Memories of how violent she'd become, how frustrated at being locked up, came rushing back. She had no way of pushing them back, even though she didn't want to be reminded of the wolf inside her. Her muscles ached as if she'd done a rigorous weightlifting routine with a personal trainer, attesting to the fact that the wolf had relentlessly clawed and scratched at the door and the walls to find a way out. But just like the furniture in this room, the walls and floor were made of concrete.

Not wanting to stare at the claw marks she'd left, Fallon tapped in the code and pivoted to see a door she hadn't noticed previously spring open. She opened it wider and entered the well-lit bathroom. Relieved to see a large shower equipped with different soaps and shampoos, she turned on the water and stepped under the warm spray. Her muscles instantly felt better.

She wasn't sure how long she stood in there, letting the water run down her body, before soaping up and then washing her hair. When she finally turned off the water and dried off with a large, fluffy towel, she felt better. She looked into the mirror above the sink, pleased to see that her face looked refreshed. There was a still-wrapped toothbrush on the vanity, as well as other toiletries. She brushed her teeth, used deodorant, and dried her hair with the hairdryer before she dressed in the clothes that lay on a small stool. The clothes weren't hers, but they fit perfectly nevertheless. The soft fabric of the form-fitting sweater and the comfortable pants felt good on her skin. Whoever had placed these items in the bathroom, had thought of everything, including underwear, socks, and shoes her size.

Feeling like a human being again, even though she knew she wasn't, she opened the bathroom door and walked back into the cell. To her surprise, Patrick was leaning against the wall, waiting for her. She met his gaze.

Patrick bridged the distance between them with three steps, and opened his arms, embracing her.

"It's so good to see you," he murmured into her hair. "How are you feeling?"

Her stomach suddenly rumbled loudly.

He drew his head back, smiling. "Apart from being famished."

"I'm better now," she admitted, inhaling his masculine scent and hugging him tightly. "Thank you for everything."

He put his finger under her chin. "I'd do anything for you." He pressed a tender kiss on her lips.

His kiss ignited something inside her, making her want more of the same. She angled her head and kissed him back with more fervor, wringing a surprised gasp from him. But he didn't pull back. Instead, he kissed her more passionately, and she suddenly felt her back being pressed against the wall, while their bodies were touching so closely as if they were one. She now regretted having gotten dressed. But before she could start undressing, Patrick severed the kiss.

He breathed heavily. "Damn, baby, you can make a man forget everything in a second."

She put her hands on his hips, drawing him closer once more. "Don't play hard to get."

He chuckled, and his eyes sparkled. "Hold that thought. You've gotta eat something first. After what you went through last night, you need to get your strength back."

He pushed a strand of hair behind her ear. "From what I saw, it must have been painful."

"You were here? Watching me?" she asked, surprised.

"Yes." He pointed to the ceiling, and she followed his direction. A camera was installed there. "I wanted to make sure that you didn't hurt yourself."

A shiver raced down her spine, and she looked past him. She

wished he hadn't seen her at her worst. "I'm sorry you had to see that. It must have been awful to watch."

"No, Fallon, don't say that," he said softly and tipped her face up with his fingers. Affection streamed from his green eyes. "You're beautiful, even as a wolf."

She knew he meant it, even though she didn't understand why he would still find her beautiful when she was a beast.

"Come, let's get you some breakfast, and I can fill you in on what we've been working on overnight."

Patrick led her outside by punching in a different code in the keypad next to the cell door. He took her hand as they walked to the elevator and rode up to the top floor. It was quiet on that floor, and she didn't see or hear anybody. The office doors they walked past were closed.

The office Patrick ushered her into was a corner office with several large windows. It was furnished comfortably with a large desk, several chairs, and a seating area with a coffee table. On it stood a tray with food and drink.

"This is your office?" she asked, surprised that it was so large.

"It's my father's, but he's still on vacation," Patrick replied and pointed to the seating area. "Eat something."

At that moment the sun was coming out from behind a cloud and shone straight onto the food, making her aware of something she hadn't even thought about earlier.

"The sun! It's gonna burn you," she said, whirling around to Patrick in an attempt to shield him.

"It's okay," he said quickly, "the windows are coated with a UV film that protects vampires from the rays of the sun. But even if they weren't, the sun can't hurt me."

"What?" Suddenly she remembered when Patrick had picked her up from the hospital and taken her home. It had been during the day. "You were outside when you... but how? Don't vampires burn in the sun?"

He took her hands. "They do. But I'm a hybrid. My father is a vampire, but my mother is human. That gives me the ability to walk in daylight, unlike my father, who has to stay indoors while the sun is up."

"Oh!" She'd never imagined that there was something like a vampire hybrid. "But if your mother is human, won't she age and die, and your father will stay young and immortal? I mean, vampires, they're immortal, right? And they don't age?"

"Yes, they're immortal. I'll explain everything you want to know, but why don't you start eating?"

He led her to the sofa and made her sit down. She reached for a piece of pastry and poured herself a cup of coffee from the thermos. "Go on."

"You mind if I get breakfast too?" he asked.

"Just take some of mine. It's too much anyway."

He shook his head and walked to a small fridge. He opened it and retrieved a bottle. When he turned back to her and joined her on the sofa, she could see the bottle more clearly. The contents were red.

"Tomato juice?" she asked skeptically.

He shook his head. "No. It's human blood."

Her breath hitched. She should have expected this.

"We procure it from blood banks. We don't attack humans to feed."

She found her voice again. "So vampires don't bite humans?" It sounded rather civilized and somewhat of a relief.

As he unscrewed the bottle, he gave her a crooked smile. "Well, it's not as clear-cut as that. My father, like all vampires who are blood-bonded to a human, drinks only from my mother."

Shock charged through her. "And she allows that?"

"Of course. She loves it. And it's their blood bond that keeps her young. She still looks the same as on the day she met my father. She also drinks his blood on occasion, while he drinks hers daily."

"But that must hurt," Fallon said, still frowning.

"It doesn't." Patrick sighed and set the bottle on the table without drinking from it. "I have to make a confession."

He hesitated, and instinctively, she froze.

"The day we had sex after you came back from the med center... I tasted your blood."

For a second, she had trouble understanding the words. She shook her head. "No, that's not possible. I would have known."

"Remember when I licked your breasts when I was inside you? You were so close to coming."

She remembered it well. How could she forget? It had felt out-of-this-world amazing.

"My saliva made sure that you didn't feel my fangs piercing your skin. I drank your blood, not much, just a taste, because I couldn't resist. You smell so good."

She still couldn't believe it. "But there were no puncture marks. I would have seen them."

"A vampire's saliva heals small wounds instantly. It doesn't leave any scars behind either. I'm sorry, I should have asked for your permission, but back then you didn't know what I was. But I wanted you to feel the pleasure of a vampire's bite."

"The pleasure," she murmured, thinking back at how hard she'd come in his arms, how long her climax had lasted.

"You remember," he said and smiled at her. "That's what the bite does. It heightens arousal. Just like it heightened mine when you bit me."

She felt her cheeks heat and didn't have to look in the mirror to know that she was blushing like a sixteen-year-old schoolgirl encountering her schoolyard crush. "Oh."

He chuckled and reached for the bottle of blood. "Now eat your breakfast."

Patrick set the bottle to his lips and began to drink. She couldn't turn away and watched him, fascinated. When she caught his gaze connecting with hers, she noticed his eyes starting to change. She'd seen this in him before and had blamed the light, but now she knew that it was his vampire side trying to emerge. Her heart began to beat faster because she could feel sexual energy roll off him in waves.

When the bottle was empty, he set it down on the table and brought her hand to his lips, pressing a soft kiss into her palm.

He locked eyes with her. "I wish I could make love to you right now, baby. But we have to go."

32

Fallon sat on the passenger seat of a dark blue Audi. Patrick was driving, and behind him sat Wesley, the witch she'd met the previous night. It was mid-morning, and the traffic over the Golden Gate Bridge was moderate. Following them in a black SUV were three of Patrick's colleagues, all vampire hybrids: Nicholas, Benjamin, and Cooper. Patrick had explained why they all looked younger than they were: a vampire hybrid stopped aging at age twenty-one.

Her head still swam with all the information Patrick had given her on the subject of vampires. She was grateful for it because it helped her push back the anxiety about where they were heading: into the lion's den. Or, more accurately, the wolf's lair.

The closer they got to their destination, the faster her heart raced. As if Patrick knew how she felt, he reached for her hand and squeezed it.

"I won't leave your side," he promised.

Moments later, he stopped the car in front of a tall iron gate and rolled down the window. He reached out and hit the button on an intercom system. There was silence for a while, then a crackling in the line.

"Yes?"

"We're here to speak to William Gallagher," Patrick said firmly.

He'd told her earlier that William Gallagher was Cameron's father and most likely the alpha of their pack.

"He's not expecting anybody."

"It's vital that we speak to him. It's about his son, Cameron."

There was a long silence, and Fallon wondered if the other person had simply severed the connection when she heard some more static coming from it. It was followed by the same voice.

"Come in."

The gate in front of them opened slowly, and they drove through it, the second car following them. It was a long, winding driveway, and Fallon guessed that it was about half a mile long. At its end, a massive old brick building rose. It reminded her of the quintessential horror movie mansion. It sported a turret, several dormers, and a couple of gargoyles sitting high above the entrance door as if standing sentry over the building and its residents. She shivered at the sight of it.

Patrick parked the car and switched off the engine. As they got out, she noticed that the three vampire hybrids had parked a few yards away from them and were also getting out. She looked back at the building and noticed the movement of a curtain in front of one of the upper windows, but there was no light behind it, so she couldn't see who was watching them.

When she heard the opening of the heavy oak entrance door, her gaze was drawn to it. A man appeared at the door, a shotgun in his hands. She recognized the man's aura: he was a werewolf.

"Vampires," he snarled. "You should know better than to show up here."

She noticed him looking at the three hybrids, who were already approaching the entrance. It was clear that the man hadn't noticed her yet.

With more courage than she thought she had, she stepped forward, drawing his attention to her. "They're with me."

His gaze shot to her, and he jerked back visibly. "What the fuck?" he hissed loud enough for everybody to hear.

From inside the house, a male voice boomed. "Byron, what's going on?"

Without turning his head to reply to the man, he said loudly, "There's a bunch of vampires here with a female werewolf."

Seconds later, a second man appeared in the door. He was older and she could clearly see the resemblance to Cameron. This was William Gallagher, Cameron's father.

Gallagher's eyes quickly roamed over his visitors, then snapped back to her. "Who are you? What pack are you with?"

She lifted her chin, steeling herself. She had to pretend to be stronger than she was; she wouldn't let him intimidate her. She let a growl roll over her lips.

"Your son Cameron attacked me three nights ago and made me into this. Against my will."

Gallagher's expression didn't change, but she noticed that Byron showed signs of surprise.

"Cameron died two months ago."

"You mean he faked his death two months ago?" Patrick interjected, now stepping next to her.

Gallagher narrowed his eyes. "I'm not talking to you, vampire. I don't know what your game is, but you should know better than to come to a werewolf Alpha's home and make accusations."

"It's not a game," Patrick replied. "We're here to get justice for Fallon. Cameron turned her; he has to pay for that."

Gallagher huffed. "Stay out of our business. All of you." He swept his gaze over the Scanguards contingent, suddenly stopping at Wesley. "A witch? How dare you?"

"So you're sticking to your story that Cameron is dead?" Fallon asked, not wanting him to change the subject. "I saw him only three nights ago. I spoke to him on the phone yesterday. He's alive. And he did this." She made a hand movement indicating her body. "I shifted last night for the first time. I hate everything about it. I didn't choose this. He needs to be punished for what he did to me."

"My son would have never done such a thing. Clearly, somebody is impersonating him."

Gallagher lifted his chin in a gesture that reeked of superiority. She saw it then: he was used to his word being law. Was it really possible that he believed Cameron to be dead? He certainly had a good enough poker face not to give anything away. But was Byron just as cunning? She ran her eyes over the younger man. There was something almost refined about him, something that made it hard for her to believe that he was a werewolf. But his aura didn't lie. His face, however, showed more than that of William Gallagher. She could read the guilty expression as if it were written on a big billboard. William Gallagher was lying.

She trained her gaze back on the older Gallagher. "Cameron won't get away with this. I *will* find him. And he *will* pay."

Gallagher's lips peeled back from his teeth. "You shouldn't make accusations that you can't substantiate. As for your vampire friends..." He cast a dismissive look at them. "They'll use you for their own interests. You don't belong with them. You belong with a pack. A werewolf on her own is always in danger. Something might happen to you, and without a pack, you have no defenses."

The threat was clear. "You think I would join your pack? Then listen carefully." Her hands began to tremble, and she balled them into fists to hide that she was close to breaking down. "I spit on your pack. You disgust me. You're harboring a criminal. Cameron is a killer."

Gallagher's face was beet red. "Lies!"

"She's not lying," Patrick interrupted. "Cameron killed two

hikers here in Marin County, and one jogger in the Presidio in San Francisco."

"That's a false allegation! Cameron isn't a killer."

"Isn't?" Patrick asked, his voice cutting now. "Didn't you mean *wasn't*?" He let out a bitter chuckle. "We can prove that he killed the man in the Presidio. We have footage. Now all we need is to find him. There's a warrant out for his arrest."

Fallon was surprised at Patrick's claim. He hadn't mentioned anything about a warrant earlier. Was he bluffing?

"Then why aren't the police here right now, huh?" Gallagher challenged. "I tell you why: because you have nothing. Just conjecture."

"So you're sticking to your story that Cameron is dead. Fine. We'll find him without your help. Harboring a murderer makes you an accessory." He tipped his head in Byron's direction. "Just like the rest of your family. You want them to pay for Cameron's crimes too?"

Gallagher growled low and dark, and she could see that he was close to shifting. She knew it because she could feel it in her own bones. With Gallagher about to shift, her own need to shift grew. As if Gallagher knew, he tossed her an evil grin. He knew what was happening to her. He knew if he shifted, she would too, and she wouldn't be able to control it.

"Patrick," she whispered. "We need to leave."

Gallagher scoffed. "Might wanna listen to the pup. Now get the fuck off my land! If you ever come back, I'll rip your hearts out myself!"

Wesley suddenly raised his arms, a few Latin words rolling over his lips, but Patrick stopped him with a quick movement of his head.

"We're leaving," Patrick announced.

Her nape prickled with tension, and she couldn't wait to get in the car. Only when the engine finally howled, and they drove back to the gate that opened by itself, did she feel better.

"It was a mistake to come here," Wesley said from the back bench.

"No, it wasn't," Patrick said. "We now know that Gallagher knows full well that his son is alive and that he merely faked his death. He probably helped him."

"How? The guy looked pretty stone-faced from where I was standing," Wesley said. "Wouldn't wanna play poker with that asshole."

Fallon looked over her shoulder. "Byron gave him away. He knows that Cameron is alive, and he also knows what he's capable of."

"Exactly," Patrick confirmed, and squeezed her hand. "We'll get him."

"How?" Wesley asked.

"What would you do if your son was being hunted by vampires?"

"I don't have a son, but, well... I would probably try to help him get to safety," Wesley mused.

At Wesley's words, Fallon relaxed into the passenger seat. Patrick had a plan, and she was grateful for it because she was close to breaking. The argument with William Gallagher had cost her more energy than she'd expected. But she'd withstood his demands and insinuations. She was stronger than even a few days ago. Was the wolf inside her lending her this newfound strength?

33

It took almost an hour to get back to Scanguards headquarters. Despite it being daytime, it was busier on the executive floor, which was reserved for vampires and their mates only, but Patrick wasn't surprised. He'd asked Amaury to put a call out to the entire vampire and hybrid staff to report for duty, even though most of them normally worked nights only. It was all-hands-on-deck to find Cameron and subdue the werewolf threat.

Whom he hadn't expected to see was Striker Reed. He and Amaury were waiting in Samson's office. He hadn't seen the tracker the vampire council had employed to find vampires who didn't want to be found for quite a while. Why he'd left the council's employ—and why they'd let the best man they'd had leave—was anybody's guess. Striker wasn't one to offer information if he wasn't forced to, and even then, he'd rather bite his tongue off than talk. Still, he liked the taciturn vampire with the grim expression, because he'd helped find Isabelle's kidnapper almost two decades earlier, and more recently, he'd helped them out when Samson and Cain, Grayson's now-father-in-law, had been kidnapped.

With an outstretched hand, Patrick approached Striker. "Striker, it's good to see you."

He nodded and shook his hand. "Patrick." Then his gaze slipped past him to Fallon. "So, this is the reason we're starting a war with the werewolves?" He clicked his tongue. "Not that I can blame the guy. She certainly has something…"

"Careful," Patrick said, his jaw tight, not liking the way Striker let his eyes roam over her body. "Yes, this is Dr. Fallon Doyle, and you'd better keep your comments and your hands to yourself."

A humorless chuckle rolled over Striker's lips. "I see. Now things are getting clearer."

Patrick turned to Fallon. "Fallon, this is Striker Reed. He was a tracker for the vampire council, one of their best, actually."

"Nice to meet you, Striker," she replied.

"Sure," Striker said, since clearly a response like *likewise* or *nice to meet you too* was too much to ask for.

"What brings you out during daytime?"

He jerked a thumb toward Amaury. "Got a call that you need information on werewolves."

"What do you know about them?" Patrick asked eagerly.

Striker shrugged. "A fair amount. I've run into a few in my time."

"Fill us in," he urged him. "We know practically nothing about them, other than that a bite will turn a human, and that they automatically shift during the full moon."

Striker rubbed his neck. "Yeah, well, not exactly. Just like vampires, they are either born into the life or bitten. The werewolves born into it don't have to shift during the full moon. They're in control over when to shift at all times."

"And those bitten?" Fallon asked, anxiety evident in her voice.

Striker shifted his gaze to her. "Like you? They're compelled to shift during the three days of the full moon."

"But I'll learn to control it like the others, right?"

"No."

"But Fallon was able to fight it for a while, after she drank my blood," Patrick interjected. "So there must be—"

"You let her drink your blood?" Striker shot back, arching an eyebrow.

At the implied reprimand, his jaw tightened. "She needed it; it helped her."

"Hmm. Well, as long as she didn't do it during sex."

His heart stopped for a moment.

"What do you mean by that?" Fallon asked, sounding panicked.

"That's how werewolves mate," Striker explained.

"Amaury," Patrick said, looking at his colleague, "I thought you said that the male werewolf has to bite the female during sex to mate with her."

Before Amaury could reply, Striker interrupted, "He's right, in the case when both are werewolves. But when only one partner is a werewolf, no matter if it's a male or a female, that werewolf's bite during sex will result in them being mated."

A gasp escaped from Fallon's mouth, and Patrick met her gaze. He reached for her hands and felt them trembling.

"I didn't mean to," she murmured, tears welling up in her eyes. "I'm sorry."

He shelved her chin on his fingers and tilted her face up so she had to look at him. "I'm not. I want to be your mate. I would have asked you once all this is over."

Tears ran down her cheeks, and his heart broke. Did she not want to be his mate? Did she not love him enough?

"But if you don't want me," he started, swallowing away the disappointment, "then I'll—"

"I want you," she interrupted, sniffling. "But you can't possibly want this." She freed her hands from his and made a gesture indicating her body. "I'm a beast. I can't control this."

Relief flooded him. Fallon wasn't rejecting him. "I love you no matter what. We can beat this together."

She nodded, suppressing the tears, then looked past him. "Is there a way to reverse this?"

"The mating? No."

"No, not the mating. Me, my condition. Me being a werewolf," she corrected him.

Striker shrugged, hesitating. "Hmm. Nah... no."

She walked closer toward Striker. "You hesitated. There is something, isn't there? There's a way."

Striker let out a breath, and Patrick noticed that he was carefully weighing his next words.

"Out with it, Striker," Patrick demanded. "What are you not telling us?"

Striker raised his hands in a gesture of capitulation. "I'm not gonna give any guarantees, and it's really just a rumor. There might be nothing to it, so don't sue me."

"What is it?" Fallon pleaded. "Please. I need to know."

"Well, there's this rumor that a newly minted werewolf can turn back to being human if his or her maker dies before the third night of that new werewolf's first full moon."

"This is my first full moon," Fallon said excitedly, the tears suddenly drying.

"And only the first night is behind us," Patrick added, feeling the same excitement. Finally, a kernel of hope. "We have two more nights."

"Hold it," Striker said, "like I said, it's just a rumor. I can't guarantee that it works."

"We have to try," Patrick said, meeting Fallon's eyes.

She nodded, but then another expression washed over her face. "I've never killed anybody. I don't know that I can have that on my conscience."

He took her hands and pulled her to him. "You won't have to kill him. I will. Or one of my colleagues. He's killed three people that we know of. He needs to be put down. There's no other solution. He could never be in a prison. He would be a danger to the other inmates. He deserves to die."

"That was never really a question, Fallon," Amaury added. "Even if it's only a rumor, it changes nothing about the fact that Cameron is a cold-blooded killer and needs to be eliminated before he kills more innocents." He paused for a moment. "Patrick, what happened with the Gallaghers?"

"Kind of what I expected," he replied. "His father claims that Cameron died two months ago and couldn't have killed the jogger in the Presidio or hurt Fallon. He was lying. His other son, Byron, kind of gave it away. It was written all over his face. Cameron is alive, and his family is helping him cover up his crimes."

Striker tipped his chin in Fallon's direction. "Do they know what Cameron did to you?"

"Yes," Fallon said, "I told them."

He grunted. "Hmm. Bad move. Now they know there's a werewolf without a pack running around. They're not gonna like it. They'll try to claim you as theirs. To strengthen their pack. You're new blood; it'll keep their bloodline strong."

"I would never go with them," Fallon gritted.

Striker tilted his head. "Yeah, well, you might not have a choice. They won't give up so easily. I'm surprised they let you leave at all."

"There were five of us, four hybrids and a witch."

Striker nodded to himself. "That means there were only two or three werewolves close by. They probably didn't like the odds, particularly with a witch in the mix."

"That's why I brought Wes," Patrick said. "So, Striker, since you're already up, wanna help us find Cameron?"

"I'm available for hire."

"And I have my father's checkbook. Let's roll."

34

The next hour passed in a flurry, and Fallon was glad for it. Patrick was busy with getting everybody organized in the search for Cameron. She watched him in fascination as he gave orders and answered questions. The Scanguards employees he worked with—all vampires and vampire hybrids—didn't need many instructions as it turned out. They knew what to do. Like the cogs in a well-oiled machine, each used their unique skills to contribute to the mission.

She met the two gay vampires, Thomas and Eddie, who were in charge of anything to do with computers and technology. From what she gathered listening to their conversations, they were expert hackers who had no qualms about hacking into any system for the sake of justice. Several teams of hybrids were roaming the city and Marin County on surveillance missions, following any clue they received from traffic cameras. In addition, Thomas and Eddie fed them information they'd gathered from banking transactions linking to Cameron's or his family's credit and debit cards. Another group of IT geeks worked on mapping all properties and companies the Gallaghers owned, and where Cameron could possibly hide out.

Fallon sat on the sofa in Samson's office, watching Patrick working the phones. She was glad to have a little while to herself to collect her thoughts. Striker's claim that she and Patrick had unintentionally mated was something not easy to digest. For starters, she didn't really know what it all meant. She'd always associated the word *mating* with, well, with making a baby. But it didn't appear that Striker or Patrick had used that word in the same context. Patrick had said that he'd wanted to ask her after all this was over, so she could only assume it meant that he wanted to ask her to marry him. This would mean that mating was the same as getting married.

Her head was spinning, so many different emotions jumping around like in a kid's bouncy castle. She tried to sort them so she could process them like she processed the results of her research studies. Oh God, she hadn't even thought of work and her research projects in the last few days. She hadn't missed it either, which was unusual for her. But who could blame her? Her entire world had upended in the last few days, and she had to figure out what this new world meant for her. What her future would look like. Which brought her back to Striker's earlier words that she could become human again if Cameron died by the end of the full moon. It meant they had two nights left before her condition was permanent.

She should feel terrible about wanting somebody dead. But no such feeling rose in her. Instead, she felt that justice would only be done once Cameron was dead. Had the wolf inside her eradicated her humanity to the point where she couldn't feel anything wrong with killing somebody?

"What's wrong?"

Startled, Fallon looked up and saw Patrick standing only a couple of feet away from her. She met his eyes, and he sat down next to her.

"Does it make me evil to want Cameron dead?"

"No, Fallon! Don't think that!" Patrick cupped her shoulders and drew her closer to him. "It's not evil to want justice, even if that means killing somebody. He brought this on himself. We'll take care of him, my colleagues and I."

His voice sounded as if this was nothing new in his life.

"Have you ever killed somebody?"

He hesitated for a moment, then nodded. "Yes, to save my family and friends from bad people." He sighed. "I don't like killing. But sometimes, it's the only way to eliminate a threat for good."

"I understand." She put her arms around him. "Thank you for telling me the truth."

"I'll always tell you the truth," he murmured.

"Then please tell me one more thing." She had to be sure. "Are you really okay with us being mated? I know it wasn't your choice."

He smiled, and his eyes suddenly turned almost golden. "Oh, Fallon, I've wanted to make you mine since the moment I first saw you."

She drew back a little, some of his words sending a chill down her spine, because she associated them with something bad. "To be yours?"

"Not the way Cameron meant it. Not like property. No. Never. I want to be with you for eternity, that's what the blood bond means for vampires. I never want to touch another woman. I never want to drink another person's blood—"

He suddenly stopped himself, and his forehead furrowed. "That can't be..." He rubbed his temple.

"What is it? What's wrong?"

He locked eyes with her then. "When a vampire mates with a human or another supernatural creature—other than another vampire—he can only drink blood from his mate. If he drinks any other blood, it will make him sick, and he'll eventually die. It makes the vampire or vampire hybrid dependent on his mate, in a way leveling the playing field. Like with my father and mother. He drinks only her blood. It gives her power over him. Not that she would ever abuse it, but he'll do anything to make her happy."

Not understanding what he was trying to explain to her, she asked, "What are you trying to say?"

"You drank my blood *before* we had sex, not during! We're not mated, Fallon. I drank bottled human blood this morning while you had breakfast, remember? And I didn't get sick."

"Oh!" She suddenly felt deflated. Disappointed. But maybe it was better that way. Maybe this would give them both time to think about whether they really wanted this.

With his fingers underneath her chin, he tipped her face up, and suddenly, his face was only inches away from her. "Yes, unfortunately. However, the silver lining is that I'll get my chance to ask you officially after all."

Her heart beat excitedly—more than it should—because wasn't that a question that she should contemplate for a while, particularly given her dating history? Wasn't it unwise to tumble head-over-heels into a serious relationship? And eternity sounded not just serious, but, well, it meant forever. It should scare her that Patrick wanted this even though they barely knew each other. After all, they'd only met a little over three days ago. So, why did she feel as if she knew him? As if she could look into his soul and see that he had a pure heart, one that beat for her?

"Ask me what?" she whispered, unable to stop her lips from moving.

"Whether you want to be my blood-bonded mate."

When she parted her lips to give him an answer, Patrick put his finger over them. "Don't answer now. I like having something to look forward to."

His lips brushed hers for just a second before the sound of the door opening startled them both.

"Patrick, we've got something."

Thomas, the blond IT guy dressed in leather pants and a casual T-shirt, entered the room.

Patrick rose. "Let me hear it."

"We think that William Gallagher called his son just after you guys left the property. The call lasted less than a minute."

"Do you know what was spoken?"

"No. We didn't have a tap on the Gallagher lines yet, but the number he called was a burner, and we must assume that it was Cameron's, because his own phone has been disconnected. He probably trashed it, knowing that he could be traced that way."

"Okay. Do we have a location for the burner?"

Thomas shook his head. "We're working on it, but no luck so far. But Ryder just called in. He's surveilling the access road that leads to the Gallagher estate. He saw an SUV passing, heading there."

"But Cameron drives a sportscar," Fallon interrupted.

Thomas looked at her. "He may have dumped it. If his father told him that vampires came for him, he wouldn't be so careless as to use his own car to get around."

"I agree," Patrick said. "Have you sent drones up to verify it's him?"

"No. Too risky in daylight. They'll spot them, and he might run before we can get there with a team. I can't send Ryder in there on his own. We don't know how many other werewolves are there."

Patrick nodded. "Alright. Then we'll have to be a bit more clandestine. I think I have an idea how we can confirm that Cameron is there without alerting them to our presence."

35

A few minutes later, Patrick had laid out his plan: he would go to the Gallagher estate, enter from a different side, sneak into the house, and scout it out to see if Cameron had returned, and how many other werewolves were present.

"Are you crazy? You can't just walk into the lion's den alone!" Fallon said in a raised voice.

"Wolf's lair," Patrick replied. "And I'm not going in alone. I'm taking Virginia."

"By daylight? They'll see you coming," she claimed. "And even if they don't, they'll smell you!"

He sighed and took Fallon's hands into his. "Trust me on this. Virginia is a Stealth Guardian. She can make us invisible, so the Gallaghers won't see us coming."

"Invisible? That's ludicrous!"

"It's not. The Stealth Guardians are our allies, and we know what they are capable of. Virginia is Wesley's mate. She'll help us. As for our scent: Wes is down in his lab, brewing a potion that will disguise our scent. We've done this before. Trust me on this. If we had more time, I would have asked Virginia to come meet me here so she could show you what she can do. But we don't have that time."

She took a few deep breaths before she nodded. "If you don't come back, I'm coming after you."

He could see in her eyes that it wasn't an empty threat, but he would make sure that she would never have to execute it.

On the way to the Golden Gate Bridge, Patrick picked up Virginia and they headed north. Once in Marin County, Patrick didn't take the main road leading up to the gate of the Gallagher property. Instead, he used an unpaved road that led around the Gallagher's estate and ended about half a mile from its western border. Across a bare field, he spotted a fence in the distance. As he'd expected, this section was a simple chain link fence, not the impenetrable brick-and-mortar wall that surrounded the land on the east and south sides. But he wasn't stupid enough to think that the Gallaghers didn't have cameras around this side of the estate. He and Virginia would approach the fence invisibly.

"Well, let's get moving. Looks like it might be a bit of a hike to get to the house," Virginia said from the passenger seat. She was a striking woman with long red hair and an even fiercer warrior, and he was glad that she'd agreed to his plan.

They exited the car, and Patrick removed a bolt cutter from the trunk. "Ready."

Virginia glanced around, then nodded. "Alright, I'm cloaking us now."

He didn't feel any different than before, and he could still see her. However, he wasn't concerned, because he knew that Stealth Guardians had different levels of invisibility. They could make themselves and others invisible to anyone or just to select people. In this case, he and Virginia could still see each other, but nobody could see them. It was essential on a mission like this, where they had to work as a team and couldn't risk bumping into each other.

They approached the fence. When they reached it, Patrick used the bolt cutter—which was also invisible to other people because it had already been in his hand when Virginia had made him invisible—to cut an opening into it. Then he hid the bolt cutter in a bush, and both squeezed through the opening. The bolt cutter would turn visible once they were at a certain distance from it because Virginia could only make things invisible when they were close by.

They walked swiftly, avoiding stepping on dry branches and other debris that would make a sound and echo in the woods surrounding the Gallagher mansion. As they walked, Patrick noticed a cottage in the distance. He pointed to it, and Virginia nodded.

"I think it's time to take Wes's potion," she suggested, reaching into the inside pocket of her jacket. "There's a chance that members of the pack are nearby."

"Yes, that's possible."

He watched Virginia spray a good amount of the potion over her face and body, before handing it to him. He did the same, emptying the small spray bottle and then handing it back to her. He set his stopwatch for one hour.

"We'd better hurry now," he advised.

"You didn't tell Fallon that the potion only has a limited duration, did you?" she asked keeping her voice low.

"Why worry her?"

There was no need for her to know that once administered, the potion's effectiveness would wane completely within an hour at the most, and their natural smells would be back, giving them away to any werewolf close enough to pick up their scent.

He pointed to another small house to his left. "Looks like some of the pack members live on the property."

"Makes sense," she replied just as quietly. "Wolves are pack animals. They want to stick together for protection. We need to find out how many we're dealing with."

"If we have time once we assess the situation at the house," he said. "Our priority is finding Cameron's whereabouts. We'll worry about the rest of the pack later."

They passed a total of four smaller single-level houses or cabins that looked no larger than a home with one or two bedrooms. It was impossible to see at first glance if the homes were occupied. However, he noticed car tracks on the narrow dirt roads leading to them. He pointed them out to Virginia, and she nodded, acknowledging that she'd seen them too.

A few minutes later, the Gallagher mansion came into view. From its back, it was clear that this house was larger than he'd first estimated. Rising three stories, there was a side wing that hadn't been visible from the front entrance where they'd encountered William Gallagher and his son Byron. It looked more modern than the rest of the house, which meant it had been added later. He counted the windows on every floor and guessed that the building most likely had ten to twelve bedrooms. It could house more than just the Gallagher family. According to Thomas who'd done a lot of research on the Gallaghers, the patriarch of the family was a widower and had three sons and one daughter. It was unclear if he had extended family who lived here too. But from what he'd learned about werewolves, he knew that families stuck together, and he had to assume that there might be aunts, uncles, and cousins living either at the main house or in one of the smaller cottages dotted around the estate.

He exchanged a quick look with Virginia. "Cell phone on silent?"

"Done."

Good. They were ready. As long as they remained silent, and their footfalls didn't reach any werewolf's ears, they'd be okay. He glanced at his stopwatch.

"We have forty-seven minutes."

The soft grass that reached as far as the terrace and a couple of back doors swallowed the sound of their sneakers. Virginia pointed to one of the doors leading into the house. He nodded, and they walked toward it. In front of it, they stopped, and Virginia gave him a sign to remain outside while she passed through the door as if it was air. It was one of the other special skills only Stealth Guardians had—walking through anything solid except for lead. However, they could not make anybody else pass through solid objects.

Virginia was back in a few seconds. "Mudroom," she whispered. "I unlocked the door from the inside."

He quickly pushed the door open and entered, Virginia on his heels. She eased the door shut quietly. The first thing he noticed was the overwhelming smell of werewolves. Evidently, this was the room where they shed their clothes before they shifted and went for a run or a hunt—or whatever they did—in their wolf forms. The floor was dirty with leaves and soil. In one corner was an open shower area, most likely used to clean the dirt—or the blood—off them once they came back from their run.

Virginia motioned to the other door. It stood open and led into a hallway. Remaining silent, Patrick walked ahead. He could now hear voices and other sounds in the house. The smell of human food wafted to him, accompanied by the sound of cutlery and dishes clanging. Somebody was cooking lunch.

They walked by a door where the scent was at its strongest, and Patrick quickly looked inside without entering. A woman whose aura identified her as a werewolf was stirring something on the stove, while another female werewolf chopped salad or vegetables next to the sink. He couldn't see the faces of either one, and they didn't turn around, confirming that Wesley's potion was effective in eliminating his and Virginia's scent.

He heard sounds from the second floor. Somebody was walking up there, and the old wooden floor was creaking. Motioning to Virginia to follow him, he crossed the large wood-paneled foyer and headed for the room from which the voices came. The door was ajar, but not open wide enough for him to squeeze through.

Without a word, Virginia understood his predicament and used her preternatural skill of walking through solid objects to enter the room. A moment later, she peered back at him through the space between the door and frame and nodded. Slowly, she eased the door open wider and stepped aside to make room. Patrick squeezed through the space and entered, when the floor beneath his feet suddenly creaked.

36

Shortly after Patrick had left to meet up with Virginia to drive to Marin County, the door opened, and Isabelle appeared at the entrance to the office. Fallon jumped up, startled. Patrick hadn't mentioned that he was expecting his sister. Instinctively, she tensed. Even though Isabelle had taken care of her when she'd thrown up the previous night and even held her hair back like a girlfriend would do, her werewolf instincts were trying to push to the surface, warning her that vampires were her enemies. She suppressed these instincts as best she could because her human side knew that Isabelle wouldn't hurt her.

"Oh, hey, Isabelle. Patrick just left," she managed to say without her voice shaking.

"I know." She turned halfway, then addressed somebody in the hallway. "Ross? Are you coming with Mummy?"

A little boy waddled in, grinning. Since she didn't have much contact with kids, she couldn't be sure of his age, but he was definitely not of school age yet. He had a full head of dark brown hair and stunning green eyes like his mother.

When he spotted her, he walked toward her, tiny fangs suddenly descending as he opened his mouth. A soft hiss came from him.

"No, Ross, stop!" Isabelle said firmly and snatched him by the back of his sweater, lifting him up with one hand.

He peddled his feet, trying to escape from his mother's grip, while he pointed at Fallon.

"You're not human. But not a vampire."

Isabelle turned him toward her so he had to look at her face. "Ross, didn't I teach you to be polite?"

"But she's not human, and she's not like us," he insisted and looked over his shoulder, pointing at her again. "What is she?"

"She's a werewolf."

"A wolf?" The little boy stared at her in disbelief. "You don't look like a wolf."

"I'm sorry," Isabelle said quickly. "But he's at that age where he's so curious."

"It's okay," Fallon said quickly, not wanting to embarrass her. "How old is he?"

"I'm four," Ross replied and showed his palm with his thumb tucked in, indicating the number four. "And you?"

"I'm thirty-five."

"That's not old," he said, sounding much more grown up than he was. "My daddy is over 100 years old."

"I think I've seen your daddy before." She shifted her gaze back to Isabelle. "Your mate is Orlando, the owner of the Mezzanine Patrick mentioned, right?"

A warm glow seemed to settle over Isabelle's face when she answered, "Yes, Orlando is mine."

The last word would have felt odd if a human had spoken it, but knowing what she now knew about vampires and their mates, she understood that the word wasn't an exaggeration or a jealous declaration. No, it was a simple statement that everybody in their world accepted without question. *Their world.* It was strange to think that way. Yet within twenty-four hours everything in her own world had been turned upside down. Now she was living in their world, the world of supernatural creatures.

"Did Patrick ask you to look in on me?"

"Not directly." She walked toward the sitting area and put Ross back on his feet. "Go find the Legos."

The little boy ran to a cupboard and opened the lowest drawer from which he pulled a huge box with Legos.

"There!" Ross said triumphantly. He sat down on the floor and started to play.

Isabelle finally turned back to her. "All families with small children have been asked to report to HQ. The others should be arriving soon too."

"Oh. Why is that?"

"Because of the werewolf threat." She gave her a quick smile. "Once Patrick and Virginia are back, they'll all be getting ready to fight the Gallaghers should they not give Cameron up to be executed for his crimes."

Executed. The word sounded so final. Yet Isabelle spoke as if this was nothing new. And maybe it wasn't new in her world.

"I doubt his father will give him up."

"It's to be expected. They'll fight back, so we're taking precautions: the human blood-bonded mates and underage children of all Scanguards employees have to stay at HQ so they can be properly protected, and can't be used as bargaining chips by the Gallaghers."

Fallon let out a breath of air. "All because of me. I'm so sorry."

Isabelle put a hand on her forearm. "It's not your fault. It's Cameron's. And even if he hadn't terrorized and turned you, he would still have to be taken out. We can't have a killer in the city. It's too dangerous for everybody, humans and supernatural beings alike. That's what the city pays us for: to keep the streets safe."

"The city knows about this? Is that because Anita is married to a vampire?"

"No, that's not the reason. The current chief of police has known about our existence for several decades, and he's kept our secret for just as long. There are only a few select police officers who know about us, and they send cases that involve vampires or other supernatural creatures to us to handle. We have a contract with the city. We patrol the streets at night."

"That must be so dangerous."

"It is. But we're all well-trained."

"Patrick said you work as a bodyguard too. Do you still do that?" She gestured to Ross. "I mean with having a little one now?"

"I do, though I don't work full-time anymore. This little boy needs a lot of supervision." Isabelle ran her eyes over Ross, who was building a castle with his Legos.

"He showed his fangs earlier," Fallon said. "Isn't that gonna be a problem when he goes to school?"

"By then, he'll understand that he can't give away what he is. He doesn't go to preschool or kindergarten because of it. Scanguards has a little informal preschool in the building where all hybrid children can play together and learn the basics so that they're ready for first grade."

The more she learned about Scanguards and the vampires who ran the company, the more normal it all sounded. They lived like normal families, or almost, because surely the fact that pure-blooded vampires like Patrick's father, Samson, couldn't be outside during daylight meant that their daily schedules were upside down. Night was day, and day was night.

"You okay?" Isabelle asked softly.

Fallon nodded quickly. "Yes. It's just... well, there's so much that's happened in the last few days, and I'm still trying to adjust."

But what she really thought she kept to herself. She didn't want to voice it. All the vampires and vampire hybrids she'd met so far appeared so civilized. She, a werewolf, was the odd one out: she didn't feel civilized. She dreaded the coming night and the rising of the moon, because it meant she wouldn't be in control of herself. And she hated that feeling. She hated being ruled by the beast inside her. And to think that this could be her future if they didn't succeed in bringing down Cameron. Could she really live like this?

37

William Gallagher who stood in front of the fireplace suddenly whirled his head toward the door, clearly having heard the sound of the creaking hardwood floor. He stared directly at Patrick, who didn't dare move. The man with him looked over his shoulder too, and Patrick recognized him instantly. It was Cameron.

"I won't do it!" Cameron said with a raised voice, picking up his conversation with his father.

The older Gallagher glared back at him, the sound from the door clearly forgotten. "You listen to me now, you ungrateful little pup!"

He underscored his superiority as the Alpha by jabbing his son in the chest.

"It was one thing killing those stupid hikers out here in Marin where I can do damage control. Do you have any idea how many palms I had to grease, and how many favors to call in to take the heat off you?"

Cameron opened his mouth, but his father continued without pause. "I can't fake your death twice! I had to find a homeless man who wouldn't be missed so I could blow him up in your car. I can't keep doing that! Don't you get that?"

Just like he'd thought: the Gallagher pack was complicit in Cameron's crimes. Patrick exchanged a quick glance with Virginia who gave a nod.

"I didn't ask you to fake my death in the first place!" Cameron snapped, snarling. "I had it handled. They didn't suspect me. I was careful!"

"Don't be an idiot! Killing two hikers on our property? You didn't think that made the cops suspicious of us? You endangered the entire pack! How many times do I have to tell you not to hunt in our woods? I don't care what you do somewhere else. As long as it doesn't put the pack in jeopardy!"

Gallagher was on a roll, dressing down his oldest son.

"But now you've done it! You brought vampires to our doorstep! Are you out of your fucking mind? Biting a woman who can identify you, and letting her live?"

He smacked his son so hard that Cameron's head whipped to the side and a loud cracking sound echoed against the walls of the living room. With defiance in his eyes, Cameron faced him again, and Patrick caught a glimpse of the violence that hid only skin-deep beneath the exterior of a man many women would have found attractive. He was sure that this was what Fallon had seen when he'd attacked her because he wasn't getting his way. Just like he wasn't getting his way with his father now.

"Fallon is mine!" Cameron's voice was but a snarl and barely human.

"You did this on purpose? Turning her?" This seemed to be news to Cameron's father, and a mask of disgust spread on his features. "You should have come to me first!"

"So you could forbid it? I'm not an idiot! I know how you feel about humans. That's why I turned her into one of us."

"Don't bullshit me! You didn't turn her for my sake or the sake of the pack! And now you've put us on a collision course with a bunch of fucking vampires! Even worse, vampires who can be out in daylight! But no, you never think of the pack when you do anything. It's always you, you, you!"

"Like you're any different! No wonder Mom killed herself!"

"Don't you dare bring up your mother!" William Gallagher yelled and lunged for his son.

But Cameron was prepared and punched him first. As they exchanged vicious blows, the scent of blood started to permeate the room, and Patrick's nostrils flared, while his fangs extended. Sounds from outside drifted to his ears at the same time: car engines as well as footsteps approaching the living room.

Virginia put a hand on his forearm, reminding him that they couldn't be part of this fight. Not with more people coming. Nodding at Virginia, Patrick looked out the window that overlooked the driveway. Several SUVs were pulling up, stopping in front of the house.

Before he could concentrate on them, somebody threw the door wide open and charged into the room. It was a woman, but not one of the ones he'd seen in the kitchen. She was dressed in riding gear.

"Dad! Cameron! What the hell are you doing?"

But the two didn't answer and continued their fistfight.

"Damn it!" she yelled and turned toward the open door. "Spencer! Owen! Get in here now!"

Heavy boots trampling on the old wooden floor followed her order, and several men ran into the room. Patrick moved out of their way swiftly, using the noise they made to cover his movement. Virginia did the same.

The three newcomers put an end to the fight between father and son, subduing Cameron who resisted. William Gallagher took a breath, while he smoothed his hair back and righted his shirt. He glared at his son.

"You're leaving on the Alberta at midnight. And you'll stay in the

Philippines until it's safe for you to come back. We'll take care of the vampires and deal with the woman, and—"

"If you kill her," Cameron interrupted. "I'll—"

"It's none of your fucking business what I do with her. It's pack business. And I'll do what's best for the pack!"

Then he looked at the men holding him prisoner, while four more entered the room. It was getting too crowded for his liking.

"Now get him out of my sight, and secure him, until it's time for him to leave," the older Gallagher commanded.

Patrick's wristwatch suddenly vibrated. He looked at it. Fuck! They had ten minutes left until their scent would give them away. They needed to get out of this room and this house to get far enough away before the werewolves could smell them and realize they had intruders. He made eye contact with Virginia, indicating the watch. She understood.

As quickly as he could, Patrick walked toward the door, but he wasn't fast enough. Two of the werewolves stood there like sentries, clearly expecting trouble from Cameron.

"You'll regret this!" Cameron yelled over his shoulder as two werewolves dragged him toward the door. He hadn't reached the door quite yet, when he kicked out toward one of the men guarding the door, thrusting the guy in Patrick's direction.

Only his vampire speed saved him from colliding with the massive man. However, the man's hand brushed across Patrick's jacket, before he hit the wall. For a second, the werewolf seemed confused. He stared in Patrick's direction. Patrick didn't dare move, didn't even breathe, worried that the werewolf realized that there was an intruder.

"Damn it, get him out of here," William Gallagher demanded with a booming voice.

Everybody sprang into action, and the werewolf who'd brushed him aided in getting Cameron out of the room. Relieved, Patrick looked at Virginia, who made a motion toward the door. He understood. It was vital that they left now, while plenty of sounds would drown out their footfalls.

In the hallway, Patrick followed Cameron with his eyes. Three pack members dragged him to a door beneath the stairs. The basement, he assumed. A tug at his shirt sleeve made him pivot. Virginia gave the sign to leave. He didn't have to look at his watch to know that their time was almost up.

Another minute, and the werewolves' nostrils would twitch and give away his and Virginia's presence. He didn't like the odds: at least nine if not more werewolves against one vampire and one Stealth Guardian. But at least now they knew what they were up against.

38

Upon arrival at HQ, Patrick headed straight for the command center on the first floor, where Benjamin was on duty.

"Hey, bro."

"Did you reach everybody?" Patrick asked.

"Orders went out to everybody to report for duty. Meeting starts in fifteen minutes. And I gave everybody the basics of what's going on."

"Good. Any information on the Alberta? I'm assuming it's a ship?"

"Correct, a cargo ship. Belongs to one of the companies the Gallaghers own. Set to ship out at midnight heading to Manila."

"That's what I thought. Easiest way to smuggle Cameron out of the country without the authorities finding out is on a ship for which you control the manifest." He took a breath. "I'm heading to the conference room. Patch in when the meeting starts. I need you to be up to speed on what we're planning."

"Sure, bro."

Patrick headed for the door.

"Oh, and Patrick?"

He looked over his shoulder.

"Fallon is still in your father's office. You want me to tell her you're back?"

"No, I'll go see her now."

He exited the room, headed for the elevators, and punched the button. The doors opened a few moments later. Two vampires were inside: Orlando and Zane. Just the guys he needed. Orlando, his brother-in-law, was one of the biggest vampires he'd ever encountered, and Zane, the bald Holocaust survivor, was one of the most brutal and cold-blooded ones.

"Good to see you guys," Patrick said and joined them in the elevator.

"Wouldn't wanna miss getting my claws into some fucking werewolves," Zane said, his facial muscles barely moving.

"You and me both, bro," Patrick replied.

Orlando grunted and only offered one word. "Yeah."

He wasn't a man of many words, though ever since he'd blood-bonded with Isabelle, he'd become a little more approachable. However, he was still the stubborn bouncer he'd worked with when Patrick and Damian had run the Mezzanine, the club that now belonged to Orlando.

"Is Isabelle here with Ross yet?" Patrick asked.

"Yeah, up in your dad's office."

"And the other blood-bonded mates and children?"

Orlando shrugged and looked at Zane.

"Scarlet's car is in the garage," Zane replied.

Scarlet was Ryder's blood-bonded mate, and they had five-year-old twins who needed protection.

The elevator stopped again, but they hadn't reached the top floor yet. Blake entered, his seven-year-old son Harrison, in tow.

He greeted everybody.

"You've got the whereabouts of all the kids and the human

blood-bonded mates?" Patrick asked, since Blake was officially in charge of hybrid security.

"Buffy is picking up Dean from school as we speak, and then they'll both stay here," Blake reported. "Scarlet and the twins are already here. And so is Katie with Jacob. They are all down in the lounge."

"And Lilo?" he asked.

"Mom is at a writing conference," Harrison replied.

Patrick winked at the boy. "So that means you get to stay up all hours of the day and night while your dad is in charge?"

Harrison chuckled. "We're not gonna tell Mom that."

Patrick looked at Blake. "Harrison should probably join the others at the lounge downstairs."

"He will. Just as soon as he gets his iPad from my office. Right, buddy?"

The doors of the elevator opened on the top floor, and they all exited.

"Blake, check that all the other humans are here too: Savannah, Nina, Naomi, Ursula. Who am I forgetting?"

"No worries, I've got the list. Everybody's been notified, and we're keeping track of where they are. I'll make sure everybody gets here safe and sound," Blake assured him.

"Thanks, bro." Patrick marched toward his father's office at the end of the corridor. "I'll be in the conference room in a few minutes."

He opened the door to his father's office without knocking. Isabelle and Fallon sat on the sofa, deep in conversation, while Ross played with his Lego set on the floor.

"Hey," he greeted them. "We're back."

Fallon jumped up. "Thank God!"

His sister rose too, a relieved breath rolling over her lips. "About time. We were getting worried."

He cast Isabelle a look. "Meeting is starting in a few minutes."

She nodded. "I'll bring Ross down to the others. Nina can watch him." She addressed Ross. "Hey, Ross, wanna go see Auntie Nina?"

Ross jumped up. "Yay! Nina!"

"Hey, buddy," Patrick greeted him and opened his arms. Ross ran toward him, and he lifted him in the air as he giggled.

Isabelle smiled, and he transferred her son into her arms. "I'll be back in a few minutes. Don't start the meeting without me."

With a nod, Patrick stepped aside, so she could leave the office. When the door finally fell shut behind her, he marched toward Fallon. He took her into his arms without a word and kissed her.

It felt good to feel her arms hug him tightly as she kissed him back. For a few seconds he allowed himself to enjoy her embrace before he severed the kiss.

"How did it go?" she asked, her forehead furrowed in worry.

"We saw him. He's at the Gallagher estate."

"What now?"

"We're meeting in a few minutes to put an action plan together. You can join us if you want. But just so you know, there'll be a lot of vampires and vampire hybrids in the room. Some of them might be hostile toward you in the beginning. Can you handle that?"

She nodded immediately. "Yes."

"Alright then. Let's introduce you to them."

The conference room on the executive floor was packed. Patrick was pleased to see that not only most vampire hybrids, but also most vampires in Scanguards' employ were assembled. Notably missing were Damian and Ethan, who were both providing security at the jeweler's convention, which was due to end in a few hours. Benjamin would have to fill them in once they returned from their assignment.

When he entered the room with Fallon by his side, the conversations stopped, and everybody eyed her with caution. He walked to the front of the room, where he turned toward the crowd, still holding Fallon's hand.

"Thanks for coming so quickly," he started. "This is Fallon. Her ex-boyfriend Cameron Gallagher bit her three nights ago and turned her into a werewolf against her will. She means us no harm, something that can't be said of the Gallagher pack."

There were a few grumbles and murmurs in the crowd, but overall, everybody seemed relaxed despite the presence of a werewolf.

"Here's what we know. You've all been briefed about the Presidio murder. We've confirmed that Cameron is the killer. And we also know that he killed two other people in Marin County. Because of these murders in Marin County, Cameron's father, William Gallagher, helped fake Cameron's death to take the heat off him. In order to fake his death, he used a homeless man, whom he blew up in Cameron's car. We don't know yet whether the homeless man was already dead, or whether he was killed by Gallagher. Anyway, the police subsequently classified the murders of the hikers as mountain lion attacks."

A few people in the crowd scoffed.

"My sentiments exactly," Patrick continued. "But the police in Marin just don't know any better, and I'm sure Gallagher paid somebody to make the whole thing go away. It doesn't matter now. We have a more urgent issue. When Virginia and I were at the Gallagher property, we witnessed an argument between William Gallagher and his son. When Gallagher found out that Cameron killed the jogger in the Presidio and turned Fallon, he told his son that he'd be sent to the Philippines until it was safe for him to return. The cargo ship he's leaving on belongs to the Gallaghers, and it will leave tonight at midnight."

Next to him, Fallon gasped. "No! You can't let him leave!"

He turned his face to Fallon. "I won't let it happen, trust me." Then he addressed his colleagues again. "For those of you who don't know, we believe that Fallon can be turned back into a human if her maker, Cameron, dies before the last night of Fallon's first full moon ends. This is Fallon's first full moon as a werewolf, and tonight is night two. The full moon lasts only three nights. I'd hoped we'd have more time to plan how to get Cameron, but we have to do this tonight, or Cameron will be gone, and with it the chance of making Fallon human again."

A few curses echoed in the large room.

"Then we'd better come up with something quickly," Luther interjected. "You're sure about Cameron's current whereabouts? Has he already left the Gallagher estate?"

"He can't," Patrick added. "When he protested about being sent to the Philippines, his father had him locked up in the basement of the house."

"Besides," Thomas interjected, "we've got eyes on all roads leading to and from the estate. All we've seen so far are more cars arriving. Nobody's left the estate."

"They're getting ready to fight us," Patrick predicted. "They know we want to punish Cameron. Not only that, they also want Fallon, because she's a werewolf. She will never be safe, as long as they consider her one of them."

"Well, then we've gotta change that," Amaury added.

Patrick nodded. And they had to get it done before midnight. The clock was ticking.

39

For almost three hours everybody in the conference room debated ideas of how to get to Cameron, kill him, and make the Gallagher pack understand that they would be eliminated if they retaliated against Scanguards or harmed Fallon in any way.

Fallon's head was spinning, but she understood that this wasn't Scanguards' first rodeo. They'd taken on other dangerous creatures —namely demons, which Isabelle had told her about—and had won. She could only hope that they would be victorious over the werewolves too. Her future depended on it. That was also the reason she couldn't just stand by. She needed to be part of this mission.

When the meeting dispersed, and everybody got themselves and their weapons and equipment ready, she tapped on Patrick's arm.

He turned to her. "Everything alright? You know we have to do this, right? He has to die."

"I know. And I need to be there when it happens."

"No!"

The firm one-word answer riled her up in an instant. "You can't keep me away from this. It's my fight."

"You're not getting anywhere near those werewolves. It's too dangerous."

"You seem to have forgotten that I'm a werewolf myself."

"How could I forget that? Didn't you listen to what we discussed here? You must realize by now how dangerous the Gallaghers are."

"That's exactly why I have to be there with you."

Patrick let out a breath and took her arm, leading her toward his father's office. "Let's discuss this in private."

A moment later, they were in the office, and the door fell shut behind them. They were alone.

Patrick faced her. "I can't let you come with us. You might be a werewolf, but you have no control over your shifting. We're going in after dark, which means the moon will be out, and you'll be forced to shift, if you want to or not."

She knew that, and it scared her, but she also knew that she could help.

"The Gallaghers won't hurt me. You said it yourself: they want me to be part of their pack. We can use that to our advantage."

"What advantage? Do you really think I'd risk them snatching you?"

"It won't happen. I won't leave your side the entire time." She put her hands on his hips and pulled him closer. It was time to play dirty to get him to agree to her request. "I'll make it worth your while."

Patrick gasped and let out a surprised laugh. "You actually think you can seduce me so I'll let you come?"

She winked at him. "I'll let you come first." She slid her hand over the front of his pants.

"Damn it, Fallon, you're manipulating me."

She squeezed him and felt his cock grow thicker under her palm. "Apparently it's working."

He put his hand on the back of her head and drew her face to him. Without another word he sank his lips onto hers and kissed her, robbing her of her breath. She allowed herself to melt into his embrace, pressing her body to his, his hard muscles crushing her breasts.

The kiss lasted only a few seconds before Patrick severed it.

"Alright, you get to come with us, under one condition."

"What condition?"

"You'll drink my blood."

Her forehead furrowed, but before she could ask why, he continued, "Last time when you drank my blood, you were able to control the wolf and hold off the shifting for a while."

She stared at him, surprised, but she had to admit that he was probably right. His blood had helped her fight the wolf inside her.

"But I can't bite you."

She showed him her teeth. They were too blunt to tear into his skin.

"Don't worry. You'll drink from me like all the other human blood-bonded women drink from their mate: I'll cut into my skin with my claws or my fangs, and you'll suck on the wound."

He brought his face closer to hers, and added, "And one more thing: if I get in trouble during the mission, don't try to save me. Run to the closest vampire you see and get their protection. Got it?"

He had to be crazy to think that she would leave him if anything bad happened to him. But she was wise enough to know that she couldn't tell him that she would do everything in her power to rescue him, or he would lock her in a cell and leave her here.

So, she did what she had to do and lied, "Got it."

She leaned in to kiss him, but to her surprise, Patrick didn't respond. Instead, he released her from his arms and turned to the door. Before she could figure out what he was planning to do, she heard the door lock click.

A breath escaped her when she realized what he intended to do. "Oh."

Patrick pivoted and approached. "Now, now, *Dr. Doyle*," he

teased. "I hope you're not gonna rescind that little offer you made me. Shall I remind you?"

"You mean right now? But we have to get ready for the mission…"

Her voice trailed off as he stopped only inches from her.

"Everybody is doing what they need to do. You and I, we've got a couple of hours."

She pointed to the door. "But your colleagues on this floor… they might hear us… or smell us."

He grinned. "And your point is?"

"I guess I don't have a point," she conceded, reaching for him.

She put her hand on his nape to pull him closer so their noses almost touched.

"That's much better," he murmured, and his breath ghosted over her skin.

"Well, then how about you drop your pants?"

Without waiting for his reply, she gripped his waistband and opened the button. He didn't stop her when she lowered the zipper and shoved them to mid-thigh. Instead, he dipped his head to the spot where her neck met her shoulder and kissed her there.

"One day soon," he whispered seductively, "I'll drink from you right here while I make love to you."

His promise sent a spear of heat through her insides. It was as if he could make her surrender to him with just a few words. But she wouldn't surrender right now. No, she wanted him to surrender to her.

She hooked her thumbs into his boxer briefs and lowered them, freeing his cock. The thick, hard rod thrust into her waiting hands, and with it a moan and a curse dislodged from Patrick's throat.

"Fuck!"

She smiled to herself and gripped him harder, then slowly lowered herself to her knees, bringing his beautiful shaft in line with her face. With one hand holding onto its base and the other gripping his hip, she licked over the bulbous head and felt him shudder beneath her touch.

She felt his hands on her shoulders then, steadying himself. Casting her gaze up at him, she noticed him looking down at her, his eyes shimmering golden.

"I love the way your eyes are glowing like gold."

"They're glowing like that because of you."

Holding his gaze, she licked over his erection once more, before she wrapped her lips around the tip. When she took his cock into her mouth as deep as she could, she closed her eyes, reveling in his masculine taste and the velvety-smooth texture of his skin. Her lips remained tightly wrapped around his erection while she drew back a little, letting him slip out but for the last inch, before sliding down on him again, taking him deep.

Patrick let out a moan. She felt him withdraw on his own now, and a moment later, he drove deep into her mouth again, his tempo still slow and measured, but judging by the strength with which he was holding on to her shoulders, she knew he was holding on to his self-control by a mere thread.

To show him that she was ready for more, she increased her tempo. Patrick moved with her, thrusting and withdrawing, while she added friction by moving her hand around the base of his cock up and down with her sucking motions.

"Fuck, babe!" he cursed, his thrusts becoming more urgent.

She felt her own arousal grow with every second she was sucking him. She loved to see that he was close to losing control. She felt power in her because she could pleasure this man, this powerful vampire until he was only driven by his basic instincts. And she realized that she loved it, loved the power he gave her by surrendering to her touch. It was as if he was already hers. And maybe he was. Maybe no bite was necessary to form their bond, to know that they were one.

When Patrick suddenly withdrew completely from her mouth and pulled her up to stand, she was surprised.

"I wasn't done."

With a speed she'd never seen before, Patrick opened her khaki pants and lowered them to her knees, pulling her panties down in the same move.

"Turn around and brace yourself on the desk," he ordered in a gruff voice she'd never heard him use.

When she stared at his face, she noticed his fangs descending. The sight sent another spear of lust through her body, and she did what he'd asked, bracing herself against the desk and offering him her backside.

He gripped her tightly with his hands, and she could feel that his fingernails had become sharp little barbs. But that knowledge did nothing to dispel her desire for him. On the contrary, she wanted him even more now.

In the next instant, she felt Patrick's cock plunging into her pussy, forcing all air out of her lungs. Before she could take another breath, he began thrusting and withdrawing rapidly. He was in charge now, and she realized that she needed this, needed Patrick to hold the reins. She could let go now, let go of all her worries, all her fears, all her thoughts about the future, and live in this one moment. The moment in which only she and Patrick counted. The outside world didn't matter.

Her body was finally free of everything that was holding her back, and she could enjoy this moment. She felt the approach of her orgasm, felt the tensing of her muscles. Patrick increased his tempo even more, clearly recognizing how close she was. Another thrust, another withdrawal, and her pussy spasmed, clenching and releasing his erection in quick succession.

A relieved sigh came from Patrick, and now she could feel him shudder, while his semen filled her, making his thrusts even smoother than before.

When he finally stilled, they were both breathing hard. Still inside her, he leaned over her back, bringing his mouth to the crook of her neck.

"I love you, Fallon, with every fiber of my being."

He sank his lips to her neck and kissed her there, his fangs scraping gently against her skin. She shivered with pleasure at the contact.

"I want you to bite me," she demanded.

"After tonight," he replied.

"Why not now?"

He chuckled. "If I bit you now, I'd have a hard-on for hours. I'd be thinking only of you, and of making love to you. I can't afford that distraction. Not right now. You understand that, don't you?"

She did. "You'll bite me when it's over, promise me."

"Nothing will be able to stop me then."

And she would hold him to his promise.

40

Patrick felt the engine's vibrations beneath him as they traveled over the Golden Gate Bridge in one of the many black-out vans Scanguards owned. They were vampire-safe, their windows coated with a special UV film that blocked out all sunlight. He sat in the back with Fallon, a metal grille separating them from the driver and the other passenger. This van was normally used to transport dangerous prisoners, the partition preventing them from attacking the other people in the van. Patrick had chosen this van in case Fallon couldn't suppress her need to shift and attacked his colleagues.

Zane was driving. Damian was in the passenger seat, talking on his phone.

Several other vans were following them. Every vampire and vampire hybrid in their employ was taking part in this mission.

"I don't understand why we can't all be going in invisibly like you and Virginia did. Wouldn't that be easier?" Fallon asked.

"Unfortunately, she can't make more than three people invisible at any one time, without putting herself in danger," Patrick explained.

"And she's the only Stealth Guardian you guys know?"

"No. We know a whole bunch of them. They've helped us a lot before, but they're dealing with some major unrest in Europe, and can't send us any of their people. We're lucky that Virginia is available at all. As a member of their council, she should have gone back to help them, but I begged her not to. She's gonna help us."

"But if she can't make the whole team invisible, how are they not gonna see us coming? We might never get close enough to Cameron if they see us."

Damian looked over his shoulder, removing his cell phone from his ear for a moment. "Just spoke to Thomas. They've hacked into the Gallaghers' security system and are ready to record a thirty-second video as soon as the sun is down."

She remembered having heard something like this in a heist movie before. "You mean they're gonna put it on a loop so that the cameras show a recorded video rather than a live transmission?"

"Exactly," Damian said. He tipped his chin in Patrick's direction. "I think it's time. Sunset is in about ten minutes."

"Alright," Patrick replied and looked at Fallon. "How are you feeling?"

"I can feel it coming. It's close," she admitted.

"Let's do this."

Patrick pushed the sleeve of his shirt up to his elbow. He let his fangs extend to their full length, then sank them into his forearm, piercing the skin. When he tasted his blood, he withdrew his fangs and looked at Fallon. She leaned closer, and he held his arm out to her.

"Drink."

She lowered her head to his open wound and began sucking. Her soft lips felt good on his skin, and he couldn't help himself and pulled her onto his lap with his other arm.

Damn, her curves pressed to him gave him all kinds of ideas of what he wanted to do with her, but he forced himself to suppress his desires.

To distract himself from the erotic experience of Fallon drinking his blood, he addressed his friend.

"Damian, did HQ get any news from Striker?"

"Not since he called over four hours ago." Damian shrugged. "And as usual he was just as chatty as this guy here."

He motioned to Zane, who cast him a warning look and grunted.

"What did he say?"

"Just that he's working on some sort of intervention."

Patrick nodded. "Yeah, that's vague. Guess it's too late now anyway. I doubt he's gonna come up with something usable in the next half hour."

It didn't matter now. Everybody was prepared for the battle and armed to the teeth. With some luck, they would all walk away alive, all but Cameron.

Fallon stopped drinking from him, and slid off his lap, her cheeks flushed, her eyes dilated. He could feel her arousal, a direct effect of his blood.

"You okay?"

"Yeah."

He brought his arm to his lips and licked over the two puncture wounds, closing them with his saliva. When he looked out through the windshield, he saw that the van had turned onto a rural road, heading for an abandoned barn.

One by one, each Scanguards van piled into the makeshift staging area which abutted a forest, just a short distance from the Gallagher estate.

"Sun's down," Damian announced.

Patrick helped Fallon exit the van, holding onto her hand to make sure he'd recognize instantly if she was in distress and unable to suppress the need to shift into her wolf form. He glanced around and ticked off everybody in his head.

"What are they wearing?" Fallon whispered next to him.

"Kevlar suits," he replied. "No silver bullet or knife can penetrate them."

"Then why are you not wearing one?"

He caught the panic in her voice.

"They're a pain to fight in. Pretty heavy and a little stiff. I need to be more agile."

He tipped his chin in Zane's direction, who didn't wear a Kevlar suit either.

"Those of us going inside the house can't be weighed down by the Kevlar suits."

She nodded, but she didn't look happy about it. He couldn't really blame her. He would have liked to stick Fallon into a Kevlar suit, but he knew that eventually she'd need to shift, and the Kevlar might trap her, making her vulnerable to an attack.

He reached into his pocket and pulled out two earpieces. He handed one to Fallon while he stuck the other one into his left ear.

"Everybody," he called out. "Communication systems on."

Everybody followed his command.

He lowered his voice for his next command. "Identify yourselves if you can hear me in your ear."

Alphabetically, like they'd learned in their training at Scanguards, they began to say their names.

"Alright," Patrick said with a nod. "All is good. Cole, you're running the command center?"

From his position back at Scanguards HQ, Vanessa's human mate, Cole replied, "Yep, drew the short straw."

He knew that Cole had wanted to join them in this fight, but if anything happened to him, Vanessa would literally skin him alive. Besides, Cole was an IT genius like Thomas and Eddie and was needed at HQ because both had opted to join them in the field.

"You're more valuable at HQ, bro," Patrick said into the mic. "Where are the drones?"

"I parked them down the road from you guys. Ready to deploy them now."

"Okay, send 'em out."

"That's a go," Cole said. "Drones are in the air. I'll keep you posted about what I'm seeing."

"Thanks, Cole. And the security cameras? Have the Gallaghers noticed that we're manipulating their feed?"

"Nope. All clear and quiet. I'm logged into their system. So far, they haven't tried to override my code."

"Good." Then he waved to Charles and Wesley. "Wes, Charles, the potions."

The two witches distributed small spray bottles among the team.

"Wait with spraying yourselves with it," Wesley advised everybody. "Once in contact with oxygen, the efficacy of the potion will last only for one hour."

He felt Fallon gasp next to him and looked at her.

"You knew this and didn't mention it when you went in there with Virginia?" Fallon asked, her voice raised.

Not that she would have had to raise her voice for all of them to hear, because she too wore an earpiece and a mic that transmitted every word she spoke.

"Somebody's in trouble," Wes said with a smirk.

Patrick cast him an annoyed look and covered his mic with his hand in an attempt to have a private conversation. "I'm sorry, Fallon, but I didn't want to worry you."

She simply shook her head. "I can handle the truth."

"I know that now." He leaned in. "Forgive me."

She sighed, but her eyes already gave him her answer.

"Thank you," he murmured.

Charles, the witch blood-bonded with Roxanne, a vampire female who'd been in Scanguards' employ for decades, approached. In his hand, he held several Epi-pens. He looked over his shoulder and waved to somebody.

"Zane? Virginia? A word," Charles demanded.

Virginia and Zane joined them.

"What is it?" Virginia asked.

"Since you're the team going into the wolf's lair, I've got a little present for each of you."

He held out his hand with the Epi-pens.

"I'm not allergic to anything," Patrick said, bemused. "You should know that better than anyone. Immortals can't get sick."

Charles chuckled. "Ah, sorry about the packaging, but I didn't have time to build auto-injectors myself, so I just grabbed a few Epi-pens from the med center."

"Still not following you," Patrick said with a shake of his head.

"I'm getting to it," he said with a grin. "So, I've taken out the epinephrin, of course, and replaced it with a potion that Wes and I concocted. It should knock out any werewolf within seconds."

"Should?" Zane asked with a tight jaw.

"Yeah, I mean, we didn't really have any occasion to test it, but we've been using ingredients that have worked on werewolves before, so, if we're correct, and I'm pretty sure we are—"

"Pretty sure?" Zane ground out.

"Yeah, well nothing is 100%."

To stop Zane from bickering, Patrick asked, "And for how long are they gonna be out, if we jab 'em with that?"

Charles shrugged. "Don't know for sure. Maybe a half hour?"

Zane shook his head. "Thanks for nothing."

"Alright," Patrick said and took one of the offered auto-injectors.

Fallon stuffed one into her pants pocket too. Virginia did the same.

"Zane, you should take one anyway, if only to have it available if somebody in your team needs a second one," Charles cajoled him. "You don't have to use it yourself."

Zane grunted something unintelligible and shoved the offending item into his pocket.

"Just a quick note on how to use it: I've rigged the pens, and taken the caps off already, so, all you need to do is jab the thing into some fleshy spot on your opponent, and press on the back end. The needle is strong enough to go through clothes. Just be careful not to poke yourself. Oh, and it's a one-time use only, just like a regular Epi-pen."

"Thanks, Charles," Patrick said with a nod.

He looked at his assembled supernatural friends. Everybody had small spray bottles in their hands and looked at him expectantly.

"It's time."

Everybody began to spray down their body with Charles and Wesley's potion, and within mere seconds, he couldn't smell any of them anymore as if the barn was completely empty.

"Remember: we're not here to annihilate the Gallagher pack. We're here to make them fear us so that they will never dare retaliate against us for killing one of theirs. Immobilize them, but spare their lives if you can."

Because the only death he wanted on his conscience was Cameron's.

41

Outside the barn, walking along a footpath leading to the main gate of the Gallagher estate, Fallon could feel the influence of the moon on the wolf she was trying to suppress. With the help of Patrick's blood, the battle raging inside her was being fought by warriors of equal strength. However, she knew that she would lose this battle eventually. Whether this was going to happen in ten minutes, half an hour, or an hour, she didn't know. She hoped it was the latter, and that by then, Cameron was dead, and the wolf inside her gone with him.

Silently, they approached the massive iron gate.

"I can see you all on infrared," Cole said through the earpiece. "I'm opening the gate for you now."

When the gate opened in front of them, she was once again amazed at the IT skills some of Scanguards' staff possessed. Hacking into somebody's home security system seemed like a breeze. For a moment, she wondered what would happen if Scanguards took those skills and used them for something nefarious, but she pushed the thought out of her mind instantly. She instinctively knew that the people of Scanguards lived by a code of ethics that wouldn't allow them to do anything evil. They were here to get justice. Justice for her.

While the team broke up into smaller groups, still heading for the main entrance of the house, her group, consisting of Patrick, Zane, Virginia, and herself, veered off to the left to make a wide berth around the house. They hurried along, staying close together.

"I'm cloaking you now," Virginia whispered into her mic.

Nothing changed. Instinctively, Fallon tapped her torso, still feeling the same. She could still see the other three members of her group, but she wasn't worried. Patrick had explained earlier that nobody else but the four members of their group would be able to see them.

"Team one, I've got eyes on you," Cole announced. "You're good to continue."

"I thought nobody could see us," she whispered to Patrick.

"Infrared can, 'cause our bodies are still here," he replied.

"Oh." That hadn't even crossed her mind. "Then I hope the Gallaghers don't have infrared cameras."

"We've reached the back of the house," Patrick announced in a whisper. "Cole? Any obstacles?"

"You're clear to advance. Remember, I'm gonna lose you once you're inside the house."

"Understood."

Patrick made signs to follow him, and their small group stayed close together as they approached the house from the back. There would be no more talking from now on, unless other sounds would drown out theirs. Fallon looked at the house. There were lights behind several of the windows on the upper floor, as well as light on the ground floor.

Fallon's heart beat into her throat, and her palms were sweaty. Fear crept up her spine, and she couldn't shake it off.

"Team one is at the back door," Cole announced through her earpiece. "All other teams, you're free to engage."

Following the command, she heard a loud howling sound coming from the front of the house. It wasn't a wolf's howl, she recognized that instantly. It sounded more like the wind howling, even though there had been no wind earlier. But she couldn't ask what it was, too worried that they would be overheard.

A small outside light illuminated the back door. Virginia was already walking through the closed door, opening it from inside. She let everybody enter, before closing it as quietly as she could. They were inside.

Fallon heard hasty footsteps, people yelling and cursing, and other sounds like those of doors opening and closing. The Gallaghers were readying themselves to defend their home.

Patrick led them down the hallway. Looking past him, she could see the large foyer with the stairs leading to the upper levels, and several doors leading into other parts of the house. A big chandelier illuminated the entry hall, and she spotted several men—men armed with guns—running into different rooms.

Despite these men crossing the foyer, Patrick pressed on, leading them right into the same area. There, he stopped, holding one arm out to the side as a sign not to advance. He gave Virginia a sign and pointed to a door underneath the stairs. It was closed.

Fallon understood their predicament instantly. They couldn't just open the door to the basement while people were crisscrossing the entry hall. A door opening and closing by itself would give them away.

Her heart pounded like a locomotive now, and she worried that somebody could hear it despite the many voices and all the other sounds in the house. After a few more seconds, Patrick suddenly gave a sign to head for the basement door, and they all ran to it as fast as they could. Virginia opened the door. She was the first to reach the stairs. Patrick was the next, then herself. Zane followed, drawing the door shut behind him.

It was dark in the stairwell, but she understood that it was better not to flip the light switch. They couldn't know how many guards were down there, watching Cameron. A light would only alert them.

Downstairs, stale air accompanied by other scents hit her nostrils. They passed storage areas, a wine cellar, a boiler room for the heating system of the old house, and finally, they arrived at a room that was definitely meant to house a prisoner.

A huge cage was welded to the ground, looking just like a cell in an old Western movie with thick steel bars and chains anchored in the concrete floor. The door to the cell stood wide open.

"Fuck!" Patrick cursed.

"What if they didn't bring him here after all?" Zane asked.

Fallon instantly shook her head. "I can still smell him. His scent is strong. He must have been here for some hours."

She inhaled, and suddenly another smell registered. The smell of another werewolf. She spun on her heel. A female werewolf—still in her human form—stared straight at her, and gasped.

"Shit!" Zane cursed.

"Intruders!" the woman yelled and turned tail.

Zane lunged for her. He tackled her, but she shifted so quickly right before everybody's eyes that he lost his grip on her. Patrick now charged toward her, but she was fast and pounced, going for Zane's throat. Not a moment too soon, Zane slammed something into her neck, and the wolf arrested in mid-movement.

Then he pushed her off him, and rolled out from underneath her, just as the wolf turned into a young woman again, her body naked now, her torn clothes on the ground. The auto-injector made a sound as it hit the floor.

Zane brushed the dust off his clothes, then glared at Virginia. "I thought we were invisible."

Virginia rolled her eyes. "I was conserving energy while we were down here alone."

Zane grunted.

"Guess the Epi-pen wasn't such a bad idea after all, right?" Fallon asked to break the tension in the room.

Zane shrugged, and grunted again.

Patrick pointed to the naked woman. "I think that's Gallagher's daughter. Let's lock her in the cage. Quickly. We've gotta find out where they took Cameron."

Cole's voice now came through Fallon's earpiece. "I see three people heading for an SUV. On the right side of the house, where the added wing is located."

"Can you see who they are?" Patrick asked.

"Negative. Can't get the right angle on that drone. I have to rely on my infrared drone instead. Hurry. Looks like the engine is already running."

"Fuck!" Fallon cursed.

If this was Cameron, they had to act quickly, or he would disappear for good.

42

"Fallon, Virginia, lock her up! Then follow us," Patrick instructed, already heading for the exit. "Zane, you're with me."

He charged to the stairs, Zane on his heels. Taking two steps at once, he raced up the stairs. At the top of it, he ripped the door open. He was fully aware that they were visible now, but it couldn't be helped. He could have taken Virginia with them, but that would have meant leaving Fallon without protection, because he couldn't leave Zane with her. He needed Zane because he was one of the best fighters Scanguards had. If anybody could handle two werewolves at once, it was Zane.

They were lucky: the foyer was empty. Through the window next to it, Patrick saw what was happening outside. Charles and Wesley were using witchcraft to control the elements around them, throwing up walls of water, wind, and fire to separate the werewolves from their brethren, preventing them from defending themselves as a collective. Through the window he could see that the Gallaghers had all shifted into their wolf forms, but Scanguards had come prepared. Whenever Wes and Charles separated one wolf from the pack, Scanguards staff swooped in with a net, throwing it over the wolf, then pulling it tight, before tying it to one of the trees out front. Their plan was working: subdue the werewolves without killing them.

Patrick ran down the same hallway they'd used earlier, Zane by his side. He yanked the back door open and hurried outside.

"Where to, Cole?"

"Turn right at the end of the new wing and go around it. They're about to get in the car," Cole informed him through the earpiece.

In vampire speed, Patrick raced in the direction Cole had given him. Once he'd rounded the corner, he saw them: two men pushing and shoving a clearly uncooperative Cameron into the back seat of the car. The engine was idling, and as they approached, Patrick realized that in addition to the two guys handling Cameron, the driver already sat in the car.

"Fuck! There are four including Cameron."

"Sending reinforcements," Cole announced.

Patrick could hear him giving instructions to the vampires fighting the Gallaghers in front of the house to send a couple of people to the side wing to help him and Zane. Patrick barely listened to the replies, concentrating on Cameron and his fellow werewolves instead.

One of the men turned around, clearly having heard his and Zane's approach despite the sounds from the fight taking place in front of the building.

"Vampires!" he yelled to warn his friends.

The werewolf pulled a gun, but Patrick was faster, and kicked it out of his hand, slamming the guy against the side of the car in the process. From the corner of his eye, he saw the other man shift into wolf form and lunge at Zane. Patrick couldn't see how Zane was doing, because his own opponent had already recovered and landed a hard punch against his chin, whipping his head sideways and sending him flying. But the asshole would have to do better than that if he wanted to win.

Patrick got on his feet just as the werewolf reached him again. They exchanged kicks and blows, and Patrick noticed that keeping him engaged in the fight prevented him from shifting into his wolf form like his colleague had done. Patrick doubled his effort, pounding him faster to gain a couple of seconds before his opponent could retaliate. He needed those precious seconds to reach into his jacket pocket and retrieve the auto-injector. The next punch hit him in the chest, temporarily knocking the wind out of him, but Patrick recovered just as quickly and jumped the guy, jabbing the auto-injector into his side. The werewolf went down almost instantly, collapsing on the ground not far from the open car door.

Before he could take a breath, a wolf jumped out of the car, slamming into him. They went flying. There was no doubt as to who this was: Cameron. His fur was black, his eyes a bright silver, his sharp teeth a glaring white, his proportions massive. They landed on the hard gravel path together, Cameron on top of him, pinning him to the ground.

"I need backup," Patrick managed to squeeze out through his crushed windpipe.

He fought Cameron as best he could from his disadvantaged position, shoving him back with his arms, trying to wiggle free of him, while Cameron's snout was coming closer by the second. His sharp teeth would rip his throat open, at first weakening him, then ripping his entire head off if he couldn't free himself.

Patrick marshaled all his strength. His fingers turned into claws, and he began to slice into the wolf's chest and arms while trying to force him to retreat. But despite the howls of pain coming from Cameron, he didn't loosen his hold.

Only an inch separated Cameron's canines from his throat now. Fuck! This wasn't how he'd imagined dying. One more breath, and it would all be over.

THE MOMENT FALLON exited the house, she could smell the werewolves out in the open. She felt the need to shift overwhelm her and knew there was no fighting it any longer. There were too many wolves in the vicinity, and it felt like an infection had taken hold of her now. She'd heard Patrick's request for help over her earpiece and knew she had to get to him.

This time, shifting into her wolf form and ripping her clothes to shreds while doing so, was faster and less painful than the previous night. As she shifted, she lost the earpiece that connected her to the Scanguards team. She didn't need it anymore, because her senses were enhanced now. Her wolf could smell two creatures in particular: Patrick and Cameron.

She raced toward the car, where the smell was most intense, and found the two several yards down the gravel path that led to the driveway in front of the building. She focused her eyes on the black wolf whose deadly fangs were only a hair's breadth from Patrick's throat. He was pinned underneath Cameron. She howled in frustration, making Cameron look in her direction. Their eyes connected, and she realized that he recognized her.

Without slowing her tempo, she barreled toward Cameron. When she reached him, she sank her fangs into his shoulder and held on. The force of the impact jerked Cameron off his victim. They went flying down the gravel path, ever closer to where the battle was raging.

Relief washed over her. She'd saved Patrick. But her relief didn't last long. She realized too late that she was no match for Cameron's strength and experience. She'd never learned to fight as a human, other than take a self-defense class in college, which now seemed ages ago. What had made her think that she could fight now that she was a wolf?

Fighting with their sharp claws, they tumbled precariously close to the driveway where the majority of the werewolves and vampires were engaged in hand-to-hand combat, and where Wesley and Charles worked their magic. Within seconds, Cameron had her pinned beneath him, growling, flashing his fangs. She stared back at him and howled. She could feel what he wanted: her submission. How she knew that, she had no idea. Maybe wolves had a way of somehow communicating, or maybe she simply saw it in his cold eyes. But she wouldn't submit.

I'd rather die, she tried to say, but only growling noises issued from her throat, because as a wolf she couldn't talk.

She could feel anger rolling off him. Why was nobody coming to her aid? From the corner of her eye, she noticed movement and focused on it. Patrick was fighting against another werewolf, this one in human form. Virginia was helping subdue him. Zane was still battling it out with a wolf, but bleeding from multiple wounds. From the corner of her other eye, she saw that the vampires who could have perhaps helped her were cut off by a wall of air and wind, a vortex of sorts, clearly conjured up by one of the witches to protect them from the werewolves.

Cameron grinned down at her, and she growled. She wouldn't go out like a wimp. She wouldn't give him that. He had no power over her anymore. He seemed to understand now that she would never submit to him, and roared, flashing his fangs again, slowly lowering them toward her neck.

A howl that sank deep into her bones sounded. A call to surrender, she recognized, even though she'd never heard it before. Instinct, she thought. Still, it didn't stop Cameron. He would kill her, because he couldn't have her. She felt his fangs at her neck, piercing her fur and skin, the pain excruciating. He would rip her throat out. Tears shot into her eyes.

In her blurry vision, another wolf appeared. The dark brown wolf snatched Cameron by the back of his neck, making him withdraw his fangs from her neck, flinging him off her. With relief and horror in equal measure, she saw the dark brown wolf rip Cameron's throat out without him getting an opportunity to fight back. Limp, Cameron's body fell back on the ground, the brown wolf standing over him triumphantly, blood dripping from his open mouth.

Suddenly, Fallon felt her body cramp and spasm. She howled, but within a couple of seconds the howl transformed into a cry, and she felt her body shifting back into her human form. Pain surged through her, and she screamed. Her neck wound was bleeding profusely, and the pain was unbearable.

"Fallon!"

It was Patrick who called her name, but she couldn't reply. She felt cold and scared. When strong arms wrapped around her, she managed to look up and recognized Patrick.

"I've got you now, baby," he murmured.

Around her she heard voices and howling, commands and cries, but it was all different now. She couldn't hear the sounds as clearly as before and couldn't smell any of the wolves or vampires any longer.

"Something is wrong."

PATRICK'S HEART had nearly stopped when he'd finally been able to subdue the driver of the SUV with Virginia's help and tried to come to Fallon's aid. She'd saved his life—and put herself in danger in the process. He'd charged toward her, intent on killing Cameron, when a dark brown wolf had come out of nowhere and slaughtered Cameron before he could kill Fallon.

Fallon was naked and injured. But one thing was clear immediately: she was human again. Her werewolf aura was gone. He was relieved but worried about her injuries. She was losing so much blood. He pressed one hand on the wound, then bit into the wrist of his other one and held it to her mouth so she could drink from him.

When she began to suck on his wrist, he let out a sigh of relief. But the danger wasn't over. The fight was still raging in front of the house. The wolf who'd saved Fallon looked at them, then raised his head and howled so loud that the entire forest could hear him. Several other wolves trotted out from the shadows behind him, howling with him.

Suddenly, the sounds coming from the front of the house started to subside, and from what he could see from his position, the fighting seemed to have stopped.

"This is Patrick," he said into his mic. "Anybody? What's going on out front?"

"They're surrendering," Amaury reported.

"Yeah, weird," Luther confirmed.

"And they're shifting out of their wolf forms," Yvette added.

Patrick shook his head in disbelief and looked up. The wolf who'd saved Fallon shifted in front of his eyes. The wolves surrounding him followed his example. One of them ran back from where they'd come and brought back a stack of clothing.

The brown wolf, definitely their leader, stark-naked and clearly unconcerned about it, made a few steps toward him and Fallon. On his chest was a wolf tattoo with something written underneath it in a language that he couldn't read. The other men had the same tattoo.

"Will she live?"

Patrick nodded. "Thanks to you."

"And your blood," he added with a nod at his wrist.

Somebody handed him his clothes. He pulled on his pants, but took the shirt and handed it to Patrick.

"For her."

Patrick took it and covered Fallon with it.

"You can call off your witches," the stranger claimed. "We won't hurt you or your people."

Patrick hesitated. "Why should I trust you?" It could all be a trick

—saving Fallon's life and then tricking them into trusting him so they'd lay down their weapons.

"Because Striker Reed does."

Surprised, Patrick let out a breath. "You're Striker's intervention?"

"That what he called it?" He shrugged. Then he introduced himself. "Jude Beaumont from the Werewolf Alliance. I'd shake your hand, but..."

Patrick nodded. His hands were otherwise busy, cradling Fallon in his arms, putting pressure on her wound, and feeding her his blood.

"Patrick Woodford, Scanguards," he introduced himself, then added, speaking into his mic, "Everybody, lay down your weapons. We have a truce."

He watched as his vampire colleagues slowly followed his command, and Wes and Charles terminated their spells. Peace and quiet descended around him.

Jude Beaumont nodded at him, then addressed the assembled. "In the name of the Werewolf Alliance, I command the Gallagher pack to kneel."

"Lupinotuum Societatem," the werewolves who'd arrived with Jude announced.

"What's that mean?" Patrick whispered into his mic.

"It's Latin," Amaury said. "Means Werewolf Alliance."

"Never!" came a yell from the crowd.

Patrick recognized instantly who it was: William Gallagher.

"You had no right to interfere in our business," Gallagher accused Jude.

With the calmness and confidence of a man who knew he would win, Jude stepped closer to Gallagher.

"We do when a pack becomes a danger to all werewolves. You should have reined in your son when you had the chance. His death is on you."

"You killed Cameron? You killed my son?" Gallagher yelled, lunging for Jude.

But two of Jude's companions grabbed him, imprisoning his arms so he couldn't lash out.

"I'm the Alpha of this pack!" he yelled, pure hate spewing from the older man's eyes.

Jude ignored his outburst and turned to Patrick. "Take your people and leave. Never come back here."

"What guarantee do I have that the Gallagher pack isn't gonna retaliate?" Patrick asked.

"It's not the Gallagher pack anymore," Jude announced. "It's the Beaumont pack. I'm their new Alpha. And we mean you no harm. In the name of the Werewolf Alliance, we vow it."

"Lupinotuum Societatem," his companions said in unison.

"And William Gallagher?" Patrick asked, furrowing his brow. "He'll seek revenge."

"William Gallagher isn't your problem anymore. He's mine."

With a nod, and with Virginia's help, Patrick rose to his feet with Fallon in his arms.

"Let's go," he ordered his colleagues. "Anybody killed?"

"No," Amaury replied. "A few injuries, nothing serious."

"Alright, Jude Beaumont," Patrick said. "As long as this pack doesn't cause any more trouble, we won't have a reason to come back."

"Understood."

He locked eyes with Jude for a second. They would both keep their word. Now it was up to the Gallaghers to submit to their new Alpha.

43

Back at the barn where they'd left their vehicles, a surprise was waiting.

"Dad?" Patrick let out.

Samson stood in front of an ambulance that belonged to Scanguards. He hadn't come alone. Maya was inside the ambulance, and Gabriel was already wheeling a gurney toward him. Fallon was still in his arms, but she was conscious. Acknowledging Gabriel with a nod, he placed Fallon on the gurney.

"Our doctor will take care of you now," he assured her.

"Buffy?" she asked.

"No, Maya. You can trust her. She'll give you something for the pain." He looked up. "Gabriel, tell Maya to give her some morphine."

He knew she would be in good hands. He'd done what he could, starting the healing process with his blood. Maya would take care of the rest.

Gabriel rolled her to the ambulance, and Patrick looked at his father again. He bridged the distance between them with a few steps.

"You should have asked us to come home," Samson said.

"Who blabbed?"

"I wouldn't call it blabbing. And it doesn't matter who called me." He sighed. "Gabriel and I could have helped."

"I know, but you know Mom doesn't like it when you put yourself in danger."

"And you think she likes it any better when you do the same?" He shook his head. "You were lucky tonight."

"I know that. But we were prepared."

"Next time, call me."

"Alright."

Samson pulled him into a hug. "I'm so happy everybody is alright. Wanna introduce me to your future mate?"

"You know about that too, huh?"

Samson released him from his embrace. "Nothing stays a secret very long at Scanguards. You should know that."

Patrick shook his head, chuckling. "Come on then. I'll introduce you to Fallon."

They walked toward the ambulance. Gabriel stood outside, handing out human blood to those vampires who were injured. The ones who were blood-bonded to a human or a vampire hybrid received bottled blood that had been drawn from their blood-bonded mates earlier, poured into bottles, and labeled with the receiving vampire's name. It was standard procedure to collect blood from the blood-bonded mates before a dangerous mission so that any injured vampires could be healed swiftly.

Patrick hopped into the back of the ambulance, where Maya was taking care of Fallon. Samson followed him.

"Fallon, baby," he said softly and took her hand.

"Patrick," she whispered, her voice weak.

"How are you feeling?"

She forced a smile. "Better."

He locked eyes with Maya.

"I gave her morphine for the pain."

"Thank you, Maya." Then he looked at Fallon again. "I want you to meet my father, Samson."

Samson leaned over her, so she didn't have to lift her head. "Hi, Fallon. I'm very happy that you'll soon be part of our family."

"Thank you, Mr. Woodford."

"Please call me Samson," he offered. "My wife is eager to meet you too. So, get well soon, okay?"

She smiled back at him. "Yes. Thank you."

When Samson left the ambulance, Maya said, "Patrick, you wanna lick her neck wound now? I've cleaned it. I wanna avoid having to sew it up."

"Definitely," he agreed and leaned over Fallon. "Baby, I'm gonna lick your wound. It will help close it so that you won't have any scars later."

"Thank you."

He shook his head. "I have to thank you. Without you, I'd be dead now. You saved my life."

He brought his mouth to her wound, noticing that it was already starting to heal from the inside. His blood was doing this. Now his saliva would help the process. The scent of her sweet blood engulfed him, and he licked over the tender flesh, licking up the blood that was still seeping from it. He deposited his saliva over the wound, making sure to cover every part of her damaged skin. When he swallowed the blood, he felt arousal charging through him.

"I'll take care of the other injured," he heard Maya say.

He appreciated her giving them privacy for this intimate moment. The shock of what had happened still sat deep in his bones. He couldn't imagine continuing his life without Fallon. He lifted his head to look at her and realized that his vision was blurry. It took him a couple of seconds to understand why. Tears were running down his cheeks.

"I almost lost you," he murmured. "I couldn't shake that other werewolf. He was too strong. It took two of us to subdue him. I tried to get to you. I tried to help you, but I couldn't get there in time. If that werewolf, Jude, hadn't come…"

"Shhhhh." She pressed a finger to his lips to stop him from speaking. Tears shimmered in her eyes. "I know you wanted to help me. I know you would give your life for mine, just like I would give mine for yours. We're both okay now."

He sank his lips onto hers and kissed her, their tears mingling, the shock of what had nearly happened slowly dissipating. Fallon was finally safe.

44

Three days later

Fallon cast a last look in the bathroom mirror. She was human again, and that knowledge filled her heart with happiness and gratitude toward everybody at Scanguards. They had risked their lives to free her from the curse of being a werewolf. She was fully healed, the wound on her neck only a distant memory. There were no scars, just like Patrick had promised. All pain was gone, all fear had vanished, and she felt wrapped in love and understanding.

Dressed in her sexiest—and only—red negligee with nothing else beneath it, she opened the bathroom door and walked into the bedroom. This wasn't her flat. It was a condo located in San Francisco's financial district belonging to Patrick's brother, who lived in New Orleans. Patrick had suggested they use it, because tonight would be special for both of them.

Patrick sat in bed, his chest bare, the duvet draped over his lower body. He let his eyes roam over her.

"You get more beautiful every night," he claimed.

"That's because you have withdrawal symptoms."

She walked toward him, stopping only a foot from the bed. They hadn't made love since before the battle with the werewolves. Maya had kept her at Scanguards' underground med center for observation to make sure she suffered no ill effects after her injury. Patrick had spent lots of time with her to keep her company. They'd kissed, but he'd refused to go any further because he wanted to give her time to heal fully. Earlier today, Maya had finally released her.

Holding Patrick's gaze, she pushed one strap of her negligee off her shoulder, then did the same with the other, so the garment fell to the floor with a soft whooshing sound.

Patrick sucked in a breath. "Babe... are you trying to give me a heart attack or something?"

He lifted the duvet off his body, confirming that he was naked beneath it.

She smiled, slid her knee onto the bed, and leaned in.

"Or something," she teased, casting a look at his cock. "Apparently a hard-on."

"You can do that anytime you want," he offered.

He reached for her, placing his hands on her breasts, cupping them, taking their weight into his palms, while she crawled onto him, straddling him.

"Perfect," he murmured and pressed his face into her bosom.

When he lifted his head again, he kissed her deeply. She let herself go, kissing him back with the same fervor, the same passion. She could get drunk on the way he kissed, the way he touched her. Her hands on her hips, he nudged her to lift herself onto her knees, before he adjusted his cock and drew her hips back down. She impaled herself on his erection, her interior muscles imprisoning him in her body.

They both gasped, and she felt the power she had over him. The power of love. As they moved in sync with each other, she saw his fangs extend to their full length. White and sharp they peeked past his wet lips. The thought that he would drive his fangs into her tonight excited her, and made her ride him faster. She loved the way his cock filled her, reaching deeper with every move.

Their bodies were covered with a thin film of perspiration making every movement smooth and sensual. Her heart was beating faster with every second, and her arousal was reaching a fever pitch.

"Bite me now," she begged and looked into his eyes.

They were shimmering golden now, their green color gone completely. He released her left hip and lifted his hand so she could see what he was doing. In front of her eyes, she saw his fingers turn into sharp claws. With one of them, he made a small incision into his shoulder. Blood seeped from it instantly.

"Drink from me," he demanded, his voice now hoarse with lust.

She brought her mouth to it and lapped up the first few drops that were trying to run down his skin, then latched onto the cut itself and began sucking the blood into her mouth. As it hit her tastebuds, she felt pleasure spread into every cell of her body.

"I love you, Fallon."

As the words echoed in her body, Patrick pierced her skin with his fangs, driving them into her neck, and began to drink from her. She could feel him drawing on her vein as if drinking from a straw.

She suddenly felt the world shift around her and realized that Patrick had flipped her onto her back and was now taking over the reins, without releasing his fangs from her neck. She loved the way his cock thrust into her, with long slow strokes so she could feel every perfect inch of him. She gave herself over to him, giving up control, while taking his essence into her so she could share in his immortality.

She felt as if floating on a cloud of pure happiness, pure bliss.

I'll always be yours.

She heard the words in her mind and knew they were his. Their bond was formed. They were one now, able to communicate on a different level.

She replied in the same telepathic manner: *And I yours.*
And nobody could ever take that away from them.

If you're interested in finding out more about the Gallaghers and Jude Beaumont, the werewolf who killed Cameron, please read the first book in my new series, Werewolf Alliance: New Blood

Reading Order Scanguards Vampires & Stealth Guardians

Scanguards Vampires

Prequel Novella: Mortal Wish
Book 1: Samson's Lovely Mortal
Book 2: Amaury's Hellion
Book 3: Gabriel's Mate
Book 4: Yvette's Haven
Book 5: Zane's Redemption
Book 6: Quinn's Undying Rose
Book 7: Oliver's Hunger
Book 8: Thomas's Choice
Novella 8½: Silent Bite
Book 9: Cain's Identity

20 years pass

Book 10: Luther's Return
Book 11: Blake's Pursuit
Novella 11½: Fateful Reunion

Same time period →

Stealth Guardians

Book 1: Lover Uncloaked

Next →

Book 2: Master Unchained
Book 3: Warrior Unraveled

← Next

Book 12: John's Yearning

Next →

Book 4: Guardian Undone
Book 5: Immortal Unveiled
Book 6: Protector Unmatched
Book 7: Demon Unleashed

8 years pass

Scanguards Hybrids

The Scanguards Hybrids will also be numbered within the Scanguards Vampires series (SV 13 = SH 1) to preserve continuity.

Book 1 (SV 13): Ryder's Storm
Book 2 (SV 14): Damian's Conquest
Book 3 (SV 15): Grayson's Challenge
Book 4 (SV 16): Isabelle's Forbidden Love
Book 5 (SV 17): Cooper's Passion
Book 6 (SV 18): Vanessa's Bravery
Book 7 (SV 19): Patrick's Seduction (2025)

ABOUT THE AUTHOR

Tina Folsom was born in Germany and has been living in English speaking countries since 1991. Tina has always been a bit of a globe trotter. She lived in Munich, Lausanne, London, New York City, Los Angeles, San Francisco, and Sacramento. She has now made a beach town in Southern California her permanent home with her American husband and her dog.

She's written 50 romance novels in English most of which are translated into German, French, and Spanish.

Tina's Online Store: https://tinafolsom.com
https://tinawritesromance.com
tina@tinawritesromance.com

facebook.com/TinaFolsomFans
instagram.com/authortinafolsom

www.ingramcontent.com/pod-product-compliance
Lightning Source LLC
LaVergne TN
LVHW091629070526
838199LV00044B/1001